Scags at 45

Scags at 45

Deborah Emin

East Stroudsburg, PA

Published by Sullivan Street Press, Inc., East Stroudsburg, PA

Cover and interior design by Scribe Inc.
Cover Image © Corey Coyle, http://www.panoramio.com/photo/80371908

ISBN (digital) 978-0-9976663-5-9
ISBN (print) 978-0-9976663-6-6

Love wins.
Thank you, Suzanne Pyrch.

Contents

Chapter One

Her name was Margaret. Just Margaret. I never thought about her last name. She had been a lesbian nun and so was booted from the convent along with her lover, Irene.

Margaret told me that having to leave the convent so precipitously was like having someone pull out a tooth without any anesthetic. And the tooth was healthy, so it didn't want to leave her mouth.

Margaret and I were lovers and then she died and then she returned. This is such an awful amount of information and leaves out so much, which is why I had to write this story.

Knowing Margaret in her life, death and afterlife made me who I am. That's an understatement and after you read this story, you'll chuckle at it like I did when I wrote those words.

My life is the basis of this book because I know it much better than I ever knew Margaret. Margaret was always something other than. More like a barometer than a person. She could gauge my life, be its moral compass, pushing me to the true north of my nature and aspirations. She tried and failed often to keep me from battling every moral dilemma that presented itself. The problem for me was that the longer I knew Margaret, the more serious the moral dilemmas became.

The real story is not necessarily how Margaret and I ended up together but how once she had died, all of the secrets and imponderables of her life came spilling out and needed to be taken care of. By me.

How I managed that is still a mystery but is the basis of this story. The other imponderable but utterly truthful part of this is that despite the particulars of my life and Margaret's, I think this is not unlike most women's lives.

That to me is the most wonderful thing about telling this story. For all the particularities, I see it as representative of all women's stories. Laugh if you must, but read on to see if I am not telling the truth.

The beginning of this story for me was on a bus in the very early morning of November 2nd. Leaving Manhattan for Fredericksburg, Maryland, I was on my way to my monthly visit to Margaret, who was serving time for entering and trespassing on a nuclear weapons facility and pouring her own blood on the threshold of the weapons storage building. This was an act of terrorism, later reduced to criminal damage of a federal facility. While the prosecutor of her case didn't want to bring into evidence Margaret and her collaborators' religious convictions, there was the testimony of her character witnesses that made her true religious convictions part of the court record.

Then, of course, the mention of her relation to me had to be brought in as evidence of her deviance from strict religious teachings. We'd been through this before, and it had failed as a tactic. It failed again. But there I was, on a cold and rainy morning on a Greyhound bus heading for my visit with Margaret.

The year was 1992. I always sat midway back in the bus with the bags I brought with me filled with food, mail for Margaret and a book for me to read on the return trip. I rarely slept on the way to the visit. I was too excited to see Margaret. On that dreary day, my mind was full of how Margaret was about to be released. Soon, she would be home and lying in my arms again.

On that day, I watched out the rain-streaked windows, the horrible highway passing by in a blur as I decided not to dread the next month of loneliness or worry about what was happening in prison but to concentrate on getting her home. I would not think, I told myself, as if I could erase the images of her malnutrition, the damage done to her body by the lack of fresh air and exercise.

I had thought about how monochromatic the life inside prison is and bought her a sweater in the most dazzling blue. It matched the blue of her eyes. Like the sea, I told myself, her eyes sparkle like the sea when the sun plays along the top of the water. The heavy cardigan lay in a box, unadorned by ribbons or wrapping paper but ready to cover her in warmth. She had grown so thin in prison that the veins on her hands popped through her translucent skin, running with a bit of darker-blue blood. She looked frail, almost a ghost of herself.

By the time the bus had escaped the urban sprawl, my thoughts traveled to where Margaret and I had decided to live next. We were giving up on living in New York City and moving to a farm. We knew absolutely nothing about farming, but it seemed like the best antidote to how we had been living till then.

Radical changes were in order. My life since moving to New York City in 1980 had been one long set of radical changes, so leaving the city and living in the country was worth doing. It meant, to me, that I would be with Margaret all the time. We had not had such a life.

Before I met Margaret, I was oblivious to the nuclear weapons our government had built and planned on using if need be. I had been alarmed, like so many people in the Northeast, when the meltdown occurred at Three Mile Island in March 1979, but soon thereafter, it was out of my mind. I had plans to move to New York City and start a new life. The dangers of a nuclear plant melting down in such a populous area made little impression on me.

Margaret wasn't blind to the dangers of nuclear power or the probability of the use of nuclear weapons. The two of us had non-complementary life views when we met. I was mesmerized by Margaret from the moment I saw her in the lobby of the Joyce Theater during an intermission. She was so beautiful and mysterious to me. So out of the ordinary of who I fell in love with. That was true for her too.

We lived in two completely different worlds and yet we lived together for several years and made each other happy in the ways that work and social engagement could not. We fell into a life and formed a bond. This bond was also a legal maneuver necessitated by her first imprisonment, which happened soon after we met.

Nothing that happened after we signed some papers putting me in charge of her estate could I have foreseen. But that moment was like signing a pact with the devil, though neither of us would have said that of it.

We were almost-married in a country that didn't allow same-sex marriages. While Margaret was the more experienced and mature of the two of us, I now controlled, without knowing what that meant, her financial estate.

When I had left Vermont to move to New York, I had not intended to do what I have spent my life doing. I was going to be a major media critic and hold to account the ways in which the corporate media influenced our lives. That ambition disappeared soon after my 30th birthday, which was spent with Margaret in court.

New York City was facing bankruptcy a few years before I moved there. I myself had a very flimsy financial outlook at that time, and when Margaret was arrested and I lost my job, we lived on her money. Little did I know how much that was or where it came from.

Youth seemed to last a very long time for me. I lived in a perpetual state of dependence.

I had a clouded vision of my future no matter how bright the sun shone. I had no idea what to do or what I wanted to do once that major ambition of mine was destroyed. That left me living in the good graces of Margaret, who had absolutely no qualms about supporting me financially and allowing me to become a helper in many causes, none of which involved her.

Max, Margaret's lawyer and the holder of the keys to all her financial secrets, became, in the beginning, just a distant but trusted friend. As things began to unfold later that same day I was on the bus, he became my most enduring link to Margaret.

It was Max's legal mind that shaped Margaret's defense and that shaped the binding contract that kept me tied to Margaret in sickness and imprisonment, and then tried to hold onto me in death too.

The defense of Margaret and her co-defendants was lost on me. I had no part in any of the talks and rarely was allowed to attend the court proceedings. Her defense being her religious views and the judge finding her sexual relationship working in direct contradiction of that, it made things easier if I stayed away.

Sitting on the bus and realizing how dark and dreary early November is, that day or two right after Halloween when the pumpkins have all imploded, I caught myself smiling at my reflection in the window. I smiled not because of the view outside but because of the hopes I had unwillingly allowed myself based on the talks Margaret and I had about living on a farm.

Margaret was about to be released for good behavior before Christmas. That plan was in the works. My smile was about the fantasies we shared of sitting on a porch in our rocking chairs watching the rain fall just beyond the eaves of the house. We were buying a farm. There we would live and love. Max had been looking for one for us in upstate New York.

That smile was also full of the lust I felt for her, the aching kind that doubled me over at night when I roamed around our bedroom sniffing out the fragrances that charged up my memories. Margaret and I had reached an ardor for each other that replaced every sexual fantasy I had ever indulged with the actuality of her touch and kiss and the excitement we shared in making love. Our love life had come at a high price. We made sure to honor that cost by giving into it fully.

The bus route never varied. Hours of tedious thruways followed by long stretches of highways running parallel to suburban strip malls, the one-level sprawling arcades of nail salons, tattoo parlors and laundromats that are surrounded by fast-food franchises conveniently nestled within the three corners of the road hosting chain drug stores. These blights were continuous, a slew of them every half mile or so. My citified eyes never grew used to these sterile stretches of road.

I never told Margaret about the ride to visit her. Our time on the phone was too precious. We got drunk on anticipation and hoped that our reveries about country living would bore the eavesdroppers and send them away.

Even before her imprisonment, we were tired of the constant surveillance, the reading of our mail, the listening in of our phone calls, the harassing of our friends and the lack of time to be alone together. We never traveled anywhere so we walked all over the city and as we walked, we talked about what we could not say at home or even around our friends. And when we got hungry, we stopped at diners for what we called our fried breakfasts.

We enjoyed sitting in diners and eavesdropping on those who didn't worry about what they said in public. Our fellow diners allowed us to appreciate the talk that was of no importance to anyone but those carrying on the conversation. Some of what we overheard was witty or silly, lewd or angry, but mostly carried on with the combined energy of people sharing stories. We told each other those stories often, the ones we had overheard, as if they were our stories.

That really must have confused those listening in on us.

When the bus arrived at the station, I caught a cab to the prison. I'd be returning to that station after my visit for the return trip home. I clutched my bags and the present for Margaret, and after paying the driver, I got in line with all the others waiting to visit a loved one.

By the time I had gone through inspection, set up our table with the food, and laid out the sweater and her mail, it was nearly one o'clock. One o'clock was the magic hour. At that moment I would no longer see the drabness of the place with its worn linoleum floors, cement block walls and the grayness of every surface. When the doors opened at one o'clock, Margaret and I would luxuriate in being together, watched by the guards so that we did not make physical contact.

On November 2, 1992, the doors didn't open punctually. The silence of the unopened doors was measured by the loud second hand on the clock above the door. Each second ticked off was one less second we would share with the person we loved. Even a few seconds of lost time seemed like a denial of justice, further injustice in a system that never treated Margaret fairly, or most likely most of the others waiting on the other side of the door for these visits, which were important to all. But there was nothing any of us could do but wait. Protests would have dire consequences.

When the doors finally opened (though no one corroborated this telling of the story), I heard Margaret screaming my name. "Scaaaags!" I raced through that door into the corridor where Margaret lay on the floor on her back. Her head was resting in a pool of blood forming a halo about her.

I stood above her. Chaos wanted to take over. The guards pulled a woman away from the scene. She screamed at Margaret. A doctor knelt at Margaret's side and then closed her eyes. I hadn't noticed them staring at me. A pen stuck out of Margaret's neck. I knelt beside her and took her hand, which was already colder than normal. I kissed it. A gurney arrived with a black bag. Margaret's body was lifted onto the gurney and then shoved into the black bag. I still held her hand. They pulled the zipper up over her body and I had to let go of her hand. In the background, the woman who stabbed Margaret screamed as they dragged her away.

After that, I remember lying on a couch whose cushions were so sunken, I thought they had buried me. Then

I saw Max and Irene standing above me, ready to accompany me and Margaret home. I know I was drugged. I know the plane made its way back to New York in a storm and that I sat between Max and Irene, who talked to each other in hushed voices. Irene held my hand. When we arrived in New York, Max and Irene took me home to the apartment on Fifth Avenue where I had been hoping to welcome Margaret in another month or so.

That November 2nd was a very long day. I don't know who that Scags was who returned home never to see Margaret again.

Margaret's sudden death changed everything. What changed? What was lost? What was I to do? Down to the very cellular structure of my being, all had changed. I was left with my name being screamed by the dying Margaret and not much else. We never said goodbye.

The apartment Margaret and I shared on Fifth Avenue was now mine. Max and Irene took me there. I hadn't made my bed that morning before I left to visit Margaret. There were dirty dishes in the sink because I always gave myself chores to do when I returned from my visits to the prison. It was my way to distract myself from the depths of depression I felt whenever I missed her.

From the moment we walked in the door of the apartment, my memories of November 2nd end. The next morning, November 3rd, I woke up in my bed alone and undressed and covered in too many blankets. The room was completely dark. I had a hangover from something. Voices snaked in under the closed bedroom door and I thought one of them was Margaret's. I got up, eager to see her. I also smelled coffee and toast. Breakfast with Margaret.

Hurriedly tying a bathrobe around me, I ran into the kitchen to find Irene standing at the sink, not Margaret.

It was uncanny how similar their voices were. She and Max had had their breakfast and she was cleaning up from that and from the mess I had left behind for me to do so I could think of other things than missing Margaret.

Irene and Max saw me enter the kitchen and waited to see how I was. I looked at each of them. Neither had been home; they were wearing the same clothes. Irene left her work at the sink and went into the bedroom to put out clean clothes for me for after my shower. Max left the kitchen for the living room where he sat before a large pile of papers, waiting for me to sign them. Irene whispered to me that people would be arriving soon to pay their respects and I should get cleaned up. Max told me to meet him in the living room after I showered to sign the papers he needed for the opening and employing of Margaret's will. I did what I was told to do and when I went to the living room to meet with Max, a cup of coffee and some toast waited for me.

As I sat across from Max, he said, "This has to be done quickly. There is money we need to have access to for the funeral and the running of this household, among other things. Please just sign the forms and I will explain it all to you later."

I did again as I was told and then Max took all the papers and put them in his briefcase and put the briefcase in the closet and locked it. All those years I had lived in that apartment and that was the first time I had seen the closet locked or even noticed that it could be locked.

Irene took over the kitchen, cleaning and then putting out plates of food that had appeared when I was unconscious. The lingering effects of the drug and the numbing shock that Margaret was dead and would never return to this apartment clobbered me, and no matter where I stood or with whom I tried to talk, I was not there, not in any place at all.

On that first day of mourning, after everyone had gone but Irene and Max, I knew I needed the two of them to keep me anchored. They were like a set of bookends to my distress, which stretched out before me in an unseeable future that I believed would never end. I needed them to keep me from collapsing.

Though as bookends, they were a mismatched pair. I often wondered how this could work but for a while it did. Irene measured in at 5′6″ tall. Though not taller than I, she had so many other attributes that were necessary then. Her contagious laugh contrasted with her quiet way of living, and having been Margaret's lover in the convent and Margaret's first true love, she meant something to me too, especially when I missed Margaret to such an extreme.

Max, on the other hand, was a short, Jewish lawyer, with rumpled clothes and hair that never was combed or cut well. He had a big droopy mustache then with a gut hanging over his belt. He couldn't dress more drably than in his gray shirts, khaki pants and corduroy jacket with the patches on his elbows. His leather briefcase was so big it reminded me of those bags that guys carried in gangster movies to collect the protection money. But Max was an old leftie and he had represented Margaret and her estate for years.

I was Margaret's primary beneficiary. She and Max had set me up as the protector of her estate. This had also involved the formation of a foundation I knew nothing about. I had no knowledge of what these entities were worth. Margaret and Max had promised me these arrangements would be gone once Margaret was out of prison. I was not supposed to be in control of all her property indefinitely; her sudden death changed every-thing. Max had inherited the awful job of having to help me to maintain the estate.

When Max sat me down to explain it to me, he also had to reveal the private records of Margaret's father's dark past. It took several days to tell me the stories of Margaret's father's criminal life. These stories led to the revelation of all the trusts inside of trusts that had been established to keep the money from the state, from Margaret going to prison on those charges and from exposing the people who had no reason to care about Margaret and her pacifist work.

I never knew anything about Margaret's father. The man I had been told about was a complete fabrication. Margaret clearly didn't want me to know what she knew about her father. It was only after she left the convent that he told her how he made his money and what he intended to do with it. That was when she came home to take care of him as he lay dying.

She asked him to remove her from his estate. He refused. Margaret asked Max to convince her father that she was the wrong person to be involved with this much money and its sources.

I felt the same way. Max told me that Henry, Margaret's father, had probably been murdered for what he knew and for the amount of money he controlled. That that was a possibility was also a shock.

Max told me it had shocked Margaret too and she wanted to give all of it away. It turned out that there were many legal reasons why such a magnanimous gesture could not be made, even though the money was mostly obtained illegally. As Max said, "When the crooks are the ones who make the laws, there are all kinds of traps for those who want to subvert their plans. And Margaret may have been a victim of that as well."

I sat back in my chair. I had never considered that Margaret had been murdered for any other reason than the woman who stabbed her didn't want her to leave. But there was this other possibility. I looked at Max who saw the horror growing on my face.

"Let's not jump to conclusions for which there is no corroborating evidence."

This was supposed to soothe me. For a while it did because I had been living under the shadow of Margaret's legal woes for the eleven years we had been together and all of that had been "taken care of" by Max. These formulations, "Let's not jump to conclusions," had become part of the fabric of my life and how I had learned to think about most things.

For example, a friend of Margaret's had turned up at the apartment door one day without being announced by the doorman. This would have been odd enough except then she proceeded to hand Margaret a letter that she said she found addressed to Margaret from someone who knew her father. The someone who knew her father was an FBI informant and warned Margaret that they knew about her plans to trespass on a military base where nuclear weapons were stored and that she should be careful because this time her prison time would not be easy.

I remember her trial. It was, as Max described it, an assassination by illogic and innuendo. The prosecutor had evidence that could not be shared with the defense, and the judge ruled that that was okay. Max never objected. He knew that she had been warned; he knew that there was a plant in her organization, and he said and did nothing about it.

Margaret too was silent during this rigged trial. She never spoke up. I never read the letter, but I was there when it was delivered and watched Margaret as she read it. I saw Margaret's face change and knew that she had retreated into a place where she prayed and stayed still so as not to let fear overwhelm her.

Margaret never shared any of this with me. I held fast to the Margaret I knew and loved. Max's unraveling of stories about why those trusts were nested in trusts and buried inside each other became like a series of word webs covering the room but not touching me.

I listened, but I was still oriented toward the Margaret who was about to come home to me and with whom I was about to buy a farm and move out of this city. Margaret was still in prison. I could not believe that she was dead. I lived within those prison walls as she had. The rigid rules and the ceaseless noise lived in me. I smelled the staleness of that life and how Margaret's calm and sweet disposition had been severely affected by confinement. I'd seen her lose weight, though she didn't have much to lose. The veins on her hands traveled their own blue highways under her skin as she tried to keep her fists unclenched.

We prayed for a Christmas release. Margaret's return home during the same season we met seemed to confer godly approval of our plans going forward.

Max talked on and on about all the ways in which money flowed, endless rivers of cash that had to be moved further and cleaned and disposed of. Margaret might have anticipated what I would do in the face of these stories. She might have been disappointed in my refusal to listen.

All I thought about was how our eyes met the first time we saw each other. Her eyes, those soft blue sparks, spoke always of love. When I first looked into her eyes, they asked me, is this what you're looking for?

I didn't know what I was looking for, but as it turned out, being with her was far more interesting than where my imagination had been able to take me then.

I remembered us walking through Manhattan as we did often, holding hands, laughing about something silly, when suddenly she pulled me to her, kissed me, and said, "I'm sorry for what I've dragged you into, but I'm not sorry we have each other." I assumed she was referring to the life we lived due to her anti-nuclear activism: the surveillance of our lives by the FBI and the wiretaps, the bugging of our apartment, the mails intercepted, even our friends interrogated about us.

We carried that together. It affected us and all we knew. Somehow, I had accepted that as normal once I had decided to share my life with Margaret. We were wedded by love, by the full acceptance of our love and all that love required of us.

Through Margaret, I became inducted into a society I never knew existed, a group of ex-nuns and priests who took their religious vows to mean saving the world from nuclear annihilation. That commitment wound its way through our lives.

When Margaret and I first laid eyes on each other, I knew nothing of her life. I fell in love with Margaret without knowing anything about her except that being near her made me feel more alive than I had ever known.

When I knelt beside Margaret's body as a doctor closed her dead eyes, a switch inside me also closed. Margaret being enclosed in a black body bag removed her physical presence from my life forever. Never again would we walk, and talk, and hold hands and tell each other silly stories. No sudden stops that ended with a long kiss. Never again.

I walked around like a ghost, unable to make eye contact or answer a question. I saw the pen sticking out of Margaret's neck. Irene, the other bookend, cared for me and protected me.

She and Max did what bookends are supposed to do, keep the books steady.

There was another terror ready to arise and that was the funeral and what would follow because a funeral is an entry point to grief.

Chapter Two

Because I didn't exist in those days, I was unable to take care of anything. I barely knew how to sign my name on all the papers Max put in front of me. But we were also at a moment in the course of world events that had nothing to do with me; we were approaching Advent. And Margaret needed to have her funeral. Funerals entail the participation of a priest.

A shift in focus then for all of us. Not just me and Max and Irene, but for all those who had known and loved Margaret.

While Margaret was in prison, our church had hired a new rector, Joanne. Margaret never met her. But she was excited that a new, young and female presence would be guiding the parish. While I was bringing Margaret news of the church, I had lost interest in the activities I had been involved in there. For weeks or months, I am not sure, my mind had been drawn to other needs. I could only process so much. But the prospect of Margaret's early release had definitely altered how I spent my time.

There were the practical things to take care of: making the apartment ready to be sold, looking at farm properties with Max, telling every friend I could what we were doing.

However, and I confess this with some shame, I more often sat alone in the living room, looking outside for no reason and with nothing on my mind. Change was going to happen, and it was going to be momentous.

I thought about Max a lot. I saw him as the man making everything happen. Max, the study in browns and straw: his suits and shoes and eyes brown; his shirts, hair, mustache the color of straw. This man had guided Margaret through the most difficult times in her life. I sat staring out the window, trying to imagine Margaret dealing with the death of her father. Her mother was already dead. I knew nothing about her mother. Margaret was an only child. Then there was Irene, her lover at the convent. I realized then, in those days of doing nothing, how little I knew of Margaret. The simple story had sufficed. We loved each other and that was clear to me.

I had been the trustee of Margaret's estate for years because she was in prison or in court or under surveillance, and it "just made sense" to have me in that role, as Max assured me. Max brought papers to the apartment for me to sign because that's what Margaret wanted.

I never questioned anything because I had no reason to be suspicious. I'm not suspicious by nature. When Margaret died unexpectedly, leaving everything to me, I returned to sitting in the living room thinking about as little as possible.

Margaret died. When Joanne, the priest, entered our home, she found the room full of other mourners beside me who wanted to help put Margaret to rest as she should be laid to rest—as a hero of our time.

Max, Irene, and I were the official mourners. Joanne came and sat with us to discuss this event. Max and I looked to Irene to be the official funeral director.

Irene and Joanne discussed the particulars of the Mass. Max sat quietly, silently computing how much of a check the estate should write out to me to pay for this final tribute. It was obvious to me how useless I was. I didn't care. I sat in that same state I had been in when waiting for Margaret's release.

Then the others in the room came forward to talk to Joanne and Irene and as they left, they turned to me, each and every one, and said exactly the same thing: "So sorry for your loss."

I don't mean to trivialize their words. They were correct because it was my loss.

I was relieved that Irene took charge of the funeral arrangements. All I had to do was pay for it. That was really a trivial act. I could sign a check or two.

As the plans for the funeral proceeded, Max took me deeper into the story of Henry and Margaret.

Max said, "Margaret didn't talk about her father because he was a problem for everyone who knew him and especially for Margaret. They agreed on nothing."

I waited for him to say more, but he waited for me.

"Max, please say whatever you have to say."

"It's simple. Henry was a crook. A big, hateful crook. That his daughter wanted to be a nun was not good, according to Henry. She needed to produce an heir. But then to discover that she was a lesbian. Oh my. The man could not believe what had happened to him. Everything happened to *him*. So he died leaving Margaret not only everything, but in such a mess that it took us years to figure out what he had done. We pulled apart each of his messes only to discover more of a mess. Trusts within trusts, so many egregious deals and scams, and the idiot documented it all and we know that because we found all his notes. What a piece of work he was. I wasn't his lawyer. Henry never would have worked with me, not that I would have wanted to be his lawyer. But guess what? He had this very expensive lawyer who was stealing from him. Everything he had touched was a mess, and then he died of esophageal cancer so could not even talk at the end of his life.

"Margaret found me. I didn't want any part of it. I was young, just beginning my practice, and I thought this is too big for me. I'm not ready yet. But she convinced me. She had a bit of a persuasive side, probably like her father's, but not mean or crooked."

Max wanted to continue talking, but I stopped him.

"Before you plow ahead, do I need to know all of this? Can I just say no, I don't want this?"

He looked at me with such kindness.

"Funny. So funny you should say that. That's what Margaret said once we had unraveled Henry's estate. She wanted to give it all away and destroy the documents and would have if I hadn't convinced her not to. As I said, I was young. And probably too young and greedy to have paid attention to what the consequences would be for hanging onto all of this. Margaret was also naive. I should have found a more experienced lawyer to guide us. I didn't. We learned together and made lots of mistakes but eventually, the messes got resolved. This estate is now pristine, except it was not intended solely for you."

I had no idea what he meant.

I hadn't expected Margaret to die. I hadn't expected her death or being this unmoored at this point in my life. I had believed so much was possible for me and Margaret.

That was where I needed help.

But Max continued talking. In answering my question about refusing the will, he said: "You can't. Simply put, most likely Henry was killed for this, and so was

Margaret. And while you may be thinking you will be killed next or maybe I will be, I think these were blood killings. Long-term and patient waiting for the time and place. Revenge. Plain and simple.

"So, please, keep this estate intact. I didn't think Margaret would be in danger, but I was wrong. That being said, there was evidence suggesting this would happen. We chose to ignore it. Margaret finally chose to ignore it and to use what she'd been given in ways that were all to the good."

Max shuffled through his papers. He avoided looking at me.

I could not talk about her being murdered or even her father possibly being murdered, so I asked the question that was guaranteed to make me feel miserable.

"Are we talking lots more money than I already know about?"

Max said yes. And that's where I ended our talk. I didn't want to know how much. I had heard enough, and I hoped he would leave me alone.

Max acknowledged that I had learned enough about Margaret's hidden past until perhaps after the funeral.

I said nothing, but inside me there was a screaming imbecile. *Perhaps? Margaret was murdered because of something her father had done? That she knew this was a possibility and that she left all of this for me to deal with alone? Perhaps?*

I said nothing.

Max prepared to leave, pulling all his files together into his briefcase, locking it and putting the heavy load on his shoulder. Before leaving, he turned to me, gave me a hug and whispered in my ear, "I'm here. I'll help."

He walked out the door followed by Joanne and Irene and the cadre of friends who came to mourn. Silence. The silence of loneliness. I sat back down on the couch and noticed a piece of paper he left on the table. It was a check made out to me from Margaret's trust for a few thousand dollars. I usually received checks from this trust to run our lives but never in such a large amount. At the bottom of the check, in the memo, it read, "Funeral expenses."

Ah yes, I thought. *The new reality of my life.* I was in charge of the business of Margaret's legacy. How was this to measure up to the love we shared?

I needed to go outside. I had been inside since we returned from the prison. I was exhausted but decided I should go to the bank to deposit the check. The cold hit my face like tiny pellets of ice, which I realized were precisely that, ice pellets falling on the pavement making the way treacherous as I walked around the corner to the bank. I imagined someone following me; I felt someone's eyes on my back.

It was, in fact, an old friend from before the Margaret years who had seen me leave the building and was trying, despite the slippery sidewalk, to catch up with me.

As I walked out of the bank, she tapped me on the shoulder. "Scags?" she asked, and I looked up, and there was someone I didn't recognize.

"Yes?" I replied.

But then she smiled, and we hugged each other spontaneously, without my even thinking.

"Do you live around here?" I nodded yes.

"Who would have imagined that? Things sure do change, don't they? I'm Natalie. We were roommates for the last year of college."

"I remember," I said but was lying. I had not remembered her name and on closer inspection, she could have been anyone from that time in my life. She just looked familiar.

My silence unsettled her. I had nothing to say. There was way too much to say if I had truly known her and absolutely nothing to say to someone I could not place.

Natalie wore a large fur coat and seemed to be accustomed to wearing it. I should have recognized that. No matter how hard I looked at her, I could not recall this roommate of mine. I decided to make a speedy retreat back to the apartment and not say a word.

I sidestepped Natalie and walked away. If she followed me, I didn't look or care. I wanted to return to the warm spot on my couch and lie down and sleep.

When I let myself back into the apartment, Irene had returned. She was cooking dinner.

That was my life. Unforeseen encounters, the steadiness of Irene, weird talks with Max. And my memories of life with Margaret.

All of that collapsed at the funeral.

The church had been an important part of Margaret's life. As an ex-nun, as a woman who wanted to express her love for women openly, she felt more comfortable in the Episcopal Church, despite its not being that open to women or lesbians at the time she joined.

By the time I met her, she was a member of a community of gay men and lesbians at this church in the Village. I learned how important it was to her that I join her, and so I joined her on most Sundays to walk from the apartment on Fifth Avenue to the church on Hudson Street. I liked the walks no matter what time of year, but if I didn't feel like going, Margaret never complained. I wasn't religious, never had been. Her religious preoccupation was of interest to me because everything about her interested me.

When it came to her funeral, a large and well-attended one, I was lost in the crowd, even though I was known as the sole survivor. Margaret had touched so many people and had done so much for people and the causes she believed in that the church was packed. All I kept thinking was, *Where is Margaret? She is supposed to be here with me.*

I don't have clear memories of the funeral. I remember large vases filled with long branches of evergreens. I remember sitting between Max and Irene and in front of Max's wife and two children, who I never knew about. I remember men in black suits, who were probably FBI agents, standing at the back of the church, looking around at all of us. I remember it being a cold but clear day with the cold getting in behind the collar of my coat and traveling down my spine, and that chilled feeling never left me during the entire month of December.

I had been to many funerals in that church, so many I had lost count. It was the AIDS era, and the church had been one of the few places in the city where gay men and their friends could come to pray, to be a part of the church and to be buried by the church. There had been too many buried.

When the Mass began for Margaret, the familiar words came out of the priest's mouth; I heard them as if for the first time and as if they meant more to me than they ever had before.

> *"I am the resurrection and the life, saith the Lord;*
> *he that believeth in me, though he were dead, yet shall he live;*
> *and whosoever liveth and believeth in me shall never die."*

The words tolled inside my head, giant bells of words.

Resurrection and the life. I heard them. Words that had never meant a thing to me now meant death and life. They summoned me, but I didn't believe in the Resurrection. I didn't await God's return and certainly not in glory. I had seen death. It was a cold and haunting form. The last sight of Margaret bleeding onto the concrete floor, her blood forming a jagged halo around her head and shoulders, the pen sticking out of her jugular. All that life energy bubbling along the concrete was what I knew of death and all I wanted to know of it.

I had mourned one other person in my life, but my mourning period had been quickly disrupted. It was a long time ago and never involved a funeral in a church. I felt that I was a neophyte to grief. Yes, there had been one other lover who died—Charles—but I was so young and ill-informed about love and couldn't understand what it was doing to me that I rarely, if ever, thought about him. Although then, like now, I sat through a church service wondering what would become of my life.

It was when I lost my Pops that I knew I entered into the adult realm, that stage of life when one leaves behind all of childhood. Pops' death had been a traumatic turning point because that was when Mama disowned me, shutting me out of her life forever. Having learned that I was a lesbian due to the salacious headlines at the time Margaret was first arrested, Mama slammed the door on me. When I thought of Pops dying, I saw the livid scowl on Mama's face.

Every time I thought of Pops, that part of my life with Margaret came bubbling up, too.

Margaret and I had just begun living together, merging our lives, because Margaret's arrest and the outing of our relationship had also caused me to lose my job. While Margaret awaited trial for trespassing on a nuclear site, I went to Skokie to say goodbye to my Pops. He was falling out of life, was unreachable, and yet I wanted him to know I came home to say goodbye. He died.

Lost in her grief, Mama's reaction to my love for Margaret became unreasonable and angry. Even my Aunt Money, Pops' sister, could not stop Mama's rage, and so I returned to New York, never sat shiva or went to the funeral, but buried myself in Margaret's life.

In the first short months of knowing Margaret, everything turned upside down and I was more wedded to her than the law allowed. I floated into her life like a body washed ashore. Revived by her love, I reciprocated that love by helping her with the practical aspects of her life. I never questioned all the papers handed to me to sign. I loved Margaret. We experienced life together. Then she was dead. I sat in a pew at her funeral surrounded by the many people who knew her and loved her. In church, like a child squirming to get up and run around, I wanted to cry out for her to just show up and stop the charade.

Her death didn't serve me well. I was the most ungrateful recipient of Margaret's wealth. I wanted nothing to do with it. I was furious at what I was learning of her life. "I should have known all of this crap," I yelled to no one when I sat alone at night in the apartment. "What kind of love was it?"

I knew that her friends thought I was unworthy of Margaret. I wanted to tell them about this other Margaret they would never know.

When I rose up from the pew to say my words about Margaret, I felt their eyes on me. They were asking, "Who is this Scags? What did Margaret see in her?"

Death does that to us all. It opens the caves that we have been walking by and ignoring for as long as possible until we can no longer avoid them. I looked inside and saw the life that I had begun building before I met Margaret. It sat inside the cave, though no longer acted on, having disappeared into the vapors of old dreams set aside to take care of the obsessive love I had for Margaret. I was in love with someone who, as I discovered in her death, I had never really known.

I stood up to walk to the podium to say my farewell to Margaret. My footsteps reverberated throughout the church. My hands sweated in my pockets as I grasped the pages of notes I had made to remind me what it was I wanted to say. What I wanted to say that day was difficult to say. How to say goodbye in public to someone who was no longer there?

"Margaret saved my soul," I began, thus opening a door to what was only partially true. I kept going down that path and said the things that only I knew.

"She taught me how to do good for people I would never know and who would never know me. She taught me how to do that as my life's work. She said to me, 'This is an expression of the love we share.'"

I thought about her and wondered, how did I live with someone who was a saint?

What else did I say about her?

"When Margaret sent me off each day to do the errands, she slipped a piece of paper into my pocket. She liked to know that I was walking around town with a note from her. When I reached into my pocket to get my wallet or a key, there it would be. Not quite a love letter. More a prayer that whatever I was doing, I would find peace and know the love she felt for me.

"Margaret believed that if we did everything everyday as if that were our purpose in life, then we would be happy. She said, 'Wash the dishes and make the bed or put some change in a homeless person's hand or take a sick friend some food, and that is where you will find God waiting for you.'

"Margaret knew I believed in none of that, and to her it didn't matter. She knew that about me. She was an ardent believer. At the same time, she held tightly to our love. When Margaret and I went for our many long walks, I always knew that in addition to being with me and talking and laughing with me, she was praying. She described that kind of prayer as joining with thousands, if not millions, who were also continuously praying. They prayed for peace. They prayed for justice. She lived and walked in prayers and just like all of us will someday too, she died.

"She accepted me, this non-believer, because she loved me. She accepted that most people never lived as she did. Even in prison, she prayed continuously. I suspect that as she was dying, she was praying.

"She carried with her the kind of love that often goes unnoticed. It's the love that puts money into a poor sister's hand and listens to her talk about herself. It is the love that picks up all the trash she encounters on the streets and puts it in the trash receptacles. It's the kind of love that, when the moon rises and sits brightly in the sky, causes her to take my hand and stand still with me and breathe in the air of that special moment in the night. She had the constant desire to be in love with everything around her and with everyone."

I said, finally, "If this sounds like living with a saint, in some ways that was true. Margaret's sainthood came with a price; she was all of this but also lived well outside the teachings of most churches when it came to who and how she loved.

"I stand before you deeply saddened to have her gone and no longer living in my arms or in my bed. I truly don't know what I will do without her."

I took my walk back to the pew feeling as if I had doled out the weight of the grief I felt fairly.

The usual slide into depression occurred after the funeral. It was like having taken down all the decorations on Epiphany and having no more lights and glitter to brighten the bleakness of January and the rest of winter.

Having said that, ironically, Christmas was right around the corner after the funeral. I took no notice of all the lights outside, all the decorations and the creativity of the season. The music didn't buoy me. The good wishes and the anticipation, all were lost on me. What was Christmas to me other than the first Christmas without Margaret? I would neither have her home nor be visiting her in prison. She was gone. Forever. That was the truth of it. Gone. Forever.

I loathed Christmas. I became an automaton. For Max and Irene, I behaved as if I was simply depressed to be without Margaret. There was much more to it than that. But my deception led Irene and Joanne, the priest, to decide that it would help me to join the Formation Class at the church and be baptized at Easter. Their spirits were full of good wishes, but since they didn't understand the nature of my depression, they couldn't understand what the consequences of their push for me to join a group and be around others struggling with issues of faith would lead to.

They read me wrong. It was even bleaker that they so misunderstood me.

The whole awful scenario began with a phone call from the rector's secretary, saying she would like to see me. When would it be convenient?

Anytime was convenient, and absolutely no time at all was convenient. I just threw the answer back at her saying, whatever worked for Joanne.

The next day, right after my lunch, I got dressed for the first time in a few days and left the apartment. Walking along the same streets Margaret and I walked together hand in hand whenever we went to church, the cold January air was hard to breathe. Steel-gray clouds lived in a steel-gray sky. The red brick buildings fronted by the bare trees were so familiar I could have closed my eyes and gotten to the church unaided by sight. But Margaret's absence was what kept my eyes open and my whole being vulnerable to an anticipated attack or maybe a sighting of Margaret who was not really dead but had been hidden from me. I hoped beyond reason. That was what grief did to me.

I walked and when I arrived at Sixth Avenue, I saw a mounted NYPD officer sitting atop a horse so tall I thought I must have shrunk in size. As I drew nearer, the animal's statue-like form convulsed from the head and neck as he sneezed. Water vapor issued from his nostrils while the bit rattled in his mouth from the sneeze. The cop sat still, but the horse began to move. The cop used his booted spurs along the horse's sides, and they moved as only a horse with a mounted man atop him can move up the street. They looked neither left nor right. I continued toward the church, hearing the horse's shod feet clop toward the Jefferson Market Library. The sky had grown as dark as it is at dusk, and with snow in the forecast, the air held onto its coldness.

By the time I arrived in Joanne's office, the darkness had settled completely. The city's lights flicked on as if one switch ignited them all. Joanne sat behind her desk with a tall stack of books almost blocking her view of me as I sat down on the other side of her desk.

"Welcome to Formation," she said, patting the pile of books in front of her. Then she looked at me and laughed.

"Don't worry. You don't have to read all of these books. Like most things Episcopal, you are free to choose. We started the class several weeks ago, but you can catch up as you can. We've already covered church history."

She handed me a book. I think I may have forgotten it that day in her office. I never saw it again.

Joanne talked the entire time. I kept looking out the window at the snow that had begun blowing in earnest.

I lived in silence in those days. I walked home in silence from the church through the storm and by the time I arrived home, my entire body had frozen. The snow had taken me over, and its swirling, blowing mess might have buried me. But because I was so well tuned to the way home, so motivated to be at home, I found my way.

As soon as I stepped inside the well-heated apartment, I passed out. The cold clothes woke me up. They were so uncomfortable, I could have been lying on the street. That's what woke me up, thinking I was still outside. I stood up. I realized I was at home but needed to get out of the clothes and take a shower to warm up. As I walked toward the bedroom, I tripped on the rug and fell again. This time I hit my head very hard.

I laughed. It was obvious that a demon had tried once and failed to do me in and was trying again. I felt warm blood flowing from my forehead and stopped laughing. I crawled along the floor to find the phone so I could call Irene.

I woke up on a gurney in the ER, with Irene holding my hand while a nurse stitched my head. Where was I?

I spent the night on that gurney. Bright fluorescent lights shone in my eyes, making sleep difficult. Irene stayed with me through the entire night. I told her what had happened and how funny I found it.

Her response was, "I don't like it."

"I don't like it either, Irene. But you have to admit there was something funny going on."

She smiled at me and handed me a cup of water. "Are you hungry?"

"I would love some ice cream."

"Of course you would," she said.

We shared a pint of chocolate ice cream. She was able to find one spoon. We passed the pint and spoon back and forth, and when it was finished, I suggested she get us another one. For a moment, she smiled, but then a resident showed up. He spoiled the newfound pleasure we had in each other's company. He told me to stand up. Was I dizzy? No, I was not. I looked again at Irene and smiled. I wanted her to know how much I appreciated her being there. He asked me if I was dizzy when I closed my eyes. I was not.

That was enough for them to dispense with me. It was time to leave, and Irene had brought the coat and hat and scarf I needed along with the warm and dry clothes I wore.

Outside the ER, I looked around. We were at St. Vincent's, the Seventh Avenue entrance and not far from the apartment. It was morning and a warmer and sunnier day. I put my arm through Irene's and suggested we walk home and stop for breakfast at Elephant & Castle on Eighth Street.

An omelette and hot tea revived me. Sitting with Irene, who also liked to watch the people around us, helped me enjoy the taste of the food. This was a first since Margaret had died.

I think Irene wanted to talk to me about the fall I had taken, but seeing me begin to have lighter spirits, she changed her mind and suggested we cook dinner together that night. At that point, she told me that she would tell me what had happened when I fell.

After breakfast, we went shopping and took the groceries to my place together. We put everything away together too. The loneliness I had felt began to subside with Irene's presence.

Over dinner, Irene said, "That was a nasty fall you had. When you hit the floor, you cracked open the skin on your forehead. The forehead bleeds a lot. You've got several stitches. I can change that bandage for you tomorrow morning before you shower. But you have to keep it dry."

Irene took over the nursing role. She told me had I not passed out, she would not have called the ambulance. I had no memory of anything past hearing Irene's voice on the phone and telling her I needed her. I had called her because she was a nurse. But she knew that with me unconscious, I needed a hospital to stitch up my head and not just her to change me out of my wet clothes.

"I'm glad I had the presence of mind to call you. Thanks for all you did."

I looked her in the eyes and saw the tears lying behind the lashes. "I know you miss Margaret too."

"Yes," she said as she helped me to clear the table and put the dishes in the sink to wash.

In that way, Irene and I became close and then closer. I went to Formation Class every Sunday after the last church service. The classes were tolerable because afterwards, I met Irene for brunch. At first, we barely talked. It wasn't awkwardness. Silence still ruled my life. Irene tolerated my silence. Her kindness was a gift.

Once or twice, we went to brunch with the rector during that Formation period. On those afternoons, I tried to be less silent and withdrawn. But as I was withdrawn and silent during the classes, she didn't seem to expect much more from me at brunch. Irene took over the conversational duties.

We took Joanne to a new place on Bleecker Street that Irene particularly liked. It made me feel good to give to her in that way. These brunches gave us time to get to know Joanne, who was not from the East Coast but from California. She told us how the weather changes we constantly experienced were challenging what she had thought was her endless amount of good cheer. Yet, even with her challenge, she was always of good cheer with us. Laughing at herself, she said, "I sound like a typical Californian—give me good weather, and I am a good person."

We laughed with her, and then Irene did what I knew to be her typical maneuver.

"I don't think that collar will keep you warm enough, though, Joanne. I highly recommend a nice wool scarf." And with that, Irene pulled a lovely cashmere scarf from her bag and reached across the table and tied it around the rector's neck.

Joanne's pale face burned with both embarrassment and warmth as the soft, comforting material settled around her neck.

"Oh Irene, what a beautiful present. I am so grateful."

"Don't thank me, thank Scags. It was her gift, but she was too nervous to give it to you." Irene grabbed my hand and squeezed it hard, daring me to contradict her.

"Scags, thank you. This is so generous and unnecessary."

We had been drinking a round of Bloody Marys, and now the ice had truly been broken. Having burdened them with my silence, I decided to ask each of them where they had grown up.

A safe topic on that winter afternoon.

Irene answered my question first by saying, "I came from right here in the Village. I grew up a neighbor of Margaret's. We started life side by side."

"I thought Margaret grew up on Long Island."

"She did, until her mother died when she was 12. Then her father moved her to the city so he didn't have to commute every day. We went to the same Catholic high school together and then off to the convent together at 19. We were inseparable. Margaret and I both lost our mothers at a young age and thought our fathers were from an alien planet and had come here for information about us earthlings, especially girls, to take back to their planet. We made up lots of stories about what their planets must be like to produce such strange life forms. We decided that where they lived was so boring that they had to come here and stay. Otherwise, returning to their home planets, they would die of boredom. It gave us lots of laughs to think of our fathers as aliens. Since they couldn't stop annoying us, there was no other explanation."

I watched Irene tell her story. Joanne and I laughed at it, but it opened a door for me that Joanne wouldn't have known was there. How wonderful it must have been to know Margaret then, when she was young, with everything yet to be, including her love affair with Irene.

The Margaret in Irene's story was funny and so unlike the adult Margaret I knew. I watched Irene tell her story. I understood for the first time how close they had been. I felt jealous but also closer to Irene.

Joanne began her story. "I grew up in LA. I was one of so many kids that sometimes I thought we were a family of feral cats that my parents took in. But we all loved each other and were the best of friends. It made leaving home difficult for me.

"I was stuck in the middle and yet was the oldest of the girls. All the boys preceded me. I never wanted anything more than to be either at home or in church. I was that kind of a very strange child, and it worried my parents.

"When I went to college and discovered that you could study theology and the Bible and church music, I felt that college was heaven. I never wanted to leave.

"I met a man while I was in heaven, and we fell in love, and that made the whole heavenly feeling more intense. We married soon after I graduated. When I moved here to go to seminary, he wasn't as thrilled. He moved with me, but we didn't last the move."

She sat silently then, too. Finished her drink and swirled the celery stick, twirling the ice cubes and staring down into the empty glass. Then she looked up at us, taking her time to look each of us in the eye.

"Choosing to be a priest caused some disruptions."

Irene reached across the table and touched Joanne's hand. "Some choices are not what others want for us. My father and Margaret's were none too pleased that we chose to lead a religious life. Of course, we didn't make it through that life. We found other ways to serve."

Joanne looked at me. There was a trap door right in front of me, and I didn't want to fall into it. My past wasn't where I looked anymore unless it included the intimate moments between me and Margaret, and that was not the answer these two women wanted to hear.

"I'm a hybrid, I think you would say. I grew up with parents who were not religious except by birth. Until I met Margaret, I never knew what it was like to attend a church. I didn't know what it meant to pray. I'd never met a nun, let alone two."

I looked at Irene. She was listening while folding and unfolding her napkin.

"I never thought about God. I had studied the Bible as a literary text. My father's parents were assimilated Jews. My mother, as far as I could tell, had no family that she ever wanted to mention. Except for her mother, who frightened her. I was an only child, and we never celebrated any holidays. Birthdays were a big deal, as well as Halloween and Thanksgiving. Oh, yes, New Year's too. But those are the most secular of days.

"Margaret introduced me to Christmas and then Epiphany. Those were the first two holidays I had ever known as religious events. I felt as if I had walked into a new world, one that had been existing alongside the one I had been living in all those years. How could I not have known of this devotion and love? It wasn't as if I hadn't seen the movies and heard the songs. But none of it had touched me until I met Margaret. Then these parallel worlds intrigued me. I could walk in and out of them at will."

Irene and Joanne laughed at my analogy. But it had been like that.

"Do you think Margaret wanted you to be baptized?" Joanne asked.

"I think she would have been greatly pleased but never talked about it with me."

That ended our talk. For some reason, mentioning me and the baptism caused us all to look at our watches. Silently, we decided we had journeyed far enough into each other's lives, and it was now time to go home. I paid for our meal, and then we proceeded to the front of the restaurant to say our goodbyes. We watched Joanne head back to the rectory, and then Irene and I picked up some groceries for dinner. I knew I would not be hungry, but it was part of the ritual after brunch, as was taking a nap.

The following Sunday, after the Formation Class, the weather turned bad. I mean, so bad that we had to get home and forget about brunch. For us to skip brunch showed how serious the storm was. Even then, what began as a heavy snowstorm quickly turned into a blizzard.

As we were leaving the parish house, Joanne asked us if we were going to take a cab home. It was obvious Joanne had not been in a blizzard in New York before. I said, "A cab could not stop long enough for us to get inside it. We'll walk."

"No, we'll run," Irene said. She grabbed my hand, and we got a fast start while at the same time awkwardly pulling our hats down over our ears and tightening the scarves around our necks.

We were hearty souls. As we headed home in the midst of the raw wind and whipping snow, the wind was coming off the river at our backs, and the force pushed us along faster than we wanted to move. The snow had already piled up, making each step more difficult than the last. When we had left the church grounds, the snow had been around our ankles. By the time we reached Sixth Avenue, it was at our knees.

As we passed Washington Square Park, with no one out of doors, it reminded me of that scene in the movie, *Doctor Zhivago*, when the main character is walking alone across the steppes of Russia in the midst of a blizzard. Had anything happened to us as we plowed our way home, no one would have heard us.

Smarter people were inside their homes, safe and warm, not risking their lives walking in a blizzard. I don't know why we didn't ask Joanne to let us hang out until the storm died down. But we trudged through the snow, helping each other to keep moving. We knew not to stop or we would freeze.

By the time we got upstairs, we were covered completely in snow. Inches of it blanketed us and our clothing. I was frigid and the heat of the apartment didn't help until all my clothes were off. We both took off everything, ran to the bedroom, pulled back the covers, jumped into bed, then threw them back over our bodies and made love. It was the release both of us needed. And it surprised us too. Even as our hands were traveling across the other's body, we laughed and almost sang with the pleasure of that moment. Finally, our bodies said, you have found each other.

I was a moody person back then. I struggled to be kind or tolerant. But while making love to Irene, that nasty side settled down. Getting absorbed in touching Irene's very white skin and watching her body respond to my touch restored a power I had lost.

The trek to get home in the blizzard hadn't tired us out. It regenerated us. We made love, jumped into a warm shower together and went back to bed to make love again.

By 8:00 that evening, we were hungry. Irene found a robe in the closet and went into the kitchen for a container of ice cream. I shuffled in behind her, wrapped in a blanket, as ravenous as she. We finished the ice cream and were on our way back to bed when the phone rang.

I looked at Irene. "Should I answer it?" I asked her.

"Why not?"

"Hello," I whispered into the phone as if I were hiding from someone.

"Oh Scags, this is Joanne. I tried calling you earlier and no one answered. I was worried as that storm got worse and worse that I should never have let the two of you leave the church. I'm glad you're fine. I'll call Irene now to make sure she made it home too."

Looking right at Irene, I told Joanne that Irene was fine and that she had come home with me. Both of us were fine. And I thanked her for her concern and hung up because Irene and I began to laugh.

"Busted," Irene said.

We opened a bottle of wine and sat in the living room and watched the snow fall. We dropped off to sleep in each other's arms and were awakened early in the morning when Max let himself in with his key and found our clothes in a heap in the hallway and the two of us cuddled up on the couch with an empty wine bottle beside us.

Max stood looking at us. We were mostly naked and hung over. Max took this in stride and went to the kitchen to make coffee for us.

What could he have said? We were adults and it was no secret that we were both lesbians. What changed for me was that I wanted Max to explain to Irene what Margaret had done. I almost added, "done to me."

When Irene went to the bedroom to put on some clothes, I followed Max into the kitchen and watched as he counted out the measures of coffee for the pot. Then I spoke up.

"I need you to explain to Irene what we are working on. She is not going to say or do anything to jeopardize our work, so please, for me, so I can talk to someone about this, please. Tell her."

Max put the percolator on the stove and looked at me. He was laughing. That surprised me.

"What's so funny?"

He took a moment to stop laughing and said, "Nothing. Go get dressed. You're standing here naked with me. I find that uncomfortable."

"Oh," I said. That makes sense, I said to myself. I went into the bedroom and found Irene walking in circles. What clothes could she wear? Hers were in a jumble in the entryway and still wet. My clothes were . . . well, my clothes. Could she, how could she, and I interrupted her confusion and pulled out some underwear and a shirt and pants for her so we could be with Max without making any of us any more uncomfortable than we already were.

I wanted Max to tell her everything. The burden of the estate weighed on Max and me because we were responsible for it. Irene's knowledge of what was going on would make her a silent partner. She had no legal claim on any of it, but it could not claim her either. I saw nothing but good news by letting Irene know what we were doing and what it all meant.

Max agreed. I looked at Irene to see if she was all right with this change in her status.

"I am glad to help, Scags."

"The most help you can be is to make sure Scags stays focused on these files every day so we can move the work forward," Max said. He looked relieved too. Not having to keep me at work by himself meant more could be done.

The files came day after day. I read them. I read them until I couldn't stand it. Then Irene brought me tea or a meal or we went for a walk. She moved in. She was always there, and I was happy about that until I was no longer happy about it.

I had intended to study for my baptism late that winter and early spring. Instead of that, I was swallowing whole enormous amounts of data about the money and where it came from and plans for how we could move it along.

I sat up nights studying the files. Irene fed me and sat with me. She slept with me and listened to my complaints. Why hadn't Margaret confided in me? I was too disturbed by where the money came from and the money-laundering we were involved in to plan how to get rid of it.

My moods became more explosive. I felt I could murder someone.

All else in my life disappeared. Irene and I lived in that box of an apartment. We went out at night for dinner at diners, and I pretended I was not among the most wealthy people in the world. I never let Irene leave my side. If she needed things from home, we went shopping instead and bought what she wanted.

I enjoyed buying her the necessities: underwear, hairbrush, sweaters, boots. I watched her brush her long black hair, which she kept wrapped up on the top of her head until bedtime. I then watched her take it down and brush it again. I liked undressing her, and watching her skin respond to my touch. She threw herself into being my lover as if she had always wanted me.

Then, a couple of weeks before Easter, things began to dissolve between us. There was that moment when one of us misspoke.

We were in bed. It was late. We were just home from a long walk in the not-so-cold weather anymore. We giggled and poked at each other, trying to ignite something. She looked at me from above, me on my back and she hovering over me.

I saw her eyes, but they were not seeing me. I knew that. I sat up, pushing her onto her back. She looked at me, wondering what I was up to.

"We never talk about Margaret."

"Yes, we do," she said.

"No, I talk about Margaret. You listen to me."

Her eyes began to fill with tears.

I held her jaw and held it hard. "I know you miss her. I bet you think that by sleeping with me, you are sleeping with her."

As soon as I said it, I knew I was right, but I never should have said it, not if I wanted to keep the peace we had established and that was keeping me sane in the midst of this indoctrination into the new economic world I now controlled. The money was filthy, and it was not ever going to lead to a clean life.

I got off the bed and went to the kitchen and sat down in the dark. A few minutes later, Irene came into the room and turned on the light.

"I'm sorry, Scags. I assumed you and I would find our way to each other by having Margaret between us. I miss her. I miss her very much. Even when the two of you were together, I missed her, but she was here, and we could all be together. That really became enough for me. I never stopped loving her, but she grew tired of me. We were too much alike, I think."

"You were nothing alike. Not a thing."

I shut up after that. I had much worse things to say, but I knew I had already said too much.

A worm entered my soul that night.

Irene went to bed believing that this storm would end, and we'd be fine. I sat up all night alone while the worm tunneled its way inside me. I was choked with anger and disgust.

Just as dawn arrived, I heard a voice that I didn't recognize speaking to me from the bookshelves where Margaret and I had long ago merged our various libraries.

Something "spoke." When I turned to hear it more clearly, a book fell off a shelf. I left it there, afraid to see which one it was.

From then on, the strangest things began to happen.

The next day, on my side of the bed, a book appeared. It was called *Lesbian Nuns*. I picked it up and began leafing through it. It was full of stories about what it meant to be a lesbian living in a closed religious society of women. Margaret had been a nun, and while she never took her final vows because of that "sin," she had never really denied her faith. It was what bound her to Irene.

I began to suspect that my baptism was part of a sinister pact that Irene had made with Margaret and then with the rector. I had no evidence for this. I just knew it was true.

I stood in Margaret's prayer room. I looked around. It was just as she had left it. I had not moved a thing. It smelled funny, and I thought it was my imagination. But gradually that smell began to penetrate the entire apartment.

I started obsessing about how faithful Margaret had been. Margaret said her faith was important to her. I told her I never understood that side of her. She only smiled. Now it seemed that she wasn't as faithful as she had said. How could she have been, with all that filthy money supporting every part of her life?

I doubted that her faith had good things to say about how we felt toward each other. Margaret could live in two worlds. She handled ambiguity and contradiction. I saw that. She started each morning in the prayer room and walked out of there with a big smile on her face, as if she had tricked God again. She walked to the bed where I still slept and kissed me on the lips. She played a big game on God and me and all of us. I saw that now.

And me? I acted the part of a good lapdog. I "worked" wherever she sent me, but always as a volunteer. We had no need of money. And I had no action plan of my own anymore. Margaret was the sun, and when she was around, I turned to her for the light and the warmth. When she was locked up, I sat still, staring into space. Or went to a museum to stare at one painting for the entire afternoon. Or to a concert, where I sat still, never moving throughout even the intermission, and hated standing up to leave the concert hall. Or I went to a movie, like the other things I did, by myself, and watched a movie over and over, from the late afternoon until the theater closed. I always had money, but I didn't know where it came from.

As the days hurtled toward my baptism, these memories took me over. Like an avalanche, crashing onto me, burying me in regret and guilt.

I knew I had not prepared for the solemn event I had signed up for. I knew what Margaret would think of how I was treating this sacrament. I was angry. I believed this would make her angry too.

Weird things kept happening at home, like more books falling off shelves or dishes falling and breaking on the kitchen floor. These things made me realize how some other force was opposed to me being baptized. It wasn't only me rebelling against this significant change in my life. Something, some *thing*, had entered into my life, into my apartment, and was demanding attention. The more I ignored it, the more destructive it became.

By the night of the Easter Vigil, the night of my baptism, I could no longer ignore this force. It wouldn't allow me to ignore it.

Irene didn't suspect what had entered into the apartment and was living with us. She went about getting ready to go to church as if this were a normal night. She ignored the scowl on my face and assumed it was nerves. Even as she and I walked to the church that night, and I wanted to talk to her, the dybbuk—the dybbuk was what I finally called it—wouldn't let me speak. I wanted to tell Irene to protect me or to take me away because it wasn't safe for any of us to be there. But just as in a bad dream, the words were in front of my face, but the power to say them had been taken away from me.

I couldn't run away or pull my hand out of Irene's grasp. Trapped and uncertain of what would be done to me, I prayed, yes, prayed, that I would survive the night. I knew no other remedy for the predicament I was in.

I sleepwalked through the entire service until the time arrived for the Bishop to ask the questions I couldn't answer honestly. I particularly could not honestly vow to not follow Satan when I knew Satan had entered me those last few weeks, and I had been unsuccessful in casting him out.

At the moment when the Bishop placed the water over my head and when the oil was seared into my forehead in the Sign of the Cross, I knew I had sealed myself into a tomb and there was no getting out. Taking Communion for that first time, I knew I was never going to find peace again if I continued as I had been. Change was necessary.

I returned to the pew after receiving Communion. Irene handed me a box as I began to sit down next to her. "This is what Margaret wanted you to have when you were baptized."

I knew what it was. It was the cross Margaret had worn as a young woman when she had left the convent. When Irene showed it to me, she told me that Margaret bought it to change the page but not the faith.

Irene opened the box and put the cross around my neck. The sound of the dybbuk took over. Like a million swarming flies, my mind buzzed with a noise that drowned out every thought except one—*Get me out of here*. I felt I would die of shame for all that I had done and allowed to be done in my name.

I ran back to the apartment and pretended to be asleep when Irene returned. She kissed me on the cheek as she lay down next to me.

I was awake next to Irene all night, breathing as if I were asleep. I knew what to do.

I crawled out of bed and packed a small paper bag with fresh clothes and a toothbrush. I put the cash I had in my pockets and left all the credit cards behind. Walking as quietly as I could, making no move that could possibly awaken Irene, I slipped out of the apartment and walked out of the building, deciding then to go to the garage around the corner to get one of Margaret's cars. I had to wake up the attendant. He was not happy about having to produce a car for me. He had to fetch it and make sure the tires were full, and none of this pleased him in the early hours of that morning. It was Easter.

The car—a VW Beetle—had a full tank of gas. He wanted to know how long I would be gone. I didn't know where I was going so couldn't know when I would be back. All I said as I drove away was, "As long as it takes."

Neither one of us knew what I meant.

CHAPTER THREE

As I drove out of the Lincoln Tunnel, heading west, the sun rose behind me, right over the city, causing a big gold light to show up in my rearview mirror. It blinded me when I looked. I took that as an omen. I kept driving west, toward Chicago, where I was born, for no reason whatsoever.

This is a story of grief. Grief is a long, circuitous journey. This chapter goes on a long journey, a road trip. Touching base in as many small towns in the nation's breadbasket as was possible with never a return visit. That was my goal, never to return to a place I had worked. That April morning, I drove toward Chicago, not calculating how close it was to my birthday.

I didn't want to look up old friends or stop at my mother's house. All that familiarity ended years ago when my mother kicked me out of the house when my Pops died. She had no tolerance for me being a lesbian. She had had years to think about having cut me out of her life. Not one word came to me from her. I took that not as an omen but as a fact.

I drove the long almost-straight road to Chicago almost straight through with few stops. You can cross the entire continental US on one highway and never get off it. In some places, it is a tollway, and in some places, it is free. But it is mostly a straight line that hypnotizes you. If you don't stay awake, you'll go flying into a field and not know how you did that.

For the entire drive to Chicago, my eyes moved from the rearview mirror to the front of the car with only one question on my mind: "What am I doing?" As I crossed the Skyway into Chicago, I still couldn't answer my question. I took the road north and decided to go to Skokie and see where I had grown up. Maybe driving through my hometown would give me a clue.

Chicago's rush-hour traffic was worse than I remembered. The manic drivers heading home woke me out of my road hypnosis. No matter how tired or hungry I was, I didn't want to die on that roadway.

By the time I arrived in Skokie, the sun had set. I had relied on faulty memories to get me there and got twisted around, lost and then confused. When I saw the moon rising in the east, I found my way. The moon rises over Lake Michigan. I remembered that and drove towards it. That got me to Lake Shore Drive and from there, going north was easy. The lake had to be to the right of me.

I cracked the window open as my anxiety had steamed up the windshield. The early spring air was bitterly cold, but that was what kept me awake until I slid along the curb in front of Mama's house, the house I grew up in. It still looked well maintained even in the dark. Lights were on in the living room, but the drapes were drawn so I couldn't see inside. At first, I was tempted to walk up the path to the front door and ring the doorbell. I imagined it reverberating through the house. But as I opened the car door, the living-room light went out. No one had turned on the outside lights, so I was stumped. Should I try to see them anyway?

I noticed a man sucking on an unlit pipe and walking a white standard poodle. I sat perfectly still. What should my next move be?

A sharp knocking on my window startled me.

"What the fuck—," came from my mouth as a bright light shone into the car, illuminating first my face and then the messiness on the front seat from my long hours on the road: empty candy wrappers, large soda bottles, browning apple cores. I rolled down the window. A policeman who looked too young for his uniform but wearing a very serious demeanor asked me for my license and registration.

"What's the problem? I just pulled in here," I said as I handed him the papers.

"Yep," he said and walked back to his patrol car. I waited. I noticed the man with the poodle standing near the cop who was leaning in to talk on his car radio.

I was annoyed at how unwelcoming a homecoming this had turned into. I waited for the papers to be returned with an apology. The papers came back though the open window, without a word, and the cop walked away. The man with the poodle continued his walk further down the street. I put the papers safely away and drove slowly to the corner of the street and made a right turn. No one else was about. I should have remembered how bleak life was in the suburbs.

I closed the window and screamed, "Shit!"

At the top of the hill, a sign pointed to a truck route. That sign seemed more promising than just wandering through Skokie, hoping for something familiar to tell me what to do.

I needed direction, ideas. I had nowhere to sleep and not much cash on me.

I stopped at a diner several miles later. When the waitress came to take my order, I hadn't looked at the menu but decided on a full breakfast. Diners serve breakfast all day long. Then I headed to the bathroom. I saw a rack of pamphlets and newspapers on the wall leading into the bathroom and grabbed everything that said "local." Back at my table, I spread the newspapers out alongside the omelette, toast and coffee. I ate quickly and drank lots of hot coffee. The want ads made no sense to me because I had no idea what it was I wanted. What kind of job could someone like me expect to find? I had borrowed a pencil from the waitress but had circled nothing.

When the waitress came by to yet again refill my coffee cup, she said, "It's a good time of year to get outdoor work. Don't apply for restaurant work unless you have to."

I looked up at her face for the first time. I saw pretty brown eyes looking down at me. Her nametag read "Sue," and she was cute, with freckles scattered across her nose and cheeks and a sardonic smile suggesting she knew more than she was saying. I wondered if she was also trying to pick me up. I was in need of a bed and a shower.

I grabbed the hand not holding the coffee pot to see if her smile disappeared. It didn't, but the eyes looked away as if to say, not now, I'll be back. I ordered a piece of pie and prolonged my stay in the diner.

That night I slept fairly well in Sue's bed. Before going to sleep, we had circled jobs that fit my circumstances: no references, no job history, no permanent address, in need of cash. Sue understood my circumstances completely.

She was also a great one-night stand. She had no expectations except to have some fun and company. An added benefit for me was the shower in her bathroom. It was almost enough of an incentive to make me want to stay longer. She had mornings off.

We sat in her cozy kitchen where the sun shone in on her clean counters and floor. The red-and-white checkerboard tablecloth was one of those first moments of recognition that I was no longer in the city. Country life was appointed differently.

We sat holding the handles on the big black mugs of coffee and each other's hands as the minutes of the day swept by.

I felt the need to push on, to get a job so I'd have a place to stay that coming night. I tried to be polite. It would have been easy to stay.

She was definitely sweet. "If you can't find a job, come back. Another PennySaver comes out next week. You're welcome to hang here for a bit."

The end of that sentence sounded like a question. I slowly turned back to her, staring only at her lips. I kissed her. She had been kind and helpful. Her kiss was brief. She knew I had left her.

Her parting words were, "Remember to have a good story to tell about who you are and why you need the job."

That was it. I felt a tug, a faint need to be the damsel in distress, but a different part of me got behind the wheel and started the car. Sue had gone inside. It may have been April, but the mornings were cold. My search for a job had to begin or I was going to turn around and drive back to New York City. It wasn't ego that kept me moving.

I knew what had scared me out of town. As I looked for work that first day, I felt the weight of those twin monsters that I could not reconcile and desperately wanted to forget—Margaret's estate and Margaret's death. Or was it Margaret's death and Margaret's estate?

I went from rejection to rejection. In most cases the jobs had already been taken, and there was no way to convince anyone of my desperation. The last job on the list was the farthest one out on the highway. By the time I reached the location, the sun had set.

In the dark, I walked from the parking lot of the Burns Family Farm to their back door, where an "Employees Only" sign had been placed in the window. The description of the job had read that they needed two workers to set up for the opening of the Farm Store on Memorial Day. Then the job ended. It meant four or five weeks of employment, a room, food and a shower.

I rang the doorbell on the side of the house where the "Employees Only" sign was posted and let that serve as an omen. A couple of dogs barked inside. I heard a chair scrape on a wooden floor. Voices speaking indistinguishable words. Footsteps. Then a light turned on above my head, and the door opened.

A woman stood before me wearing a heavy plaid shirt and dungarees. On her feet she had heavy green socks stuck into a pair of battered clogs. Her cheeks were all red, as I later learned, from standing over a hot stove making dinner. She didn't smile at me; she looked all business. I had been unable to convince anyone that day to hire me, so my plan was clear: she had to hire me.

"I've come about the job," I said.

She motioned me into the mudroom, but the cold air followed us inside. We had to stand very close to each other because the room was packed from floor to ceiling with boxes.

She noticed me noticing and said, "This will be out of here soon. Our winter clothes. Time to change."

She paused and looked at me. I wore a pair of jeans, a heavy sweatshirt and sneakers. I didn't look like a farm worker.

"I'm looking for work. I work hard. I'm happy to do anything . . ." My voice trailed off, waiting for her to say something, anything.

She stood silently beside me. I took deep breaths.

Finally, having made whatever calculations she needed to make, she said, "It's hard work with no days off until Memorial Day, when the job ends. It's room and board plus cash when you leave. If you can't finish, no cash. We have no room for error, but you look smart. Right?"

"Right." I didn't know how to read her or what she meant by me looking smart.

She smiled at last. "You don't look like those who come here looking for work."

She waited for the story. The story Sue said I would need to secure the job.

"I'm a widow." I paused to see if she had any reaction at all. She did, a slightly more relaxed face. I continued, "I needed to get away and do for myself."

She put her hand on my shoulder. "Get your things. Dinner is almost ready, and we can get you settled in the room after that. Just leave your stuff here."

I had found my first job. Ruth Burns had no idea who she hired but my blunt storyline, which was not totally a lie, worked. She went back to the kitchen and I brought my one bag indoors. I wanted to stand outside for a minute and say something of my gratitude for this job and this bed and food. But dinner waited, and I didn't want her to think I had taken off.

We ate in a large kitchen at a very long table, although there were only four of us at that time. The dinner was hearty and hot. I hadn't eaten all day, not since breakfast with Sue. And breakfast with Sue now seemed like it had happened to someone else. I was no longer that Scags, though I still used my name. I could not imagine how to be someone else, named something else; being on my own like this was disorienting enough.

Working at the Burns place, I learned about carpentry and stocking shelves but also about the fate of these farms that lay along the secondary roads. They were in bad shape; the farmers had sold off portions of their land because of taxes, mortgages and loans on farm equipment and seeds, and they lacked cash.

Farmers like Ruth and her husband Steve, who had no heirs, had no reason to hang onto everything. Their plan was to hold on to as much as they could until retirement, so they could sell off the rest of the farm and live on that money. These plans lived inside Steve more than Ruth. The farm had been in her family for generations. The house was a set of tacked-together additions to the main house. Everything was made of wood. But each addition had announced a greater number of people to work the farm and to keep it going from generation to generation. Ruth and Steve were the end of the line.

From prolific farm life to a mostly bare-bones existence, the Burnses were like so many people I met on my road trip. They cherished these fire traps, kept them going as best they could until their bodies began to resent all the work and lack of sleep.

As I jumped into bed that night, I set the alarm Ruth had put on the nightstand. It was an old collapsible travel alarm. You pulled these tiny knobs to set the time (4:30 am) and turned a little crank to wind it up. Its leather case was now cracked and the original color a lost memory, blackened by decades of hands winding and setting it. My Mama had one of those alarm clocks. It was meant for the trips she never went on.

Each morning, as soon as I got up, I took the shower I craved, but the water was usually cold. Then I clambered down the long flight of stairs for breakfast and the day's assignment, which was posted on a board near the door as we left for work. Lunch was brought to us. Dinner happened after sundown. Every lit hour of the day was used to squeeze as much work as possible out of all of us.

Ruth assigned all the work, cooked all the meals, washed all the clothes, and cleaned the house. Then she was in the fields, delivering lunches and working almost until we finished. Then she set up our dinner.

My job was to refurbish the store. Clean, paint, plant, put in the shelving, clean the refrigerators and freezers, and then finally start stocking the shelves.

I worked alone. Occasionally Ruth stopped in to assess my progress. She said little but kept moving, leaving my lunch on the counter. Her comments about the weather meant nothing to me. I had not yet lost my city view. That sensitivity to daily changes, anticipating frosts, smelling incoming storms, tracking snowfall, all that weather knowledge and concern grew with me as I kept to these secondary roads throughout the Midwest and then into the Mountain States. This first job meant only a bed, food, a shower and an envelope of cash at the end of it. I watched the calendar and not the sky.

Yet my past soaked through. Spending the days mostly alone, as well as the nights, I encountered varieties of memories that came completely unbidden. Shooting out of the night sky of my inner life, they flared brightly and then faded. More came and faded.

Living in silence for most of the day, I saw patterns in my life that had been there before I had taken to the road. I realized that my life had been a series of fortunate connections to wealthy people who had provided for me. Always the recipient of unasked-for sums of money that I wouldn't even have known how to ask for. My dead fiancé's family had been handing me envelopes of money since his funeral. It wasn't about the immediate pain, I soon understood, but about the future pain, when I would not be married to a very wealthy man.

Then I had met Margaret. Our affair became the topic of the tabloids for a short while, a supposedly lurid story leaked to the press to prejudice the judge against Margaret.

Charles' mother got hold of the story and wanted nothing more to do with me. In her slurred speech, having now had a minor stroke not helped by her drinking, she disowned me. Her "disappointment" in me could not be expressed adequately. But Margaret's finances ended up surpassing what Charles' family could have ever provided me. I kept living very well even in the face of Margaret going to prison and my own family disowning me. My orbit around Margaret "paid" off, as Charles' mother told me. I was the sort of person who landed on other people's feet, she told me. I don't know if she knew who she was quoting. But it made me smile as I hung up the phone on that last call with her. Margaret had been sitting right next to me and stood up from the bed as the call ended and patted my hand.

"I'm only too happy to catch you."

I thought about all those fortunate falls into money throughout my life. And then, I had decided to run away from the largest money pile of them all. Eventually, I would be cleaning toilets and picking up trash from the road, among many other paying jobs.

The days mattered to me as Ruth marked them off on her calendar. The closer we got to Memorial Day, the closer I got to leaving. I felt a fear of this new life. I had no confidence yet that I could take care of myself. All I knew was this long road ahead of me with the terror of looking constantly for jobs into an indefinite future. I started thinking, if only I could find a way to convince Ruth to adopt me, then none of this existential dread would take over my life.

The salient points were that I had added nothing of any substance to the stand and how it was run. I had no interest in any of the stand's work. I hit upon the change that would be required of me when each job ended. Nothing about the work I was setting out to do would ever make me indispensable to anyone. None of these new and future employers could be a substitute for Margaret. Once I recognized that, things got simpler.

The first thing I learned was the need to never set down roots. I had to keep moving. There was a Faustian bargain at play were I to feel that urge to stay put. I couldn't risk being found.

By the time the farm stand was almost completed, and Memorial Day was at the end of the week, Ruth came to the stand to take me for a ride with her. I had actually beaten the deadline. I hoped she would give me a bonus because I had no idea where to look for work next.

We rode in her Jeep out to where her husband and the other temporary worker, Dave, were in the fields, planting and working the ground.

She had her basket of sandwiches and three thermoses of hot coffee, one for me. No road existed out to the fields. The ground was muddy. We'd had so much rain I no longer feared that their house would go up in flames but that it would float away. When the Jeep was obviously not able to go any farther in the mud, we got out to walk. Having spent some of the money I hoped to get at the end of the job on proper work clothes, I had good boots that kept my feet dry and dungarees that were sturdy enough for all the work stress I put them through.

As we trudged up the hill to find Steve and Dave, Ruth talked about the ways things had changed on the farm since she was a girl.

"When I was a kid, a young girl didn't think, 'I'm not a boy so I can't do these things.' I milked cows and dug out stalls. I buried the dead calves and wrung chickens' necks. We went hiking far out into the back fields if we needed to get up early the next morning to get to work with the sunrise. I never thought at all about being a woman. I did my work, that was what I thought about. I don't understand these folks moving in here. Do you? Maybe you know more about this need for a hair salon and a nail salon every 100 yards. It seems like a waste of time and land to me. People pay now for all kinds of things that if I wanted to do them, I'd do them myself. The thing is, I hate thinking about these people and what they are doing around here.

"They live in houses that all look 'alike. They drive hours to get to the city, which they just left to live in the country. They want an 'authentic' country look, but they don't like the country and the mud and the animal stink. It's like they got sold something that was an idea, if you know what I mean, and not an actual thing."

"I think you're right. Living in the country is different from moving to the country."

She looked at me as if I had said something both too intellectual but also very good, and she was glad she understood it.

"I never got to say how sorry I am about you losing your husband. I don't know what I'd do without Steve. He is the real boss, you know. He wants something done, we do it. How'd he die?"

Her bluntness caught me unawares. I asked her, "What?"

"Your husband? How'd he die? Was it cancer or something?"

"Heart attack. A sudden one, in his sleep. I found him dead in the morning."

I stopped. This story was a total lie, and I didn't know how I was going to live with it.

"Oh my," Ruth said and took my hand. "I am truly sorry for that."

I looked away and then walked faster. She may've thought I was going to cry but I really wanted to scream at myself for betraying Margaret in such an awful way.

I ran ahead of Ruth and found the men sitting under a tree waiting for us. She caught up quickly and gave the men their sandwiches and we headed back to the Jeep. We didn't talk anymore about my dead husband.

On my last night at the Burns Family Farm, I stood outside in the parking lot. The lights were off, and the sky above me filled with stars. I craned my head all the way back to look at as many of them as I could. In that awkward position, I apologized to Margaret for how I had lied about her and her death.

Silence, the vast silence of the black sky came back at me. She was having none of my apologies. I had misrepresented her—and me too.

I had calluses and scraped skin to prove what work I had done. I had learned a great deal and didn't even know how much I had absorbed.

Memorial Day arrived, and the farm stand stood ready to meet and greet the customers arriving from the city for the long weekend, the start of summer. Ruth would be selling the goods I had stocked on the shelves, all the fresh jams and jellies along with the honeys and cookies neatly arranged with small signs telling the price of each. Tourists were needed to fill up the parking lot and to buy out the store.

Dave and I received an envelope filled with the promised cash for having completed the jobs the Burnses hired us for. We stood side by side saying goodbye to Ruth and Steve as if we were going off to war, never to return. I don't know if Dave returned, but I never came back. I never returned to any of the places I worked over the years I was away. That became a promise I made to myself—never return. That promise started then. I didn't want to be the returning widow.

As we walked to our vehicles, Dave turned to me and stuck out his hand to shake mine. He said the most amount of words he had uttered since I met him in April. "It was nice to work with you. Maybe we'll cross paths again."

He climbed into his truck and started the engine. I had the money in one hand, the one bag I owned in the other. I watched as he turned left out of the parking lot and headed north. I was heading north too.

I threw my bag into the back of the VW and climbed into the driver's seat. For one moment, I allowed myself to look wistfully around the parking lot at all the cars and the tourists pulling in to get their first taste of summer. I turned on the motor and pulled onto the road. I headed north for about 60 miles and realized it was a holiday, no one would be hiring. I needed a place to stay. I stuck to the blue highways because they reminded me of the veins on Margaret's hands. Because they weren't the major roads, they led me into small towns where I learned I would always find work.

Even on that hot Memorial Day, I found work. Sitting in my car, eating a sandwich I had bought in a previous town, I saw a sign on the church lawn right in front of me. They needed a groundskeeper. "Apply within." Okay. The church doors were open, so I went inside and looked for someone to ask about the job.

They were having a picnic for the holiday. The church entrance was filled with a knot of people picking up food and taking it to a lawn at the back of the church. I spotted a woman who seemed to be in charge and decided to ask her about the job. As I approached her, she came right to me. She took my hand and shook it, saying, "My name is Jane."

I decided to be as forthcoming. "My name is Scags," I said, "I saw the sign about the job. I need a job."

"Oh," Jane seemed flustered but quickly recovered. "It's a gardening job. Well, more like a groundskeeper job."

I was much taller than Jane, and I had not taken my eyes off her eyes. Maybe I was being a little too direct, I thought, and turned my head to look around the hall I had walked into. There were long tables filled with food and many different things to drink—more food and drink than I had seen in a while. Ruth Burns had fed us well, but it was not with an overabundance of food. And certainly not with the amount of cookies and cakes this church had laid out for their Memorial Day feast.

"Scags, is it? Quite a name. Quite an unusual name," Jane said as she tried to get my attention back.

I turned to look at her again. It was clear she had enjoyed the eye contact. I cleared my throat to remind her that I had asked about the job. I needed that job.

"Where you from?" Jane asked.

"I just finished working a job about 60 miles from here, at the Burnses' farm. I can give you their number if you want to call them for a reference."

Jane's eyes looked me up and down as if figuring something. Then she turned to the tables and said, "Load up a plate or two, get yourself something to drink. We have a small cottage out back for the groundskeeper, if that is what you want. The job is yours. We've had that sign up for a few days now. You're the first to apply for it. I hope you'll be okay with that."

"I'll be fine with it. Thanks."

I walked to the tables and smiled at everyone I met. I was giddy with the ease with which this new job had been found and then acquired. No lies. Lots of food. A little spot of my own. I felt confident in my work clothes. I didn't feel like I had come home, but that I had found what I needed. I had no idea how long this job would last or what it paid but it was already giving me what I basically required while on the road.

In those early days of my second job away from New York, I woke up happy to get to work. I didn't know how much I liked working outdoors, so it came as a wonderful surprise to me. I was my own boss. Other than Jane, no one at the church took notice of me, and that was fine too. There was always plenty of food around. I didn't need to spend my money on that. I learned quickly to always save my money, to put it away in case of some emergency. The car, for example; I wanted to always have a good car. I had lots of cars while I was on the road.

My job was not difficult, but it was strenuous. All the tools I needed were kept in a shed. They weren't put away in good order, so I spent some of my workdays taking care of them. No one bothered me there either. Once the priest came by as I was taking the tools out of the shed to clean them, and he asked me what I was doing.

"Sorry, I am at work here. I'm the groundskeeper."

He looked me up and down. I was taller than him and much younger.

As he walked away, he said, "Carry on then."

That was it. The women who always hung out in the kitchen were not eager to include me in their chatter, which was fine with me. They were generous with the food, and if I hadn't come in for lunch when they had lunch, they put a plate in the fridge for me, covered with aluminum foil. For dinner, I was on my own, but that meant I raided the fridge and ate whatever I wanted.

I picked up my check on Friday afternoons in the office where Jane worked. After a couple of weeks, I received an invitation from her. She asked me over for dinner that night.

Our sexual relationship began then and there. And like the way all things were done in that small town hugging the border between Illinois and Wisconsin, we wanted as little notice as possible of what we did on those weekends we spent together.

I liked my work on the grounds of St. Peter's Catholic Church. Jane was one of the two women who ran the church. I never went to Mass and neither did Jane. Her qualifications for her job were that she was very good at running things and keeping everything in order. No one had a bad word to say about her. Her religious views were not an issue but of course her sexual life could have been. She had to stay in the closet to maintain the equilibrium she had established in her life.

My work consisted of raking up dead leaves, carting trash, planting new trees and bushes, sawing down dead branches on the trees, and mowing the lawns. In those early days of my road trip, all I could think about was how I had done what I set out to do. Though that may not have been true. I don't think I could have envisioned doing all this tedious work, day in and day out, and set that as my goal. But my body didn't object to it, and I was able to take care of myself. That seemed to be a good-enough goal at the start.

I fell in love with the smells: the refreshed earth; the deep, black, wet soil drying in the sun; things buried underneath beginning to pop up; leaves popping on the bushes. Then there were the sounds of the birds flitting about, and the distress calls of the squirrels as I unburied their treasures. Bugs almost invisible to the eye nuzzling at the sweat on the back of my neck, real smelly sweat seeping out of my pores like a spigot had been turned on, making me feel as if I had been baptized again but in the salt and sweat of my work, not the pomp and ritual of an established church. The surprise at the end of each working day was that, though I badly needed sleep and food, having slept and eaten well, I wanted to get up and do it all again.

I didn't design any of the landscaping that spring; I followed orders. The church had a committee that oversaw the maintenance of the grounds. Anything they wanted me to do, I did. Mow the lawn weekly? OK. It didn't need it that often, and the sound of the big seated mower was offensive, as was the smell of the diesel fuel that ran it. But that was what they wanted.

Put out the sprinklers every Thursday night? OK. But the soil got too soggy. Moss began growing instead of a lawn. But the committee never looked at the grounds except to observe that they looked neat and maintained, so they were content. And I was content to have the weekly check that became cash as soon as I explained to Jane the need I had for it. I told her the truth. I had no bank account or credit cards. I needed cash. She didn't ask me questions and handed me an envelope with the cash every Friday. Along with the money came the cottage, and because Jane found me attractive, I also had a sexual partner.

Another benefit of life in that town was the movie theater. Movie theaters are wonderful places to be in the summer when you have no AC. There were other places to go to when the weather was too hot. The library was a great place to hang out, as was the one diner in town. No one bothered me in any of these places. Jane would never appear with me at any of them either. I was an anonymous person enjoying the peace and quiet of being tired enough from my job that I had very little troubling me.

I began a journal. At first, I only listed my earnings and expenses, the towns I lived in and the dates I was there. It was like a ledger because that was how I thought about my life. The pluses and minuses of my financial situation and the passage of time in places I had never heard of until I showed up in them. Then I began describing the new skills I learned and where I had used them.

The journals then became more than a ledger. But I have run ahead of myself here. During my time with Jane, I still viewed my life as if I were an accountant. Was there enough money for me to live on and take care of the car? That was all that mattered.

Being with Jane, I began studying what life was like for women stuck in these small towns who also were stuck in the closet if they were lesbians. Though, from my observations, too many women suffered from being stuck in those towns, and their sexual preferences didn't matter.

In that early period of the trip, while working at St. Peter's, everything was so new. The work I did, the people I met, none of that had any relationship to what I had done before heading out of town and trying to stay alive on my own. I had no basis for comparison between me and the people I met and what their upbringing had been like. Women in those small towns who liked to be with women lived deeply in their closets. Jane was one of the braver women I met.

What I observed early on, even as I worked for Ruth and Steve, was how deeply conservative the people who lived in the farming areas were. How this affected women was one of the slowly accruing lessons I learned. I began to see that five men ran each of these towns. They controlled the banks and the food and the distribution of all goods, as well as the real estate and the local government, including the police department. It doesn't take many people to run a small town. But that patriarchal control was firm, and it worked like a hand inside a glove—nothing worked outside of that glove.

Women suffer the most with that kind of financial and governmental control. It wasn't just the women they controlled but the animals as well. The brutality meted out to the animals could be seen as a warning to the women. I worked on dairy farms for a while, and then I had to stop. That work also convinced me later on to become a vegan.

I couldn't have known what was to come as I traveled. While living and working at St. Peter's, I believed that I had found the perfect locale and that I should find ways to make it a more permanent spot. And even if I had to leave for some reason, that was the kind of job and town I should be on the lookout for. But then I began to see the flaws, and how those flaws could affect me.

First, there were my encounters with Hunter. Hunter worked at the only movie theater. His father owned it, but Hunter did all the work that was necessary, from opening it in the afternoon to closing it at night. He ran the projector and popped the popcorn as well as cleaning up between shows. He must have been 19 years old.

On my days off, I went out to a diner for a quick lunch before heading to the movies. I sat mostly alone in the dark and cool theater with a bag of popcorn between my knees and a large bottle of iced tea at my feet.

I don't remember one movie I saw. I do remember the cool air and the salt of the popcorn and the sweetness of the iced tea. I remember Hunter. He was very tall and very thin. He looked like it hurt his spine to have to stand at his full height. He wasn't that much taller than I was, but he tried to pretend he was much shorter. I was one of the only people there on a regular basis. He needed someone to talk to, and a stranger in town who looked like she was not going to stay seemed safe to him. He didn't want what he said to get back to his father.

He told me about his life. About the sick father who owned the theater and never came to it. He complained the way someone who is proud of his ability to do what he does but doesn't want to do it complains. In the winter, business was much better than it was in the summer, which made staying at the theater harder on him. He wanted to be out swimming and hiking with all his friends, not stuck in the cold movie theater running films for a mostly empty house.

He wanted to convince his father to sell the theater. They owned the building but the taxes on it were too high for the business they did. What he wanted was to leave town.

"Where would you go?" I asked casually, thinking he had probably only known the world through the movies.

"I have an aunt in Rome. She always said I could visit. I'd like to see her and that city and all of Italy. I have been studying Italian. No one knows. I've taken all these books and tapes out of the library and been very diligent about my project.

"My father doesn't know anything. He hates his sister. He thinks she is living above her station in life and that she should have been here to take care of him."

He sat quietly in the seat in front of me, turning to confide his family history to me.

"I can see why that might not be what she saw for herself," was what I finally said to him.

"Right? See? I say that all the time to him." He practically jumped out of his seat that he had found someone who thought exactly as he did. "I say to him all the time, 'What do you think she wanted? Do you think keeping you happy was what she wanted out of her life?'"

The kid got silent. I could see what he was thinking. Anyone could have read his expression.

"I'm 19. I've graduated from high school. I'm either going to lie to my father and say I joined the army and leave, or tell him the truth and say I saved enough money to go to Rome to live with Aunt Edith."

"What's your name? I don't know what to call you."

"Hunter," he said, and when he tried to stick out his hand to shake mine, he found himself with a broom in one hand and a garbage bag in the other. His face was washed with the redness of the realization of the difference between what he wanted and what he was doing. We were still in the movie theater. He had to clean up before the next showing, which would be the last one for the day.

I shook his hand. Hunter was not a dreamer. His handshake made that clear.

"I'm called Scags," I said, and got up to leave.

"Thanks," he said to my retreating back. I raised a fist in solidarity and continued onward to dinner with Jane and maybe a sleepover.

A fixed regularity took over my life in sync with the regularity of the town's life. We do this on Friday because it is Friday, and that ethos was what kept things chugging along. Friday was our date night.

Jane made dinner. The same dinner every Friday. The exact same dinner, including the same brand of every item included in the meal. There was only one brand of dinner rolls and one brand of ice cream for dessert and one flavor of ice cream, and one did not add anything to the ice cream such as chocolate sauce or nuts.

We ate dinner, watched a movie on TV and then went to bed. We had sex; it was nice and made me feel good but not great, not inspired enough to tempt me to move in or to make this a long-term affair. If we got hungry in the middle of the night, Jane got up and made bologna sandwiches, and we washed them down with a can of beer. We spent our weekends like this, locked in a routine that never varied, and at first, as I accustomed myself to it, I was fine.

Jane's life was precisely laid out. A stranger like me added variety or maybe a spice. Jane was happy with this arrangement. She whistled all the time during the weekend. When Sunday night came, I packed up my small bag and left. Nothing was said. I walked out the door and as far as I could tell, I walked out of her mind too.

I returned to the little cottage behind the church. I liked walking back in that soft summer air. The week ahead had its regularity for me too. I worked. I went for walks, went swimming, saw a movie, read a bit and wrote in my journal. At the end of that, I walked to Jane's place for the weekend and settled in.

I had never experienced this routine way of living before. I didn't pick up the cues from Hunter, for example, that he became hesitant to talk to me so frankly again. I became too cozy at Jane's and offhandedly suggested that we try something new as I left her place one warm Sunday evening. I meant it as a suggestion.

Jane's head jerked back and forth. Her eyes said one thing and her mouth another. The eyes said, "Over my dead body."

She said to me and then turned away, dismissing the idea while seeming to leave the door open, "We can talk next week. Good night."

She never said "good night."

I walked home excited about the next weekend. Maybe things would get spicier, and we could leave her house, go for a walk, to a bar, to a movie. It had hit me when talking to Hunter that everyone's life was too stultifying. Everyone was in need of something more, or something different.

Jane and I never talked about ourselves. I was fine with that. I didn't want to have to make up a story or tell the truth. But that meant too that I had no idea how what I had only suggested the previous weekend had affected Jane.

When I arrived at her place the next Friday and walked into the kitchen, another woman sat at the table eating the same meal Jane and I always ate. I didn't know the other woman at the table, but she obviously knew about me. Certain things hung in the air like an invisible line of old underwear.

Jane didn't introduce us but only said, "This is a friend of mine. We're spending the weekend together. Sorry I didn't let you know. But you said you wanted to change the routine."

She sat down at the table and went back to eating her dinner. No one said another word. I turned around and left her apartment. The silence that followed me out the door reminded me of how little I knew about any of the people I met every day.

I took my time heading back to the cottage. A certain relief and giddiness came over me. I knew I could get along without Jane on the weekends. There were always things for me to do.

When I got to the cottage, I saw an envelope tacked to the door. I took it down and stuffed it in my pocket, thinking it was a note to say they wanted the sprinklers turned on this weekend. I felt exhausted for no good reason and wanted to sleep, even though it was still early.

I woke up very early the next morning and pulled the envelope out of my pocket to do whatever the committee asked of me. I opened it and some money fell out, not much, but a bit of cash. I read the note. I laughed out loud. They had fired me. It was time to get back on the road. My suggestion had shaken things up. "They fired me!" I said over and over. I couldn't believe it.

I showered and dressed in clean clothes and put everything else neatly into a duffel bag I had bought. I threw it into the car and then stashed all the money I had with me into my cash box. I had no idea how long it would take to find the next job. It was mid-summer.

I had had no time to do any research for which town would be the best after leaving the job at St. Peter's. I drove farther north along the country roads and hoped for a sign advertising some work.

I left that town without regrets or nostalgia or even sadness. That became the pattern. For whatever reason I left, I didn't feel bad about leaving or wish things had been different. The back roads of the breadbasket states have pockets filled with little towns and villages that were once thriving hubs of industry or mining or manufacturing and now were only remnants of what had been vital a long time ago.

That Sunday morning after I left Jane's town, I sat in a McDonald's. Folks were holding a prayer meeting over their Big Macs because all the churches were gone in that town. Even the churches had died along those roadways; it was a rough life all of us lived then. I continued moving, and despite the warning regarding working in restaurants, at some points along my circuitous routes I had no other options. Indoor work had its benefits. My journal filled up with all kinds of insights I gained working for cash—"living very small," as I called it. No matter where I was, I made sure that I could leave anywhere at any time.

A year or so later, on a different swing through Wisconsin, farther north, I had a new misadventure. I was in dairy country, but the area had not been dairy country for that long. The farmers were dependent on a migrant labor force that had originally come to the US to pick vegetables in the fields. But that way of life in Wisconsin had died and been replaced by the dairy industry. That industry, in order to make the profits it wanted, had begun milking cows three times a day. In order to do that, they needed a consistently large workforce to handle the work schedule.

The constant milking was brutal on the cows. It was also enforced on the workers in such a way that even though many of them had been born in the US, they could not find their way to citizenship because the dairy association stood in their way. The cows were miserable being kept to this schedule, and as their udders became sore and then bruised and infected, they were not easy to handle as they were rounded up to be placed into the stalls where they were tied to machines that pumped out the milk.

I knew nothing about migrant labor in Wisconsin or the effects of the milking schedule on cows until I arrived in the area. I had not worked on a dairy farm. I had worked in the fields picking crops on small organic farms. That was backbreaking work, as you can imagine, and hot and tiring. I didn't last very long. I was too tall, too leggy to get that close to the ground for long periods of time. I was better suited to running machines and then learning how to fix them.

It was late fall, and the nights were getting much longer and colder. I spotted a woman walking along the road far ahead of me, but the roads were straight lines, and I knew soon I would catch up to her. She carried several bags of groceries. When I pulled up even with her, I slowed the car down and rolled down the window. I asked her if she wanted a ride.

She stopped in her tracks and looked at me and sighed out loud with relief. Her face showed me how much she needed a lift, and even if she only needed to go another 500 feet, she needed a ride. She spoke little English; I spoke no Spanish. I let her settle into the car and took the bags from her and put them in the back seat. I rolled all the windows up and turned the heat on higher. No one was on the road but us. She could have died walking back to her village and no one would have seen her. I didn't want to stare at her as she caught her breath and warmed her body. The skin on her face looked ancient and sacred. I had never seen skin like that. The color reminded me of terra cotta, and the lines running through it spoke to me of tears, lots of tears flowing like a rapid stream finding its way into a country of discontent and misery.

She realized I was staring at her, and she tried to cover her face with the scarf she had around her head.

"It's okay," I said in the way of an apology. "Show me where you live."

She was a good navigator and knew how to signal the way even as the sun set and the roadway turned completely dark. There were no streetlamps in rural areas.

The most light you could hope for was from the moon when the sky was clear or briefly lit moments when passing a lighted farmhouse close enough to the road. Otherwise, all you could see was what the headlights lit up in front of the car.

I had ditched my old VW Bug and its conspicuous New York plates. I was then driving a small truck. It had enough room in back for me to sleep if I needed to. It was my home on the range. I offered the woman water. It helped her stay awake to guide me to her camp.

I drove slowly. The sun had set, and I didn't know the roads. By the time we reached the camp, I realized that she had been sent to buy the groceries for a large group of workers. They lived on a dairy farm, and the stench of cow manure, urine and mud overpowered me as I got out of the car to retrieve the groceries.

Her name was Josefa. She took my hand and led me to the fire where the entire camp was gathered for the warmth and the cooking of food. As I approached, another woman stood up to offer me her upside-down bucket to sit on. The fire danced around the shadows and onto everyone's face. The fire etched out the tired lines on their faces. Even the children looked as if they needed a long sleep. They didn't run around as children usually do but hung onto the adults and crawled into their laps like small animals in need of petting and food. I didn't know if anyone spoke English. There was so little chatter except to tell a child to be still or to instruct someone who was cooking to stir the fire more.

I remember Josefa's face. Her face was repeated on all the women's faces in that camp. I stayed with them, but only for a very few days. Their exhaustion became mine very quickly. The smells, the kindness and the harsh routine to milk the cows overwhelmed me. Everyone shared a bed. A watering hole that was used by the cows was where we all bathed.

I tried to keep up with the work, but I couldn't. It was brutal, and the cows were angry and sore from the constant abuse. I remember the angry looks in their eyes as we herded them to the machines to hook them up for the milking. Their nipples had large open sores, bleeding and tender. Hooking up the machines to milk them caused them to panic in anticipation of the pain. While we pushed the cows into the slots where the hoses were, my body acted strangely. It didn't want to do the work. It refused.

The men and women I worked with had taken a huge risk to allow me to work with them. I was not on the work roster. They were sharing space and food with me and there I was, acting as if this work was beneath me. They were deeply insulted.

I could not keep up. I would not keep up. I ran around looking for a salve to put on the cows to alleviate their pain, but there was none. If a cow became too much trouble to milk, she was separated out and sold for meat. The routine was the routine.

The man in charge, a white man, always shouted at us to keep the cows moving, keep the machines milking.

I became a liability. I could tell that Josefa worried that I would make trouble. She asked me to leave. No white woman ever worked with them.

I had been trapped there by my worry for her. But given the extreme poverty of the place where we all shared beds on a rotating basis and the food supply was minimal and the toilets were permanently backed up, I had to agree with Josefa that I was indeed a burden on them.

I had a luxury none of them had. I could quit without being paid. They knew that and weren't sad to see me go. All I had to do was get in the truck and drive off, which is what I did.

I didn't say goodbye. What could any of us say? "Thanks for not needing to be paid, thanks for eating our food and causing us to cover for your inexperience?" And would my reply be, "Thanks for making me see a world I never knew existed and that I am powerless to change?"

I knew I was wealthier than any of them would ever be; they never would have believed how much money I had walked away from in New York. As I headed to a main highway searching for a diner where the food would be hot and plentiful, I hoped not to see another Josefa along the road. I wanted to live in my relative wealth that day and order a fried breakfast and drink too many cups of hot coffee.

I pulled my journal out of my bag. The journal had not seen me in a few days, but I thought the events with Josefa deserved words. I didn't want to lose whatever it had been that made me want to work with them. I didn't understand it then. I heard my stomach growl so loud that everyone in the diner must have heard it. The place was packed with people off work having their dinners. Plates of fried chicken and mashed potatoes and corn covered in gravy came past my table. There were huge chunks of beef hanging off the sides of plates, red and bloody-smelling, with gobs of creamed carrots and big steaming baked potatoes filled with butter and sour cream.

I might have been in a horror show the way my stomach then turned on me, reminding me where I had been, what I had been doing.

Despite the cost and my hunger, when the food arrived on the table in front of me, I couldn't eat it. I looked at my plate and then at the plates of all the other people gorging on animal parts served up with varieties of dairy, and I could not put one forkful in my mouth.

I had never felt such a kinship with the animals before. I looked at my plate and saw Josefa's face. I knew she would have cried to be able to eat what I was going to throw away. I put my journal back in my bag and asked for the check. The waitress wanted to bag the food for later. I assured her I would never eat it.

"I hope you aren't sick, dear," she said and walked the plate back to the kitchen. She looked as if she would never uncurl her nose from the disgust she felt for me. I understood.

All day long, she was pushing plates of food like I had just refused to eat and believed that she was doing a good thing. I understood that.

I left the diner and got into the truck to look for a motel. I had only stayed at a motel once before, but this was an emergency. I had no job, I was exhausted and I needed to sleep and shower. I also needed to figure out what had happened to me and what that would mean as I moved on.

I pulled into a motel thinking I was going to stay one night, but there was a "Help Wanted" sign in the window, and I got a job. It wasn't my first experience working in a motel. Being a maid was hard work but left my mind free to do as it pleased.

I needed the money, and I also needed a break from the farms and being outdoors. I hated the smells of the cleaning fluids and the way they made my hands dry up and the way they seeped into my mouth, making me gag, but it was work.

Then one night, I had a dream. The dream was more like a memory of what I had done to a cow. I held a cow's head in my hands. I was pushing her into a stall so she could be milked. Her head was large, and she had trouble breathing because she was frightened. I heard her shortness of breath and smelled her distress. I felt her weight pushing against me. Cows are big, and when they don't want to move, you have to use force. I put my shoulder into her chest, my arms wrapping themselves around her neck. Everything I did was wrong. She refused to move.

In my dream, I held the memory of my shoulder against her chest and my arms embracing her, as I wished her to move and needed her to move. She put her head on my head. Then she jerked her head up and down trying to end my thoughts that she should move against her will. I stood up and pulled her face into mine, looking right into her big, fearful eyes. Out of me came a roar. I had given up trying to convince her to move. I roared because I couldn't stop what was about to happen to her. She watched me watching her as they dragged her away to kill her. A look resembling compassion crept into her eyes. I took a step forward to rescue her but instead someone handed me a stick to beat her with, to move her along. I wanted to go back to hugging her, but instead I had to beat her.

She shouted out with pain and despair. She had been tricked. Again. She went mad, full-out mad at all of us. She screamed and screamed, and when she fell to her knees, crying, as if begging me for help, I woke up. I couldn't stand it any longer. In life and in my dream, I had not saved her.

For a few moments I lay in my bed, and when I fell back asleep, I was still standing between her and the men who wanted her dead. I watched the cow on the ground. The men walked away, throwing their sticks into a corner of the stall. She was exhausted and covered with wounds. I slept with my head on her head, listening to her breathe. Soon she was dead. They dragged her body off like she had never been alive and threw it into the back of a truck to be taken to a meat factory, cut up and sold off. She was gone.

For the next few nights, when falling asleep, I felt her chest again. I heard her heart beat. I felt the breath coming out of her onto my face and neck. I kept dreaming about that bulk of her, how broad her chest was, how strong her legs were, and how beautiful her eyes were.

Farmers weren't usually willing to hire women because they thought the work was too hard. The work was hard. I had learned on the job how to keep myself healthy and safe. Working on a farm with animals meant looking into the eyes of those who were going to be killed.

When I had learned how to kill and clean chickens, I had sung to myself, "If Margaret could see me now."

I had learned how to milk cows and to load them onto trucks to take them to slaughterhouses, seeing the looks of terror in their eyes but refusing to pay attention. I was still learning and while learning, I had allowed every atrocity to be committed in front of me and had said nothing.

The brief time I worked with Josefa on the dairy farm changed it all.

I realized at that point that what Margaret and I had imagined was to be our life on a farm was nothing at all like what life on a farm was. We had shared a hazy dream of our perfect, bucolic life, where flowers bloomed effortlessly and food appeared on the table without ever killing an animal.

But I no longer was the same person who I had learned to depend on while on the road. I now felt so guilty about my complicity that I burned myself at the stake for my own involvement in this barbarity. I was overwhelmed with self-disgust. I still blamed Margaret for the sad state of my life.

This revulsion cost me in terms of what jobs I could take and how much money I could count on making.

But work was the answer to every problem. As a motel maid, I moved from room to room along the floors I was assigned, and my mantra became: "No milk, no cheese, no ice cream." I laughed. I could survive just fine without them. No more chicken, no pig, no cow. No longer eating meat would not be a problem, I told myself, because I rarely had the money to buy a hamburger.

I was like a child who had recently discovered a big secret and wanted to hold tight to it because it made her feel special. I worked my shift and then went to the little closet of a room the motel let me use and made myself a pot of rice and beans. I had been eating like this before my big discovery, but my conviction made it new, all new to me.

No dairy. No meat. No eggs. Like so much that has happened in my life, I met a woman who helped me learn how to live this new life.

I left the Midwest and that motel job and many more until I was in Wyoming.

Cheryl lived in a small town in Wyoming. I lived with and near her for a long time as long times went in my life on the road. She was my first vegetarian.

She was younger than me, but with an older person's acceptance about things she knew she could not change and an understanding that she could not change others to see what mattered. While she seemed vastly experienced in the ways of the world, she had never traveled more than 10 miles from the town I met her in. But she was a songwriter, an artist with a vast imagination, dreaming of places she had never been. Saying that she sang from her imagination neglected to mention that she also hit on those deep places we all want to live in. She aroused great feelings in many in that town. For some, I thought, her songs were a way to go away and never have to pack a bag. Cheap tourism was the kind most of the town could afford.

Cheryl was buried deep in the closet for her own protection. But we knew each other the moment I started my job at the restaurant where she sang on weekends.

Cheryl didn't dream of being a recording star. She was at home where she lived and wanted never to leave. She enjoyed the constancy of her performing life and the time she had to write new songs and the friendly audiences she had to try them out on. Her songs were like clothes that were changed based on the season. And then when that season ended, they were put away. She wrote hundreds of them and was meticulous about storing them. She had two three-drawer filing cabinets in which she organized her work. In labeled folders, she kept track of the constantly evolving music she wrote. The filing cabinets sat covered in plastic tablecloths in her kitchen. They served as her kitchen table and the counter where she chopped and prepared her food.

She lived above a coffee shop. Her small place was as organized and neat as the arrangement of her work in the cabinets. She had rudimentary sound equipment. Her guitars, banjo, ukulele and mandolin hung from the rafters. The window sills were covered with potted plants, herbs and small sprouts, as well as ripening vegetables and some of the stones she had collected from the shore of the river that ran through the town. Baskets of onions and apples and potatoes hung in front of the windows.

The first time I walked into her place, I couldn't believe how organized a life she led, and it wasn't one of drab sameness and routine meant to keep her real life at bay. She lived her artistic life, her culinary life as fully as possible. It was her real sexual life that had to be kept out of sight and that caused the problems.

Her small town was organized around the "five guys" principle: five guys owned everything, and they decided who would survive and who would not. They too were very organized, and that organization made them powerful.

Cheryl had survived by keeping her true sexual desires a secret. She gained further protection by having a sexual liaison with a son of one of the five guys. It helped that he was married.

When I met Cheryl, she was singing on weekends in a restaurant at the golf club. I washed dishes and when needed, filled in for the busboy. I could not have been in a more lowly and therefore invisible position, but Cheryl spotted me right away and came into the kitchen during one of her breaks to get a glass of water. I think she was there to check me out. I didn't look like much when I washed dishes. My face was flushed from the hot water, and my hands and arms covered in long blue gloves, with a messy black rubber apron covering me to keep me from being burned by the hot water. I was not quite the sex toy she might have been looking for.

Cheryl slid into the kitchen and looked around, making sure no one else was in sight. She walked up to me and stood there. I looked at her. She looked like she sounded when she sang. I had trouble hearing her voice fully through the filters of the water and other kitchen noises, but I fell in love with her voice immediately. For the first time in a long time, I felt love without hesitation.

When I saw that she too was feeling that way, that her eyes reflected that same startled sensation, I almost cried.

Cow towns were brutally masculine and conservative. I was tolerated because I worked hard, and no one supposed I wanted to hang around. Cheryl took a chance even standing next to me. We both knew that. But she took that chance. It was wonderful to stand next to a woman who smiled so fully at me.

"I need a glass of water and maybe later a bit of the potatoes and salads that are left from tonight's dinners," she said to me as a way to explain why she was in the kitchen.

She confused me. She wanted the same food I relied on. Not many meat-and-potato people actually ate their potatoes and few ate their salads.

She saw the startled look on my face and laughed.

"Ah hah, you too?"

"Me too what?" I liked her laugh.

"You don't eat meat? You're a frigging vegetarian, aren't you?"

I wanted to say something that would keep her laughing. But I had nothing to say other than, "Oh, yeah."

"Stick around after I finish work. I'll make us something better than potatoes and a salad. You'll see, I'm a great cook as well as a great singer."

Then she left the kitchen with a big glass of water in her hand. But she managed to wave at me as she headed back to the stage, and I resolved not to count on a meal cooked by her. It had been enough, I assured myself, to spend those very few minutes with someone like her.

She went back to the stage. She sang songs about the difference between loneliness and loving to be alone. She had a couple of songs about the emptiness of love that made me wonder if she was singing to me. She ended her set with songs about her love of the sky and mountains, something everyone listening to her knew all about. I only knew that I wanted to know her better.

I couldn't be open about my interest in her. I couldn't go into the bar and wait for her. But she did return to the kitchen as she promised and did cook dinner for us. She made a big bean dish filled with spices and greens and a lot of vegetables, which she got from a farm in the morning to collect for her dinner at night.

As we sat eating what was at that moment the most delicious meal I had had in years, she talked. I had nothing to say about my life.

She was pumped up from performing. I was hungry. She talked about her music, and when the manager came into the kitchen and saw us having dinner together, he made nothing of it; he was eager for me to close up for him so he could go home. I lived in a trailer behind the clubhouse. What he'd overheard of our conversation was insignificant. We both enjoyed eating vegetables and had been listing the ones we liked best. That soon became our cover. We were the only vegetarians in town.

Part of my pay included that trailer behind the clubhouse. That way, I was available for deliveries and for closing up at night. The trailer was small, but I had very little to put in it and only used it to sleep. The surrounding country was beautiful, and I hiked in the mountains during the day.

At first, I didn't care how long I held onto the job, so I was careless about my responsibilities. If I missed a delivery or I was slow in opening the place up, I had no guilt. I had stopped in that town to rest from my travels and because I wanted to explore the mountain trails. I put up with the bad pay, the bad food included in my pay, and the trailer because of the mountains. They put up with me because I did a halfway decent job without complaining and because, since I ate no meat or dairy, I was actually putting money into their pockets.

Meeting Cheryl changed everything. First, she was my food buddy. We cooked together at night after she finished working.

Then we began going on day hikes and swimming in the streams. As we increased the amount of time we spent together, we began going to the farm to pick up the food for the night's dinner, and sometimes we stayed for a while. The farmer was coincidentally named Ruth. I began to learn about what made food organic. My life became filled with the time I spent with Cheryl. Picking up food or hiking or swimming, we began a fling with the start of summer, and what I had thought was a brief rest stop became a longer sojourn.

I learned to cook better for myself. I learned how what I ate affected my health and my emotions, though the emotional part may have been a subsidiary of the feelings I had for Cheryl.

While Cheryl enjoyed spending time with me too, she also needed to work. She needed to practice and to write music. Her place was too small for both of us to be there then.

I went to the library. Every town had a library. They became my home. They offered shelter when it rained and bathrooms and free information about where I could find work next. I could read and read and never have to create a library of my own.

Libraries were churches. The safest refuge from any storm and the place to go when trouble mounted. Nothing soothed me like reading a good book. Libraries offered a sanctuary where I could sit for hours.

That year on the road, the year in which I had fallen in love with Cheryl, I began keeping much better track of what it was like to be an itinerant worker. I carried with me a composition book that I began filling up. I liked composition books because they had mottled covers in a variety of colors. I wrote my name in big block letters in the square in the middle of the cover. I liked the blue-lined pages that were the same color as the blue lines on the highway maps. These books were cheap and could be found in any place they sold school supplies, which included drug stores, dollar stores and even post offices.

As my journal-writing took on a more demanding presence in my life, I stopped writing about my life as if I were an accountant and began to tell the stories of the people I met and the things I had learned from them. I noticed the size of towns and if they were large enough to buy a pair of pants. If there was a post office and how many gas stations they had. Was there a liquor store and a grocery store. Was there a doctor or a lawyer. How about a good mechanic? In this documenting of my life and where I had been, I recorded what it was like to wash the floors of post offices and sheriff's offices, clean up the parks after motorcycle gangs came through and trashed the latrines, or how heavy the metal trash cans were that I lined up on a Sunday night for the local sanitation guys to remove and empty and return for me to place back where they had been. I got paid in cash, always, and moved on when it was time to go. The cash filled my cash box. It kept the gas tank full and bought me rice and beans along with some beers on occasion.

On some days, it bought me the time to sit outdoors with nothing to do and nowhere to go. I sat in a field from sunrise to sunset. With some bread and fruit and a bag of nuts and maybe carrots, the crunching of my food was the only sound I made.

I heard the grasses blowing. I heard the sun warming the rocks and the leaves whispering to each other. Snakes swooshed through the weeds and around the rocks. Birds dropped in to watch me eat and waited for some of the food to be shared with them. Breadcrumbs, apple cores and ends of carrots never went to waste.

The slow-motion light show of the sun kept me company. I'd sweat and swallow water, feeling the coolness slide down to my gut. Those were still and placid days. I'd sit, not thinking what my life meant or how to make good use of it. Nothing mattered.

When I taught myself to sit still on the not-so-nice days, with the rain and cold falling all around me, what captured my attention was how the mist covered up most of what lay before me. At those times I listened to the drops hitting my poncho and the rocks at my feet. My poncho became a tent as I sat on the cold ground, eating the same food. With each bite, I saw my breath curling out of my mouth. No bird sat patiently waiting for a handout. I got cozy with my loneliness.

I wrote about those experiences in the library. I discovered through this accounting of my finances and my experiences that I had learned to do a number of things I had never known how to do. The skills I picked up while working from job to job were vital skills. At that time, I had no idea where else I would use them, but they saved my life.

I began the practice of assessing my life in the library. It was easy to do and made the time go quickly before it was time to return to Cheryl's for dinner and some cuddling. If I implied we had an easy affair, that would be false advertising.

In addition to spending time with me, Cheryl had a boyfriend, Steve. He was a necessary part of her life. He gave her cover for what we had between us. Though he didn't know that at first. He also had lots of money and could provide Cheryl with the instruments she loved to play and the sound system she required. His father was one of the five guys in town. He owned the golf club where Cheryl sang and where I worked. Steve was much meaner than his father, and he was also possessive. Though married, he kept a tight hold on Cheryl.

We, therefore, had to be careful about being seen together. I learned quickly to honor the space she lived in. It was there that she could be the complete Cheryl. If I showed up to have dinner with her and there was a red scarf in the window, I scampered away quickly. That meant stay away and don't even breathe her name. Steve was with her.

Cheryl built a space awash with her creativity. It flowed from her. The light that rushed in off the mountains at the end of the day heated up her herb garden. The herbs scented her home and spiced her food.

Though her life was circumscribed by the poverty of possessions and the lack of access to more female lovers, she made music, and that was what mattered. She needed money for the recording equipment, her instruments. None of that could be bought with the tips she made singing in clubs. Steve and she had a bargain, and I was a threat to that bargain. I knew that. The time we spent together also made her happy. We were trapped and thought we could beat the odds, which were not in our favor.

I loved seeing Cheryl naked. She loved holding and touching me. She had a tough and beautiful body that had scars, bigger and more awful-looking than mine. Mine came from working. The burn scars came from stoves, and the puncture wounds on my side I got falling off a tractor. Her body was more delicate than mine, and her scars were not ones of pride of work but ones of abuse. I didn't care about my scars. They were not awful and not that multiple. Her scars, which she finally let me kiss, came from the violence of a man who didn't know how to love.

I knew we needed to be careful. But I was careless because I thought I was invisible. Who sees the dishwasher in a club, a transient whose name no one knows?

It wasn't obvious to me how brazen I had become. Two-plus years on the road, most spent in towns like that one, and I should have known better. Worse than that, I had not learned that no one was going to voluntarily leave these towns with me no matter how much I loved them.

One night, sitting at the bar after work, I was too obvious about how much I loved her. Steve sat next to me at the bar. He watched her, and he watched me.

When Cheryl said, "Steve looks at me like I'm his prize steer," I misheard her as pleading with me to take her away.

I didn't become jealous on the nights they spent together. I believed she was sleeping with him but fantasizing about me. I didn't listen to her or to the vibes in the town around me.

I lived in my own world. The experiences I had in cattle country, of seeing the brutality cows were subjected to, I had not wanted to see the same brutality come right out of the barnyard and into the bedroom.

One night a few weeks later, I sat side by side with Steve at the bar, listening to Cheryl's last set. I knew all her lyrics. He jabbed me with his knee and when I turned to say something, he looked at me, laughed and offered me a beer.

I said no, and the no was said in a way that made him suspicious of me. He watched and saw me get lost in her. I wasn't careful. I didn't want to be careful.

I was planning our escape. I was going to tell her that I needed to leave. I needed to be where I could get better work. Staying around was costing me money.

I wanted to move on. I wasn't happy leaving her, but I didn't like how Steve treated her, and I thought she should leave with me.

We talked that night about me leaving, and I considered telling her that we could go to New York where she would never worry about money or Steve again. But I never said those words. We made love and fell asleep.

My car was packed. It had been packed for days. I wanted us to go in the morning.

That night, while we soundly slept in each other's arms, Steve crashed through the door and into Cheryl's place. As soon as Cheryl heard him, she told me to take my clothes and get into the closet. I moved from her embrace and leaped off the bed into the closet with what I knew were my clothes, and lay on the floor, listening to him tearing up the apartment, and her. He trashed everything—the instruments, the plants, the kitchen and the recording equipment. She screamed, but she knew no one would save her, and I did not save her. I stayed curled in a ball while he destroyed as much as he could.

When the noises stopped, I stayed in the closet, not daring to move, terrified he was waiting for me to emerge and to then pounce on me too. Slowly, I put my clothes on in the closet. I opened the door and crept across the floor, looking for Cheryl. I didn't dare to turn on a light, but the floor was covered with the shards of her life, making little cuts on my hands as I tried to find her.

When I did find Cheryl lying naked on the floor, she was unconscious and broken in ways I could not explore in the darkness.

I pulled her body into my lap. Then I realized I needed to move her. She was alive. She was breathing, but I had no idea what damage he had done to her. Despite all the noise Steve made destroying the apartment and Cheryl's screams, no one had rushed up the stairs to save her. I was going to have to get her help or she'd lie in that busted place and die.

I bundled Cheryl up in the blankets from the bed and carried her to the doorway. I tried to see what I should take with us. I saw nothing but the ruin of the place and the pieces of her life scattered everywhere. I picked her up and waited at the top of the stairs to make sure no one waited for us.

I carried her down the stairs, across the yard to my car. It was out of the way but ready to leave town.

When I got her into the car, she was still breathing. I lifted her blood-soaked hair away from her eyes and told her we were on the way to a hospital. I don't know if she heard me. My hands shook on the steering wheel, and I didn't turn on my headlights until we were well out of town. I kept my eyes on the road behind me as much as the road in front of me. I needed to make sure no one watched us leave.

Five miles out of town, I turned on the headlights. I drove in the direction of a hospital based on a sign I had seen as we left town.

From time to time, Cheryl moaned. She was alive. I put my hand on her forehead to let her know I was with her. It took thirty minutes to find the hospital. I drove straight to the emergency-room entrance.

A nurse came out. I think she wanted to tell me not to park there, but when she saw Cheryl, she ran inside for a gurney and others to help her.

They lifted Cheryl in her blanket carefully from the car and put her on the gurney. She never made a sound. I hoped she was still alive. From the way they were dealing with her, she was, and they asked me to follow them inside. I knew I needed a story.

I wanted to run away. Looking at me, they saw I was drenched in sweat and covered in her blood. I had been a coward all night, and I needed to know if she would live. There was no one else in the ER. Cheryl got their immediate and full attention. I watched them slowly pull back the blanket once they had her in a small examining room. Her naked body shone with the bright purple bruises and the deep red of the gashes where blood still burbled out of her.

A nurse stood beside me with a clipboard in her hand and asked me if I was okay. I looked down at my bloody clothes and hands. I told the nurse I found Cheryl lying in the road and put her in my car to bring her to the hospital.

I said, "But I'm fine."

I wasn't fine. I was high on adrenaline. I could have made up line after line of a story for that nurse all night long. But then she wasn't standing beside me. She talked to a doctor. Then she returned to me and asked, "I don't suppose you know her name or where she's from? Did she have any ID with her?"

"Nope. I just saw her in my headlights lying on the road and she didn't have a thing with her. The blanket's mine."

"That's it? That's all you know?"

"Yep. She never talked, and I didn't know if she was alive or dead. I didn't know what to do but bring her here."

"All right. Take a seat. The sheriff is on his way to take a statement."

That changed everything. I could not give a statement. I was not going to lie my way out of this. As soon as the nurse walked away, I left the hospital. I never said goodbye to Cheryl. I have no idea if she survived that beating, and if she did survive, where she went after she recovered. I never went anywhere near any of those towns again.

That night, I drove into the woods and got out of the car. I felt like I was sleepwalking, and when I woke up in the morning with the sun peeking over the horizon, I was lying with my head on the flank of a deer. I don't know how that happened, but I appreciated the warmth she generated. Her gentle breathing must have kept me asleep. But waking up, I could see the extent of the blood from Cheryl on my clothes and on my body. I took off the clothes and found a stream nearby and soaked in it. I then burned the clothes and buried them in the ashes of the fire I had built. It was time to trade in the car.

I was haunted for months by Cheryl's screams and Steve yelling at her to shut up while he destroyed her and the apartment. I managed to find someone willing to take the car off my hands and sell me a piece of junk I could drive for a while until I had more money for something more reliable for the winter.

While I changed the plates on my car, I had the radio on and heard the news about a woman found alone on the road naked and badly beaten up. There was no mention of whether she was talking. Maybe Cheryl woke up and could tell them what happened. I didn't want to wait around to find out. I needed to get far enough away that news of Cheryl would not be of interest to anyone.

I headed south and then east again, toward Nebraska. Nebraska isn't only a flat state. It can be quite beautiful in the summer when the corn is growing.

I worked on some farms. I was feeling too much and needed to feel nothing at all. When I finished work, all I did was drink beer. I wanted no food. All those weeks with Cheryl, eating healthy and enjoying the making of good food, led to those days and weeks of that summer. My mind wouldn't turn off the past. On the one side of my haunted brain was the deer who had let me sleep with her that night. She was a miracle. I didn't know how she allowed me to sleep with her, but I knew counting on miracles was dangerous.

In another part of my brain, I heard the voice I knew too well. It screamed, "MY fault, MY fault."

I saw Steve offering me a beer. I heard Cheryl screaming at him to stop hurting her. To stop destroying her things. I saw me on the floor in the closet, naked and frightened, refusing to jump out to save her. He knew I wouldn't save her. He did all that to show me who was in charge. Well, he showed me.

For months after the beating, I beat myself up. All day and all night. By the time I was entering the third year of my life on the road, I left Nebraska and headed farther east. I was like a punch-drunk fighter. I made little sense to myself. My balance was off.

I decided I needed to do better with myself and get healthy again.

Then I was in southern Illinois, in horse country. I got work on a place owned by a very wealthy man. Wealthy men can take any place on the planet and transform it into anything they want. In this case, the man tore down most of the trees to build up a sizable horse farm, a large mansion with a lot of gardens to maintain, and a pool to be kept clean so that the woman he also bought could play in it some days.

I worked on that man's farm. It was the end of winter, beginning of spring, and I was cleaning out the garden beds and putting the grounds in order for all the annuals he wanted set out in big planters. I had to shovel the mulch he'd bought over the areas he wanted the large planters put on. He liked annuals, I was told by the very gossipy boss I had, because he had seen movies where large houses had them so there could be lots of different colors everywhere. The gossipy boss told me that was why he planted a maze behind the house. He'd seen one in a movie and thought he should have one too. Truckloads of mulch waited for me that year. I was happy about it. I was healing myself. I needed work that was steady and repetitive. The solitude also promised to heal me.

The problem with liking to work alone was how often people thought you wanted company. The boss was one of those people. He burst into where I worked and started stories about everything that went on in the house. I had no interest in any of the gossip. It infuriated him that I never asked a question. He would finish a story and leave again as suddenly as he had appeared.

He was fascinated by the wife. He assured me that things would change as soon as she returned. I didn't ask him where she was returning from, so he had to tell me. She was in Austria with her family.

"But," the boss said, "that's the cover story. She isn't in Austria. She's in a sanitarium. That's where he puts her for the winter so he can travel wherever he wants. Then, during the warmer months, they are here, at this beautiful hacienda, as he calls it. He and the wife and then lots of friends come to visit, and he can slip off and visit with other friends."

I had no idea where he found all this information. But he enjoyed talking about our employers as if they were the only other people in the world. He invited me to his home after work so he could tell me more stories. I always declined. Gossip is a dangerous tool. Living off the flotsam and jetsam of other people's lives is dangerous for workers. Being told too much of the lives of those I worked for made me nervous. Most of the information was untrustworthy, but once it was in my head, I tended to perceive things through that information, and I didn't want to know anything about them. They didn't know me, and I didn't want to know them.

When I finished work, I kicked off my work boots and shoved them behind my seat in the car. I drove to the small room I rented in town. The drive there was along a straight highway right into the setting sun. Every night, I stopped at a market for my fruits and vegetables. I also bought a six-pack of beer.

I liked this routine, and I liked having my own place away from the farm. I explained to my financial manager—the one who lived inside my head, counting beans—that having privacy meant more than the extra money I might have in the cash box if I stayed on the farm. I bought a small TV at a local thrift store. It got three stations, which was sufficient. They didn't come in clearly, but I didn't care. They were the noise in the room that substituted for a roommate.

I made dinner for myself and then sat down to rest and watch TV. I rested all night, and some nights, I didn't make it to the bed. On the weekends, I rested more. With the TV on, I stared into the void of all that could be and never was.

I also took good care of myself. I ate healthy meals. My clothes were clean. I touched no one. I was the steadiest of all souls. I found a way to not feel pain.

In mid-March, Frieda, "the wife," arrived. Among the staff who were permanently there, like my boss, there was a general dread of her return. It was of no interest to me. I did my work. I didn't know she had returned until one day, when I was on my hands and knees, crawling around the flower beds near the swimming pool, a shadow moved over me. I had been enjoying the warmth of the sun and hoped the shadow would pass quickly. The shadow didn't move.

I twisted around, putting up my hand to shade my eyes. All I saw was a tall figure blocking the sun. The sun-blocker didn't move. I stood up to get a better look. It was then that Frieda introduced herself to me, in her own way.

"Who are you?" she asked.

"My name is Scags. I work here."

"Mmm," she said, and walked away.

I got back down onto the ground. Her odd appearance meant nothing to me. I was happy cleaning out the flower-beds. I was obsessive about this work. I didn't mind being down on my hands and knees. I didn't mind the mud, or the way things smelled or even what I might find in the dirt.

I was still working when the shadow returned. This time I knew who it was. I continued working.

But then I had to move from the spot I was on. She blocked my path. My hands were full of the nasty stuff I had pulled out of the ground.

I took a step back to see how I could navigate my way around her. As I stepped back, she pulled me toward her and kissed me. Caught off guard, my thoughts went to what work I had to finish before I could leave for home.

My feet lost their place, and I started to fall backward. She grabbed me by the front of my shirt to hold me up.

"I like the mouth," she said.

I steadied myself but said nothing. I stared at her.

"You're supposed to say something, like thank you, or I like your mouth too or welcome home. . . ."

I continued to stand and stare. She tired of the game and walked away.

As she left, she turned back to me and said, "My husband will be away tomorrow. Clean up and come see me first thing."

With those words trailing out of her mouth like some smoke blown by a cigarette smoker, she walked away.

The wind took over the conversation. It kicked itself up, and I was left to put all my tools away before the storm hit.

Early spring storms came up quickly, I knew, and it never paid to doubt that one was on its way. One minute the sky was clear, and if you didn't pay attention, you got caught, like Frieda and I did then, in a heavy downpour. She may have had a long walk back to her house, but I didn't care. I had to put the tools away and then get into my car soaking wet for the long drive back to my temporary home. In the heavy wind and rain, I drove straight to the market as I always did. I bought a six-pack, nuts and an apple. It was a long night of staring into the void. When storms kicked up like that, I lost TV transmission.

The next morning, I got ready for work as I always did. Nothing Frieda said made me think that I was needed for anything other than what I did every day. I wiped the kiss from my mind. Staring into the void had that effect.

I arrived at work and went about the start of my day as usual—I put my food in the refrigerator in the shed and put on my work boots.

Something began tugging at my mind before I could grab a tool. I had reached for a rake and then put it back. Out of curiosity and tiredness, I headed up the long front walk and knocked on their big front door and waited. Their housekeeper, Constance, opened the door and let me in. She didn't look surprised to see me. In fact, she showed me into the living room, where a table had been set with coffee and sweet rolls and fruit and a large plate of eggs and bacon. Most of this I no longer ate, and besides, I had had breakfast.

Frieda arrived through a doorway off to my right. I hadn't noticed a door there. It was by a wall of books that were not books, I realized at once, but cardboard facsimiles of books. I'd never seen a fake library before. Who installs rows of cardboard boxes made to look like famous English novels arranged alphabetically?

Frieda seemed both annoyed and pleased that I was looking at the fake books rather than at her.

"As you can see, my husband only likes to look educated. I've never understood this fascination he has with appearances."

She looked around the room but then grew bored with what she already knew and sat down near me. She wore a riding habit. It looked very new and freshly ironed. I couldn't smell a horse on her.

"I have work to do," I said. I wanted to leave as soon as she entered the room.

"Ah, do you really want to work outside in the dirt when you could sit inside here with me and still get paid? I'm quite lonely."

I looked at her and thought I had walked into one of her husband's favorite movies. This had to be a line from one of those films.

Frieda began to eat and drink even though the coffee was cold and the other foods seemed to have dried out or gone stale. It was most unappetizing.

"Why won't you eat anything?"

I stood near the table. It seemed too personal to say I was a vegetarian. Any word of who I was or what I liked or didn't like would make me an accomplice in this pathetic melodrama. Yet, just standing in the middle of this fake library, doing and saying nothing, also seemed to become my own pathetic little drama. So, I sat down across from her.

"Look, I can't help you not be lonely." What does one say to such a request?

"But you can," she interrupted me. "All you must do is sit there and talk to me."

I spoke honestly to her. "I haven't had a conversation with anyone for a long time. I wouldn't know what to tell you."

"See, that wasn't so hard, now was it?"

She waited for me to respond to her question.

"Yes, it was."

She sat farther back in her chair and drank her cold coffee. She put the cup down and picked up a stale Danish with a big red dot of something artificially sweet, which she then cut and offered me half of. The entire stack of Danish sat on a chipped platter and looked as if they had been store-bought past their prime date.

I didn't want to look like a snob, but I could not eat that stale piece of fake food.

The temperature in the room rose. I unzipped my jacket and tried to sit more comfortably in the chair.

"Why don't you eat?"

"I can't. I'm a vegan."

She looked at the plate of sweets as if seeing them for the first time. She inspected them and then looked up at me. "What's wrong with them?"

"There's nothing wrong with them, for you. I don't eat eggs or butter."

"That's what makes you a vegan?"

"That's what's in the Danish that I can't eat. I don't eat anything that comes from an animal or that was an animal."

"How is that possible?"

"It is easy. And it makes me happier than eating these sweets. I'm sorry. I should get to work."

"If I were to cook for you, what could I make?"

"I don't want you to cook for me."

"But you're hungry, you must eat something."

We went to the kitchen, and I opened the refrigerator and began pulling out what I could find to make for the two of us. She insisted on eating whatever it was I ate. Even though what I made then was peanut butter and jelly sandwiches.

That was how the day progressed. With each moment of need, she pushed herself closer to me. She cleared boundaries by being persistent and not seeing any reason for us not to, for example, take a nap together. That was because I had yawned. I had yawned because I was bored. I was bored because she was more like a cat than a person.

I did fall asleep. When I woke up, in the dark, I thought I was alone and stood up.

"Where are you going?" The voice came straight at me as if she were hovering alongside me. She sat five feet away, snuggled up in a chair, her legs tucked under her. She had been watching me sleep.

"How long have I been asleep?"

"Not too long. Maybe an hour or two."

I jumped up. How could that be? Two hours asleep in the middle of the day. When was the last time I had done that?

"Don't worry, my darling Scags. You are being paid, and you must have needed that sleep. Come on up to my room and we'll cuddle in my bed and watch some television."

I could see clearly enough to find a lamp and turn it on. I put on my shoes. I no more wanted to snuggle with her than I wanted to be shot by her husband.

I raced down to the fake library to retrieve my jacket and made my escape.

Behind me, I heard her whining, "What have I done?"

What had she done? What a question.

I walked quickly to my car and kept my work boots on. My financial manager was beside herself because I just gave up a lucrative job at the best time of year for that kind of work. And, she reminded me, I had not been paid for the week yet.

In the morning, I packed my car, left the keys to my home on the kitchen table and decided to head farther east, out of southern Illinois. I ended up in mid-Indiana and rented a room at a Howard Johnson's motel. Not long after, on another stray spring night, I stood in the lobby, looking out the large plate-glass window. What I wanted to do at that moment was walk right through the window and out into the rain.

CHAPTER FOUR

Grief doesn't like to travel, and it certainly doesn't like to be a passenger. It wants to be in charge, pick the route and if possible, hang out in old motel rooms and sleep through life. But when I got on the road, I had a limited amount of money in my pocket, no credit cards, and that meant needing to work at whatever I could get that paid me in cash.

I was lonely all the time; grief did that to me. I wasn't always aware how grief ruled my life. Yet, starting with that first summer, driving through Wisconsin and Minnesota, I had felt a pain so severe that I'd pull off the road, get out of the car and find a tree to hang onto. I'd lean my back against the tree and force myself to breathe. I'd breathe so deeply that oxygen raced to my brain and made me dizzy. When the pain stopped, I'd hold my hand against my side, just below my rib cage as if I had been stabbed. It never occurred to me who had been stabbed.

For three years, I roamed all over the Central and Mountain Time zones. I worked in so many small towns that I lost count but never returned to any of them. I didn't have to. There were more than enough of them to keep me on the move and with work.

Work of the kind I was willing to do was easy to find. I washed dishes, tended bar, did landscaping and general farm maintenance. I cleaned hotel rooms and I cooked in hospital kitchens. No job was too menial so long as it either offered a place to sleep with a shower or I made enough money to supply that for myself. Eating was an option. At first, I lived on crap and suffered for it. Later, that changed.

I'd been on the road for three years. Round and round I went with the changing of the seasons. How or why or when to go home had not entered my mind.

As I stood in the lobby that night in April, 1996, not too many days away from my 45th birthday, watching a rainstorm whip and whirl outside, my mind was at work, making my next plan. I was in small-town Indiana. All I could see through the rain-smeared windows of the Howard Johnson motel were the lights of the gas station across the street and beyond that the lights on the trucks charging down the highways, oblivious of the weather and its dangers. Thunder rattled so loud that the plate-glass windows shook, and the lightning made an eerie blue of the night sky. The trees and electric poles surrounding the motel held strong. The scent of the sulfur merged with the scents of the sweets the two women, also in the lobby, were eating at an enormous pace.

The two women, Lorraine and Candy, were a mother and daughter who had taken over the lobby tables and chairs with their large selection of cereal boxes, plastic bottles of soda and a large container of candy that Candy had swiped from the back of a truck making deliveries to the gas station across the street. They were in sugar heaven and behaving like two adults high on a sugar fix.

"You want to split the Trix with me?" Candy asked Lorraine.

Lorraine, equally as high as her daughter, replied, "Don't trouble yourself sharing. There's more than enough right in front of me."

Candy turned off her sharing self and said, "You know, Ma, this candy is mine. I found it and I brought it here. I don't have to share any of it with you."

Their conversation was the background music to my thoughts about where to go next. What to do next. My brain frazzled like wires exposed to water and the juice of a live socket. If I was going back on the road, I had to pack my gear. I had only stopped to wash clothes and get some sleep and take a long hot shower. The place I worked and lived before stopping at the motel was like a cellar in a rancid dumpster. This costly stay had helped me remove the bad smells in my clothes and the awful taste in my mouth. I couldn't move, though, from that spot in the window. I liked watching the trucks on the road as they swooshed by, throwing off the rain into the winds that preceded them as they sped along the nighttime highway.

Then Margaret appeared. That is, Margaret's ghost appeared. She stood next to me. I felt her presence before I saw her. I hadn't been with her in years, and all I wanted to do was grab her and hold her.

"Don't try," she said. "Be still. I'm here."

I had no idea what that meant, that she was there. I knew tears were there. My cheeks wanted them. They were eager for them to stream down and slide off my chin. I wanted to shout with joy that she had not left me, but she had. I knew where her remains were—in a columbarium in New York City. Yet I also knew she stood next to me because when I turned toward where I knew her to be, I saw her. I saw her as she always had been to me, beautiful and sweet, and there were those coral-blue eyes and the small dimple in her chin, and the hands, though no longer emaciated, were her hands, the hands that I wanted to hold in mine.

"You can't."

I didn't know how to be or what to do.

"I know," she said. "I know how you feel."

I stood beside her, staring at her.

I squinted and stared some more. How did this happen?

"I am a ghost. No one else can see me but you."

"Why are you here?" I shook my head. I had finally gone crazy.

It seemed perfectly natural that we stood side by side watching the rain come down, listening to Candy and Lorraine bicker about their food.

"I'm taking you home. We're going back to New York City."

I believed her. She was Margaret's ghost.

"Margaret," I said. I repeated her name many times. I had not said her name in years. Saying her name felt like I was quenching a big thirst. It felt so good, I decided to do whatever she said.

I laughed. Margaret asked what was so funny.

"I'm wondering how the FBI will deal with you as a ghost."

"They don't believe in ghosts."

"Or angels," I said.

If we could have held hands, we would have held onto each other as we walked back to my room and packed my bags to leave the motel. The storm left the area as soon as we pulled out of the parking lot. Heading east, I knew we would have a long morning of staring into the sun. The storm had left pockets of deep water on the road but also very fresh-smelling air. I opened the window. Foolishly, I asked her if she was cold.

"Really, Scags? I am a ghost."

Yes, this was a big change in my life. Margaret's return as a ghost meant she didn't have anyone else to focus on but me. Margaret had never given me her total attention. But now, we fought. That was a shock because we had never fought. Yelling at a ghost was pointless.

We fought about why I had left town as I did, why I had treated Irene as I did, and why I wouldn't take care of her estate as she had hoped I would. Having to think again about that part of my life, the part I was on my way to resuming, made me angry and I kept yelling at her to stop questioning me.

"Then what do you want to talk about? This is a long ride."

"I want to know why you are here."

"Really?"

"Yes," I said.

"It's almost your birthday."

"I know, but you didn't come during any of the other birthdays. Why now?"

"I think for this birthday, you need me. I think the time was right to be here with you."

That was the exact thing Margaret would say, were she alive.

We drove back to the city singing to the radio, whatever music we could find. We sang loud until my voice cracked. I stopped to pee and to buy food. Margaret needed nothing. When I needed to nap, I slept. She wanted to drive and offered to drive. Repeatedly. I couldn't let her because no one could see her but me. I didn't mind pulling over to sleep and then driving on. Three years of living on the road were coming to an end. I wanted to savor every last moment of it with Margaret at my side. I also thought I could not trust her to drive. These were all new ways to think about Margaret.

I had run away from New York, I realized, chased by the devil, and was returning to New York holding hands with a ghost. Three years is a long time to be away from anywhere, but also those three years had changed how I lived day to day. I had focused on my survival: food, shelter, a car to keep me on the road and a place to sleep. I had made myself as invisible as possible. My days had started out one of two ways: I got out of bed and went to work, or I got out of bed and left town.

The vagabond route I had chosen was an indefinite one. Small town USA. Driving through the northern sections, into its midsection, living deep within the guts of the country where a good deal of the food comes from.

This area was also mining country, but like all areas of the country, things were changing rapidly. New York City too had changed while I was away.

After the disaster of the Reagan years, farmers were wary and scared, and with good reason. Clinton's North American Free Trade Agreement, begun by Bush, became another slow-moving disaster for those who worked with their hands and hearts at jobs that most people living in big cities didn't want to do and didn't think about except when a strike affected the price of food. I learned while doing that work that city people rarely considered how important that work was and what it took from a person to do that daily work and also what it could give back.

Living in the smallest of places, in towns that were called towns because they had a post office, I got to see things that jolted me out of the romance my road trip had begun with. City life itself was a romantic enterprise. Full of dreams of success and stardom. The real life of rural America was more about work and the conservative nature of work that was dependent not only on diligence but on the vagaries of weather and the rising and falling prices of crops not yet planted. While I had my own romantic fantasy about what it was like to live and work in the country, those raised in small towns couldn't wait to get to the cities.

It never occurred to the city people and the rural folk how interdependent they were. I flattered myself that I saw both sides.

Arriving back at One Fifth Avenue on the day of my birthday, with Margaret's ghost at my side, was not how I had imagined my return. The building's lobby had had a major upgrade. It now wanted to look like a library. Filled with fake books on shelves that spanned two walls, with deep-green carpeting and big brown leather chairs, the difference jarred me.

The look on the concierge's face at the desk as we walked in reflected what I think everyone walking into the lobby while we stood there must have been thinking—I didn't belong at the front desk but at the service entrance. I held onto my keys, and in my other hand, I had my old driver's license.

The concierge's name was embroidered on his jacket. This was another upgrade from the old name tags they used to wear that pinned on and could be used on anyone's jacket. Fred, the new concierge with the suspicious look, took a peek at my driver's license and then said, "Excuse me," and went into a back room.

My driver's license photo no longer looked like me. I now looked older, weathered, and I had cut off my long hair. The license needed to be retired, but it was all I had as New York ID.

When Fred returned, his demeanor had changed. He smiled and offered to take my bag, the old duffel bag, which was on my shoulder. It held barely more than I had left with.

Margaret watched the concierge. His changed behavior worried her. What had he learned when he went to the back room? Fred was obviously a toady. We both knew that. While my clothes had set off all kinds of alarms in the lobby, class divisions can make strange alliances. Fred should have, in my opinion, seen that my stained and old work clothes said absolutely nothing about who I was.

As Fred relieved me of the duffel bag and guided us to the elevator and up to the apartment on the top floor, Margaret and I looked at each other; we were concerned about old Fred.

When Fred opened the door, using a key that was unlike the one in my hand, I realized that no one had lived here the entire time I was away. It looked like a ghost village with all the furniture covered in white sheets.

Before he left, Fred asked where I had put my car, and I told him I returned it to the garage where I had always kept the cars.

"Okay," he said. "I'll move it tomorrow. Mr. Max has rented a new garage. I'll let him know."

As he left, he turned and said, "Welcome home."

I went into the bedroom where Fred had left the bag. I opened the drawers to find all my old clothes lying there. Everything had been kept for my return. I emptied the duffel bag and then went into the rest of the apartment, removing the white sheets and touching everything to make it alive again.

I opened all the window shades and noticed that there was no dust anywhere, which meant someone had been taking care of this place as if I might return at any moment.

I sat down to think about being home and what to do now that I was there. Why had I returned and who needed to know?

Before I could even think through how to find the people I needed to contact, the door opened and in walked Irene and Max. Fred had called Max. Max had called Irene, and now I was back where I had been when I left this town. Except for one difference—Margaret.

She stood back and watched as the two of them came into the living room and tried to give me a big hug.

"Happy birthday," Irene said as she put her arms around me. Some things had changed. Irene didn't like me.

"How nice of you to return on your birthday," Max said. "It makes a celebration more appropriate."

They each carried bags of food and drink. The cupboards were bare, and these offerings were meant to be helpful. Their feelings toward me had changed, and so had my diet. I didn't want to slap them in the face again by rejecting what they brought, but I ate very little, and that could be explained by saying I was too tired after the long ride home.

They were solicitous of my exhaustion and volunteered to leave quickly. They wanted to just toast my return, and they promised to come by the next day. We raised a glass of champagne, and Max said a couple of words of birthday cheer. But neither of their hearts was in it.

Their bodies became illuminated with relief and offense as they gathered their things to leave. I heard them speaking to themselves: "Typical behavior of this spoiled woman. Too tired to be polite. Too exhausted to appreciate the meal we brought her. Too special to apologize for disappearing and then reappearing."

I didn't blame them. How could they not be angry at me?

I wanted to know what Margaret thought. As Max left, he set down the new set of keys. Margaret observed this and waited until the door closed and then waited a bit longer.

"You've changed a good deal."

I started to speak, but then she interrupted me, "Oh, don't worry about them. They'll get over it. Don't you worry, they missed you.

"Come on, I have a real birthday present for you. We are going to celebrate you as you have never been celebrated before."

Margaret never talked that way.

"Don't worry," Margaret said. I had not gotten used to her hearing my thoughts. "We're going to sit here and wait for the darkness to fill the room. Close your eyes, my dear Scags, and breathe slowly and deeply."

"Hah, I will fall asleep."

"No, you won't. But it might seem like a dream, so don't try to stand up or open your eyes. I'll be right here with you."

"Do I have a choice?" I thought I was joking around.

"No," she said, and it was a firm no, a command, in fact, to be quiet.

I tried to relax but couldn't.

The room got darker. Even with my eyes closed, I saw the darkness painting the room. Breathing deeply, my chest opening more, I wanted to know what was going on. I heard things. Strange sounds that also were scented.

There was a moment I would call the beginning of the show. It was as if I could hear colors waking up. Then I located where I was: I was standing on top of the world, holding on to the planet's axis. With my eyes that could see while closed, I saw the colors pop out like flowers, but they weren't flowers, just colors: the pinks bled into lavenders, and the blues became greens.

Though I continued standing at the top of the world, the planet flattened out beneath my feet. Little villages filled up with varieties of me, representations of me, as a child, as an infant, as myself at as many moments in my life as I had been in. Little villages filled with lots of me. I stood holding the axis and watching myself, but I was not active. I was in position, getting ready for something at every moment but not yet in motion.

As the villages became larger, more life-sized, there were more people inside the scenes, people I knew and people I didn't. Or maybe people I had forgotten. I could look around and see scenes that I knew well, and even some scenes of dreams I had had.

Past, present and future lay out before me, but not quite in chronological order. In viewing them all at once, I knew what my life consisted of. I mean, I knew my life in that intimate way that blood flowed through me and carried with it all that I needed to live and removed all that I no longer needed. It felt like a transfusion, in fact, a transfusion of knowledge about me.

I called it a miraculous vision. I wanted to stay in every moment that saw me living; I wanted to be where I could not be yet; and more than any of the other moments in the show, I wanted to be where I had forgotten I had been.

One image that caught me up was of me sitting with Pops as he died. I thought I knew that scene well. But I hadn't noticed his yellow skin or how that skin felt like wax, ready to be lit, with a wick running through his body waiting for its match and a prayer that would send him into a peaceful place. Was he at peace? The answer caught itself in my chest with the beautiful resonance of a sibilant yes.

Margaret rose up before me again, dead on the cement floor, with the blood spurting out of her neck soaking into her hair. Was I going to hold on to her forever? A voice flowed in, saying, "You two will always love each other." Those words became a river expanding beyond the banks, and I saw it flowing into the fields and then taking over the roadways, washing small farmhouses away, only to turn around, finding its way back to its banks. The water receded, slowly dragging with it all the objects that life accumulates, that are not tied down and can be easily swept away.

More and more images appeared, like a never-ending Rolodex rolling past my mind, swirling and never stopping. At some moment, I don't know when, the feeling of satiation overtook me. My mind could not hold on to anything else. Did I fail a test of endurance for my life? Had I seen my death but not truly observed it? Was that why I stopped taking in any further images? I had seen my life, backward and forward, in multiple images now contained in something resembling a visual card file. "Now what?" I asked.

Before anyone answered that, I was asleep, tucked into bed like a child. I awoke with an aching head. Perhaps that was the effect of having that large data dump; my head became so much heavier, I could not move it.

Looking back at that night, I see it was a "celebration." In the moment of its occurrence, I was as naive and unaware of what it meant as I had been when I experienced all those events in my life. Self-awareness had not been my strongest weapon in dealing with my life. That night was a turning point. The ways in which I skimmed over life, as if nothing could touch me, were replaced as though by a new set of clothes. These clothes determined the way I looked at the world and the way I expected myself to be in the world.

I may have stepped back into my old clothes quite literally as I got up that morning, but the Scags who put them on asked herself new questions, and the answers she gave herself startled her.

I was living in the midst of transformation, and that was too uncomfortable for the indoors.

I picked up the keys Max left me and took the elevator down to the lobby. How odd, I thought, this is where I live and have lived for many years. The times changed, owners changed, and the decor had been altered to reflect a much more upscale life. If anyone had wondered, I was among the wealthiest people living there. I knew that, but no one else did.

I laughed to myself. What time was it? I didn't know. What was the temperature outside? I didn't know. I also didn't have to wonder about the time or weather because I didn't have to look for work or get on the road to leave a job and find new work. I didn't have to count the money in my cash box and ask my financial manager for permission to use any of it. No emergency could ever again be so big that I could not pay for it to be remedied.

I walked outside and turned the corner and saw a bank that displayed in bright green neon letters and numerals the date and time and temperature. It read "April 25, 1996, 10:03 am, 67 degrees." Next to the bank was a deli. I walked inside and ordered a cup of black coffee. Where was Margaret? I hadn't noticed her since the celebration.

As I ordered my coffee, I felt a woman looking me up and down. Thinking it could be Margaret, but it wasn't, I looked back at the woman to see that she was startled by my appearance. I was a different me than the one I had been yesterday. She couldn't have known that. But

I knew things that I had never known before, and this new knowledge made me into a new person.

I knew my physical appearance was shaped by the physical work I had been doing. Menial work changed my entire physiognomy. My arms and legs had gristled down. I looked like I was capable of lifting more than my weight. My short hair and tall muscular body gave me an androgynous look that could have confused anyone who didn't know me.

Walking out of the deli, I whistled because I had nowhere to go. I whistled and walked myself to Washington Square Park and found a bench to sit with my coffee in the sun. I whistled as my coffee let off some of its heat into the morning air. I smelled it. It smelled like the coffee from the bottom of a pot that has not been washed well. I laughed, thinking about that and what I now knew to do that I had not known how to do the last time I sat in the park. I knew so much, I told myself, since Margaret still had not appeared. I knew how to plant seeds, wash dishes, mow lawns, clean toilets and oil traps, all while listening to the abusive words men uttered while they worked. I knew when to stay silent.

I looked at my hands. I saw their strength and the multiple scars from burns and scrapes. I knew I had a strong back, could stand for hours and lift weights heavier than me. I knew how to keep a 10-year-old truck on the road. I had delivered calves, planted seeds on sharp inclines, shuffled through multiple short-orders and got them out of the kitchen quickly and hot. I had skills, and they now sat in my brain like reference volumes in my home library.

Sitting on the bench, I recognized that Scags, and she was not at all what that woman in the deli would have seen before. I didn't know if she found me attractive or was just curious about me, but as she had begun to speak to me, I'd thrown my money on the counter and left the deli.

The afternoon air began to chill, and my coffee was long gone when Margaret appeared. There was no use asking where she'd been. I hadn't needed her. I had been enjoying living inside myself and happily wandering around. The gift she had given me was indeed a gift that kept on giving.

"Clear your mind," she said. "We need to go home."

I didn't want to go inside. But she looked at me in such a way that I could not argue with her. I didn't want to argue. I did as she said.

When we returned to the apartment, Irene and Max were in the kitchen talking. While it may have looked like the morning after Margaret had been killed, so much had changed that that thought didn't enter my head until later. There was no way for either of them to know me as I had become while away and then after the celebration of the previous night. I needed to learn to be patient and for them to catch up with me, and as I started to learn that day, that time had come.

I entered the kitchen and sat down at the table. Max stood next to the stove drinking a large cup of coffee. Irene was cooking something on the stove. It was a lentil soup. Good move, Irene, I said to myself.

"Are you hungry?" Irene asked.

"Of course, she is," Max answered for me.

Food appeared in front of me. The soup smelled delicious.

"Irene, this is beautiful, and my vegetarian soul is grateful." The steam wound its way into my nose and then the soup's sumptuous taste swam down my throat. It was invigorating.

"Thank you for restoring my energy."

Max said, "Fine, good, glad you have so much energy. We have to get to work. You've been gone so long that I need to teach you all of this estate's entanglements all over again. I am exhausted from handling it alone, frankly."

The frustration in Max's voice made what was going to happen next difficult for all of us because they watched me to see if I was going to bolt out the door again—and I was.

They couldn't see or hear Margaret. They didn't know what she was telling me.

"Don't bother about the food or the way Max is talking to you. They don't understand what is about to happen. The phone will ring, and then we'll leave again."

Chapter Five

The Scags who went barreling down I-80 with Margaret no more than 48 hours after returning from her three-year road trip was a different person from the one who had raced towards Chicago three years before. I was not bedeviled by images of unholy dybbuks ruling the house or fears for my sanity were I to stay in New York. Margaret, who had then been dead about six months, had become unlovable. Max introduced me to a different Margaret. What I learned about her from studying the estate that she had thrust into my unwilling hands had undone all the love I had felt. That love lived shattered in Max's files. In death, Margaret and I were reintroduced, and I never would have fallen in love with that Margaret and therefore would not be in the position I was in.

Who aspires to a life of wealth and criminality? All I wanted in that previous life I had been thrown out of was to do good, and when I couldn't do good, I wanted to help Margaret, and when Margaret died, I wanted to find relief.

My abrupt departure in 1993 was what had saved me. Because I fell in love with Irene, my life was about to become wedded to Margaret all over again, and in ways I had never wanted. Irene and I loved each other because we had both loved Margaret. There was no future in that. Leaving town had been the best decision then.

Traveling with Margaret's ghost on that springtime ride back to Skokie had the smell of freshly washed sheets. We were headed to Skokie to help Mama and Aunt Money.

I wasn't running away this time. I wasn't confused about my life. I had Margaret beside me. I felt like I had been reborn. Every move toward something since the "celebration" confirmed that I inhabited my body, and my mind enjoyed that habitat.

I wanted to look forward. I didn't know then what it was Mama wanted. When she had called me, asking for help, she didn't specify what it was she needed. She only said, "Scags, please come home. I need some help."

Choking out those words cost her a great deal, and it was evident in her voice that she was about to cry.

I pissed off Max, who thought I was home for good. I disappointed Irene for the same reason. But when I said it was my mother calling because she needed my help, what could they say? Still, they weren't happy and left soon after the call.

I finished the soup Irene made and packed up to leave. In the morning, I had to ask the concierge where the cars were kept, and I walked there, Margaret close beside me.

"Scags, it's time to think about what will happen and how you will handle it when we get to Skokie."

I laughed. It was a good thing that the streets were relatively empty. The attendant at the garage may have assumed I was happy to be heading out of town. When he asked how long I would be away, I could honestly say that I was on my way to Chicago but didn't know how long I would be gone. I told him to bring me Margaret's oldest VW Bug.

It was a fine car and may have sounded a bit like a lawn mower when it was pushed to go fast, but it drove well, and I liked driving it. Margaret's one weakness was that she collected cars. That was something that surprised me about her when I first met her. "How was it possible?" I had asked her, before I knew she was wealthy. The car-collecting had been a strange hobby because we rarely went anywhere. I felt bad that I had had to sell one of her cars while I was away. But given my circumstances at that time, it was impossible to keep. I had needed the money and I had needed a car not registered in New York.

Margaret and I were on the road, heading toward another homecoming. What a strange one, too, I thought. My body in motion again, having barely stopped feeling the motion of the car after arriving in New York and now turning around, pushing toward Chicago. My need to travel disappeared later, when everything I needed I gathered to me.

We sped along I-80, the superhighway that cuts across the entire country. I don't recommend taking it cross-country. It's much too boring a ride. And, as in past trips, I stopped seldom. I made bathroom and fuel stops. I napped in the car in rest areas. I stocked up on fresh fruit and nuts and bottles of water and waited for a real meal until I arrived at Mama's. I didn't think at all of what Margaret suggested I think about.

A long drive, like the one we were on, one third of the way across the country in early spring, was like the one I had taken when I left New York. This time, my eyes were more prepared to see what was going on in the fields and how the trees were progressing with their leaves. I anticipated the warmth of the sun that lasted into the middle of the afternoon. Migratory birds sloped past, heading north for the cooler weather.

My "celebration" had rearranged my mind. Watching the road, observing the seasonal changes, and noticing the memories triggered by the sights and sounds of this road trip made me happy. That was not how I had previously felt about those years on the road. I had been handed my role in life, and it was not a bad part. I could live with what I knew.

I was on my way to help Mama and Aunt Money. I wasn't upset with this new job. I experimented, though, to see if I could upset myself. I reminded myself of how Mama shunned me after Pops died.

I checked myself out. My hands didn't grip the steering wheel any tighter. The back of my throat didn't feel raw; I wasn't angry. My heart rate was the same. I breathed easily and was enjoying driving.

"Good for you, Scags," Margaret said.

"Damn, Margaret," I said. "I was enjoying the change in me."

"Okay."

Margaret's comment didn't interrupt my experiment or how good I felt. I lived in this astounded stage when so much newness has entered me and made everything feel wonderful, purposeful.

Margaret and I had to evolve a way of being together when we were with Mama and Aunt Money. She didn't need to breathe but would feign taking a deep breath to signal she wanted me to know what she was thinking. I was learning to adjust to her presence; it could be constant for a while, but then she would disappear for a long time. I had no way to know what she intended. But I had to adjust. She had taken up a space in me, that was clear.

For how long, I didn't know. That much I had not seen during the "celebration."

As we approached Chicago and its crazy traffic, I simply chose a lane heading north and stayed there. It was much easier to do that than to try and beat the other cars.

We were on our way to Skokie. Not everyone was headed there.

Not everyone or anyone I knew lived with a ghost of their dead lover sitting beside them. After all the years I had been with the living Margaret, this new manifestation of her posed many problems. But better her as a ghost than not at all.

I kept seeing that river that I had seen in the "celebration" and knew it represented our love. The "celebration" came with no Cliffs Notes. I was left to interpret as I chose.

As I blended into the flow of traffic, staying in my lane with no need to weave in and out of other cars, I felt her beside me. We were locked into this tin can of a car. My legs cramped. My back needed to stretch. I wanted to lie down flat on a bed. Beside me sat Margaret's ghost, whose silence and presence gave off signals. I perceived essential communication happening, but it was not verbal or physical. It manifested itself in me, nearer to my gut or heart than to my brain. It might have been regulating my breathing and heart rate. Or purely passing signals of another kind between us.

But by the time we pulled into Mama's driveway, I was tired of driving and being trapped in the seat belt. It was time to change the tune and get to work.

I stepped out of the car, noticing that the only noise in the neighborhood was the barking of dogs. Against that quiet, I slammed the car door shut and walked up the front walkway and rang the doorbell.

I noticed how high the shrubs were that separated Julia's house and Mama's. Where was Julia? I thought as I waited for the two old ladies. What had she done with her life?

A light came on above my head. The first sign of life. I eagerly waited for the door to open and for Mama and me to face one another. The door opened with the swooshing noise of a door that was rarely opened. It seemed to take a special effort to open it, and it worried me that the two of them had become so feeble.

But the woman who stood in the doorway facing me wore a blue sari and raised her right hand to her heart as she looked quizzically at me. Through the closed outer door, her voice dimly asked who I was. What it was I wanted.

Then behind her, a young man appeared. He was dressed in Western clothes, but his white rolled-up shirt-sleeves revealed long, dark arms that wound themselves around the woman's shoulders.

"Yes?" he asked. "Can we help you?"

The sari-clad woman looked worried, but he looked curious and interested.

Then, as soon as I was ready to answer their concerns, a man appeared, towering over the woman and the young man. Not rudely, but with some authority, he pushed them aside and also asked what it was I wanted.

"I am looking for my mother and aunt. This is their house?"

I had to say my sentence as a question. This was the house I grew up in and where I expected to find my mother and aunt. Who were these people, and where were my old ladies?

Shaking his head, the man tut-tutted that he understood what had happened. He knew who I was looking for.

"Ah, you mean the Morgenstern ladies. They don't live here anymore."

The mystery was only partially solved.

"Do you know where they live now?"

The young man started to speak up, but the older man spoke right over him.

"They moved not far away. On Davis, there is an apartment building. You have to go around the corner and make a right and then go one block and make a left, and there in the middle of that block is the building. It is all white, you cannot miss it."

As I started to thank him, he closed the door, and the light went out above my head.

I turned back to the car with only one thought: why didn't Margaret tell me they had moved?

It was clear to me then that while I had accepted Margaret as a ghost, I could not expect that her powers were always going to be in service to me.

That insight required a deep breath. I jumped off the front stoop as I had often jumped off it as a child, aiming not to land on a crack in the sidewalk. I followed the directions given to me. I said nothing to Margaret; she knew what I was thinking sometimes before I thought it.

We pulled up in front of the white apartment building.

Margaret said to me: "Just because I am invisible doesn't mean I am inscrutable."

I laughed: "I wouldn't be so sure of that if I were you."

I parked the car. It fit into a small space right in front of the building. Once again, I headed to the front door, but there were three front doors in this building. They all looked alike and were located in the middle of each part of a large U-shape. Standing in the middle of the courtyard, I looked at the entrance on my right and intuitively moved in that direction. Margaret said nothing.

I opened the outer door and stood in a tiny vestibule where a row of mailboxes had the names of tenants written on small white pieces of paper. I saw the name Morgenstern, and the buzzer number was the same as the mailbox number. I rang the buzzer.

Within a few seconds, I heard a click inside the device, a scratchy sound, and then Mama's voice, "Hello?"

"It's me, Mama, Scags."

She said nothing else. The scratch of the intercom ended our talk. Then a different noise, the blaring of a buzzer as it released the lock to the front door. I opened it and walked into a dimly lit hallway where there were two apartment doors, one to the right and one to the left and a staircase leading to another floor.

I observed all of this and then the door to my right opened, and there stood Mama. She was fifteen years older than she had been when I last saw her. Me too, older by fifteen years, but not looking, I hoped, as shrunken and defeated as my Mama looked at that moment. She stood aside to let me into the apartment and there was Aunt Money, sitting strapped into a wheelchair.

My breath would have been taken away had I been able to breathe the air in their apartment. It held the combined smells of grease, old bodies seldom washed, and dirty clothes, towels and sheets piled on the floor. The ammonia whiff of urine gave the apartment the scent of decay beyond anything I could have imagined Mama and Aunt Money living in.

Before I could hug them or kiss them, I toured the place and opened every window I could open. The rush of fresh air into their rooms made breathing more bearable.

I returned to the living room where they waited for me. Mama stood next to Aunt Money's wheelchair.

I had not imagined their lives during the years we had been separated. I could not have dreamed of them living as they were.

I stood in the middle of that dismal living room, surrounded by filth and failure and tried to envision what it was I could do.

Mama and Aunt Money had become two shriveled-up old ladies.

Mama suffered from malnutrition. She had an extended belly, and her flesh was pulled tight across her face. I was afraid to touch her, not because of the filth, but because of her frailty. I towered over her. If I had met her on the street, I wouldn't have recognized her.

Aunt Money sat in her wheelchair, tied into it like a toy, a belt holding her in place like a pretend old lady whose legs were too short to reach the ground, whose hands were frozen as claws. Her toothless grin and the paralyzed muscles in her face distorted who she had been, but she made eye contact with me and smiled. She was pleased to see me. Clearly this was her work to have Mama call me. They were at the end of their road without help. It didn't take much imagination to see that.

Then Money surprised me. Out of the blue, she asked me who my friend was. Margaret walked to her and put her hand on her cheek. Something passed between them, and then Money said, "Very nice to meet you. Stay as long as you like."

Mama snapped at Money. "Oh come off it, you know Scags, and you know she'll stay just as long as she wants and no longer."

Money reached for my hand and tried to give me a squeeze. But her dexterity had been destroyed by arthritis and a stroke.

I set my bag down in the corner of the living room. I looked around me. What good would it do to ask how things had gotten to this point? The question was what to do to make things better.

It was obvious they needed to eat better. Mama must have been cooking for them, but she was a terrible cook even when I was a kid. Their malnutrition spoke to that. There couldn't have been much money. The apartment was in such disrepair that I feared they would be evicted.

"Stop it, Scags," Mama shouted as she watched me looking around the apartment, room by room, looking at the filth everywhere and the piles of clothes not washed but left to rot. "I didn't ask you here for a critique of our lives."

"I'm sorry, Mama, I wasn't thinking that. Are you hungry? I haven't eaten in a while. I'll get food and make us dinner."

Mama was in a mood, and it was enhanced by needing to eat. I needed to eat, too, and I thought if I cooked for them, they would calm down. Or rather, Mama would calm down. I didn't look to see what they had in the refrigerator or in the cupboards. I knew I needed to start from scratch, to reinvent their kitchen, the meals they ate, and then to get them to drink lots of water and to sleep.

I had no medical degree, so talking to them about my plan was pointless. Mama wouldn't trust me to know as much as I knew. But I knew it was imperative to get good food into them and to clean the apartment and wash up as best we could. That was how we spent the first 24 hours I was back in Skokie. I shopped for cleaning supplies, clean clothes for the two of them, and food. I bathed both of them. One was more grateful than the other. I changed the sheets on their beds and put blankets out in case they got cold. Their stashes of sheets and blankets sat high up on the shelves in Mama's room, too high and far enough out of reach that they remained clean.

By the time they had eaten dinner and gotten into bed, I knew they were pleased I had come to their rescue, no matter what the rescue might look like. Mama and Aunt Money could sleep soundly because they weren't left alone to figure out how to head off the full-scale disaster they were in. I heard Mama's gentle snore from the living room where I set up camp for myself. She was free to sleep without worry about Aunt Money during the night for the first time in years.

I was too exhausted after getting them to bed to look at their stacks of mail on the dining-room table. I wanted to know what lay buried there that might spell trouble. I had no energy to talk to Margaret. Margaret sat with Money all night, talking to her as she drifted off to sleep and then kept watch.

The couch was a poor substitute for a bed. Too lumpy, long enough but too narrow. I could stretch my legs out but could not turn in any direction. I had to choose to lie on my back or on my side for the night. The most important thing was not to fall off the couch onto the hard floor.

My sleep was fitful; my body was still in the car bouncing along as I sped here from New York without a full night's sleep.

Again, I became focused on time. I had work to do and needed a clock. I heard one. Mama had saved the clock that sat on my Pops' desk. It was loud. The steady ticking and tocking of its metronomic beat interfered with my sleep. Probably, neither one of them could hear it, so it sat plugged into the wall, a reminder of him, one of the few things left of his, it seemed, in the barren apartment the two old ladies had wound up in.

I fell asleep and then woke up with the rising of the sun. I didn't know where I was until I saw Margaret near me, watching me. She wanted me to get up.

"Why?" I asked.

Margaret didn't sleep; she didn't need to sleep. She couldn't possibly be lonely or hungry.

"There's work to do."

"Oh boy, you're no fun."

"Nope. Let's talk about the plan here. How will you manage this?"

Ghosts must not remember the benefits of coffee or the need to pee or the desire for a little less pressure first thing in the morning.

"I'm not pressuring you. I'm concerned. They aren't getting younger."

"I won't get much older if you don't let me get myself going in my own way. When did you become so bossy?"

I took a breath and turned to her again. "This isn't home to me. I've never lived here. I don't recognize the old ladies."

Then I stopped talking. I had awakened. I took another deep breath and went into the kitchen to make breakfast.

Thoughts pinged through my mind that needed not answers but reassurances: This will be different? Won't it? Nothing about being here is familiar, yet you are here, Margaret, and. . . .

The rest of my thoughts hung in the air. Margaret walked away. She'd heard Money calling, and I followed her into Money's bedroom. I lifted Money out of bed and into the wheelchair and pushed her to the bathroom and set her on the toilet. She was light but not flexible. Her body was like a mannequin's that had few working joints.

"Thank you, Scags. You can leave now."

Money looked barely awake, and yet the softness in her voice and the sweetness that I remembered from long ago waffled through me. That voice reminded me of home.

Margaret and I stood outside the closed bathroom door waiting for Money to call us back. I stood upright against the wall, my back perfectly straight, maybe needing to counteract the effects of the lumpy cushions I had slept on.

Mama slept for many more hours. Money and I had breakfast together and laughed that Mama could sleep so soundly.

"I think she has not slept this well or long since your father died and the two of us were left alone to manage. As you can see, we didn't do so well at that."

"That's okay. We'll try and sort things out now and get you two in better shape."

"We'll never be young again. Or—"

"No, but youth is so overrated, you know. We'll get you eating better and get this apartment looking better. Maybe we'll get you to see your doctor and have him check out how you're doing? What we could do better for you?"

"That sounds like a plan," I heard Margaret say. "See, simple, easy, and we'll get it done quickly."

I liked Margaret reassuring me that this visit to Skokie would end soon.

I began cleaning. I looked at the pile of letters sitting on the dining-room table and opened them. All kinds of bills had not been paid. Electric bills had been ignored too. I didn't want to talk to them about their finances. It seemed a waste of our shared good feelings. Who wants to talk about their failure to pay up? I was grateful they still had a place to stay and the lights were on.

That's why I just wrote out the checks for each bill and added a note explaining the circumstances for nonpayment and thanking them, whoever "they" were, for their services. None of the bills was so large that it put the two of them in some extreme financial situation. They had simply gone beyond what they could handle for themselves.

After a couple of days, I established a routine for them and for me. I took care of them as early as possible and then seated them in the kitchen to be out of my way. The novelty of having me at home and working on the apartment kept them quietly entertained. They had a portable TV in the kitchen and watched their programs and drank the tea I made them, and we began our new life.

At night, after the two of them were in bed, Margaret and I walked through my old neighborhood. It wasn't like the two of us walking the streets of Manhattan until all hours of the night and stopping at a diner for a fried breakfast. Those days were long gone. I talked to Margaret about my life growing up in Skokie. I discovered I didn't need to say a word out loud, I just had to look around me, register the sights and remember the stories, and she heard it all. The ghost became a divining rod. She sourced out of me what I had hidden, and I presented it as if she, too, had been with me. Sharing my past in this truly unbelievable way caused us to become partners in the telling of the story of Scags.

This shared remembrance opened up my memories to look at as if we had a screen between us to see me as I had been and to hear what I had thought and felt. When I talked to her about how I had started running on these same streets we walked at night, I remembered myself vividly as a teenager, needing to be free of all that adolescent anxiety. Running set me free. There were no running teams for girls. I walked these streets before I had the courage to run along them. At night, I eagerly waited for the rain or snow to come. I loved being out in that wildness when the strength of the storm matched the violence swirling inside me.

The walking led to running. I always walked alone, so I ran alone too. I ran when I wanted to. I continued running until I met you, Margaret. You didn't run but liked to walk, so I went back to walking with you, which was so much better than walking alone.

As the memories about running bubbled up, Margaret informed me that there was a track not far from Mama's. How did she know this? Living with a ghost meant accepting that someone with superior intelligence worked for you.

One afternoon, I took a break from my normal shopping for supplies and food and bought a pair of running shoes. Running shoes had changed a lot. The varieties and prices, the colors and the features, a whole market had grown up around this sport, and it was as accommodating to a woman's foot as to a man's. The next morning, I took my new shoes out for a spin to see what they could do. I had to get going very early, before the old ladies woke up and needed my assistance.

That first early morning run to the track and back set loose a cascade of memories. The memories came bursting forth the way I remembered spring flowers would become dazzling eruptions. It was a mystery to me why that flowering didn't take place in Skokie.

Time might have stopped in Skokie. The houses looked like they had when I left. The streets had not become busy thoroughfares but remained as desolate as when I was a teenager. Even my memories of the treeless lawns remained in line with what I saw as I walked back and forth to the track.

I walked back and forth to the track because time had not stood still for my body. The running was difficult. I walked more than I ran. I may have looked like I was in good shape, but what I needed from my body in order to run was not there. It had run off with my age. My breathing was awful, and my knees ached. They did more than ache, they squealed with each step I took.

Once I remembered how to stretch before and after running, I had a better time on the track. But running had always been a mental game for me too. My body resisted the efforts at first, but then when I knew how to do what needed to be done, my mind stepped in with these lists of complaints. The trick was to shut down the mind and trust the body to do what had to be done.

By running, I had entered into the hallowed halls of adolescent sexuality. By running, I walked again through the sham veil of normalcy and compliance. I had come to understand the environmental disaster caused by removing and not replacing trees and by maintaining lawns with pesticides and increasing amounts of water, and those were only the tip of the iceberg of what had gone wrong when I was growing up. There had been a collective moment when we walked through those suburban valleys of death and saw all the evil that had been unleashed, and as we took our turns confronting our parents and their sisters and brothers, friends and colleagues, what we got was not the thank-you for telling us the truth we desired from them but these uncomprehending stares.

Their eyes said, "What is it? We did all of this for you."

We looked around us and laughed. Why could we see that their efforts to please us had produced vast wastelands of rusted-out factories and abandoned towns whose occupants had rushed to join this "heaven on earth" existence that was, as we kept telling them, a sham. Many of us left these barren towns. Unfortunately, too many of us returned to live the exact life we had previously rejected.

By running every day, I visited the crumbling scenes of my adolescent disillusionments. I saw how I had become a teenage romantic. Wallowing in the despair of my life, which was actually pretty dreadful, I had become attached to images of dead things. Where the running track was now, a swamp had formerly been. A lone dead tree stuck out of the middle of it, looming over the water and doing nothing else. It did hold up some crows from time to time.

By replacing the swamp with the track, they had gotten rid of valuable wetlands. But it was inconceivable that any of those who had raised the money for the track gave a moment's thought to what good a wetland does.

For me, the swamp had been an altar to despair that I worshipped at. The running track attracted a lot of moms with strollers. They were too young to remember the swamp. They probably had not grown up in Skokie.

I returned home from running to shower and then to get the two old ladies' day started. As had become our routine, I parked them in front of the TV or with games they liked to play at the kitchen table, then I cooked, shopped and cleaned. I wanted them to have nice things to wear and to start the day feeling fresh, comfortable and well fed.

The necessary renovating of the apartment began well. No matter how this chapter in their lives was to end, I told myself, I wanted to return the apartment to its original order and cleanliness.

The work wasn't difficult. The apartment wasn't cluttered with the remnants of their previous lives. It was sparse. I searched for Pops' belongings. It was his large record collection, turntable and speakers, his books and the photo albums he had kept that interested me. I saw them nowhere. I had access to every area of the small apartment, and it certainly was small in comparison to the house Mama had sold to the family I met on my first day back in Skokie. All that remained was the clock on the dining-room table.

While working, I told myself the stories Pops had told me about his work and his travels on the road. Pops had been a salesman. He traipsed around the Midwest selling ball bearings and springs to the manufacturers of farm equipment and washing machines, dryers, and refrigerators. Pops worked in a time when manufacturing took place in the US and right in the heart of the country. I knew how upset he would have been to see how all those factories had closed. All that remained along his routes was a dust bowl of rusting, derelict factories and warehouses with grass growing between the cracks in the cement of the empty parking lots, and window frames without any of their glass remaining.

The factories closed. At the same time, family farms went broke too. Pops missed the great destruction. He had a fondness for the people and places he visited, often peppering his sales pitch with lots of stories about the entertainment world, the kind of news only he could provide. Pops gave them a show in talking to them about show business. They loved him because he was not just a man in a nice suit with a smart business card. He had a unique approach to his work, and it put him at odds with his boss, his father, the man I called Boomer, but it made him an eagerly awaited visitor to his customers. To my Pops, this was what he had been able to salvage from his ruined dreams of going into show business himself. He was a good salesman. His customers were loyal. But even those customers had moved on, gotten into other businesses or retired and died. The world of the sleazy traveling salesman had ended. Those areas became the sales territories of pharmaceutical and medical-device reps rather than manufacturing reps. These men and women were of the marketing age, their briefcases filled with shiny brochures and samples and pens. They offered free lunches and often trips or cruises. The stakes were higher for these salespeople than they had been for my Pops. Numbers meant more. Data counted for something in the age of mass-delivered pain relief and relief from mental anguish as well.

At first, I was angry that Mama had thrown his stuff away. I wanted to put my hands on it all; his books and the photos I would have taken with me. I rationally knew it was simpler to have all the clutter gone; it certainly made my work easier. Not having to keep moving stuff around, out of the way, so I could work, was a good thing, I told myself. But why had she done that? Did she even know that his belongings were gone? The dual erasures of his world and his life felt tragic. The consequence of inconvenience and anger?

Was Mama angry that he took great joy in telling the stories of American royalty, celebrities like Marilyn Monroe and Arthur Miller, the hotshot playwright married to the bombshell actress being of more interest to him than their own marriage? He told endlessly the stories of what he called the only royalty Americans knew and cared about—the movie stars and their fairy-tale lives. He loved to sing all the new songs he heard on the radio while driving from small town to small town and then home. He'd pull Mama's apron off and dance with her around the house, pushing her to enjoy herself until she got looser and danced with him as if I were not there. Pops was capable of creating such magic. Why wouldn't she want to hang onto that?

Maybe Mama had been smart to let go of Pops' dreams, all those reminders of his make-believe world. Maybe once he was dead, she couldn't create the magic on her own and let it go.

On our walks at night, I tried to explain to Margaret the danger and the charm of Pops' fantasy world. But then the words left me. I began to relive the fantasy world I created as a teenager when I had walked alone at night dreaming about what life could be like for me once I left home. The pent-up sexual glee and fear had needed to be set free. I had had to be quiet about these feelings. There were no safe places to talk about who I was becoming. A huge egg sat in my throat. I stopped talking.

Until I lived with Lauren in Vermont and we loved each other as two women love each other, I had never talked to anyone about these sexual feelings. I had let it be a secret river coursing through me with no beginning and no end. My fear of coming out to Mama and Pops had as much to do with my embarrassment at discussing sex with them as it did with knowing what it would mean in their rather closed society to know and have it known that their daughter was a lesbian. I learned to keep secrets. I became extremely good at protecting people from me.

Out of the darkness, Margaret said, "I know what that feels like. And now, there is a sense of triumph?"

"Yes, at 16, 15, 14, I wanted to be with someone like you, only I didn't know that. I also didn't want anyone to know that was what I wanted.

"Now little land mines of memories are going off. All the things I never let myself think about: the crushes, the big desire, the fear, the lust. I remember the smell of that lust; it was this springtime scent, both the mud and the new growth. I hated that smell and tried to wash it off. It followed me, and I thought everyone who smelled me suspected me of wanting to sleep with a girl, even when I couldn't say those words to myself."

"Sort of what nights were like when you were on the road? Overcome with desire, not knowing where to turn?"

"Yeah. It could be like that."

As I spoke, I saw myself in a town I was about to leave. "You know, in those places where loving women is dangerous for a woman, I'd be in bed with a woman who was desperate to have a woman run her hands along her body. She was usually so aroused by the time we went to bed that it was what desperate sex is: fast. And sometimes satisfying. But it was nice to know that there were women in every place I stopped who needed to be with a woman."

"It must have been nice, right, to know that there were women just waiting for you to show up?"

"What? You don't believe me?"

"No."

"Why? Don't you think there are women more locked in a closet than those nuns you lived with?"

"Perhaps. I'm just trying to knock that cocky strut out of you."

"Are you jealous?"

"Jealous? Of what?"

"I'm not trying to upset you. I spent three years with no one to answer to and no cause to give my life to. When did you ever have that opportunity?"

We walked in silence, breathing in sync. Then Margaret said, "Scags, you were in mourning. You traveled in circles, doing work to numb your mind. Grief took its toll. Watching you grieve was one of the most harrowing sights I have seen. You were like a demented cat, licking her wounds and on the prowl for prey because you had to stay alive. You made it. You could have kept spinning through town after town until you were too old to go on like that."

I stopped walking. From a nearby yard, we heard a howling cat in heat as if she had been silently shadowing our footsteps. The empty cry for relief seared me open and out of my mouth came more of the truth than I had told myself before.

"It was different from how I've tried to remember it. Some days, I was like an icebreaker determined to cut a path through frozen seas. Other times, I could not get out of bed. I'd be driving and have to stop the car and hold onto the steering wheel as hard as I could. I needed to wait for the desire to drive over a cliff or into oncoming traffic to pass.

"One night, I'd had too much to drink. I sat in my car, clutching the steering wheel. A cop tapped on the window. I couldn't talk or move. They pried me out of the car and put me in an ambulance. They found Max's name in my wallet. I kept his name there just in case I did kill myself. They called him. I spent 72 hours in a psych ward being observed rather than in a jail, and they let me go.

"I talked to someone there. Rather, she talked, and I sat still. That was the best I could do. She asked me some questions and from that, she guessed what was going on. Or she had talked to Max. I don't know. Eventually, she said to me, 'Go home, Scags, and be with the people who love you.'

"I liked the sound of her voice. I agreed with her that I should go home. I didn't, but I often heard her voice at night when I needed to be soothed.

"I couldn't say your name then. I thought if I put that word, Margaret, out into the world, I'd go insane and kill someone. Grief was a disease I contracted that there was no cure for."

"Yes. There's no cure for grief. I watched you and trusted you'd get yourself ready to come home. Time means nothing to me. But watching you in so much pain, that was truly a time-stopper. The eternal ache. The wound that was always open and bleeding. I never left you."

"You could have fooled me. I looked for you everywhere, and that was the cruelest part. How could you be so absent?

"Margaret, we were supposed to buy a farm."

I was crying by then, wiping the tears and snot on the bottom of my T-shirt. Ghosts are immaterial. There are no hugs, no caresses. No touching of tongues as you draw your mouth to hers.

Margaret and I talked this over for a number of nights. It was a drawn-out discussion about how I might not have made it home. Interspersed with the work I did for Mama and Aunt Money to get their apartment and their lives in better shape, Margaret and I talked about life and death.

Each night as we walked and talked, the love I had for Margaret kept me grounded. The move from the physical realm to the spiritual world we met in gave me room to look into other feelings and greater concerns than what I had been dragging with me for those years. I stopped focusing on what Margaret and I were going to have had she not been killed.

I was happy all of a sudden. It wasn't from the work to get Mama's apartment back into a better condition that made me happy each day. It was the running and being with Margaret.

I became more organized. I wanted to put Mama's apartment back into good shape within two weeks and then get them to the doctor, and then I could move on with the rest of my life. I picked up a pad of paper and went from room to room, making notes on all that needed to be done and adding to each page the supplies I needed. I plotted out my work on a daily basis so that it would be finished in two weeks.

I decided that fixing the kitchen first was the priority. Once the kitchen was finished, they could sit there all day while I worked elsewhere and have everything they needed without being in my way. The kitchen also was in the best shape of all the rooms. Working to get the kitchen cleaned and stocked made for long, grueling days, but when I finished, they were pleased.

Mama looked around her tidy kitchen and smiled. The first smile of my visit.

"Scags, Scags, look at what you did. How did you know how to do all of this? Your Pops was never good with his hands this way. Look, Money, isn't this lovely?"

Mama walked around the kitchen touching the new curtains I had hung in the window and the new cream-colored paint on the walls. The stove and oven had been thoroughly cleaned as well as the refrigerator. All the cabinets had the knobs replaced, and they almost looked brand new from the layer of varnish I had applied. Their kitchen table had been thoroughly scrubbed down. I knew they would be happy to sit there and listen to the radio, play cards, read, have their cups of coffee or tea.

For me, the kitchen renovation meant they would be out of my way as I worked on the rest of the apartment. For a short period of time, they would have to sleep in the same room, but surprisingly, neither complained. The miracle of seeing results they liked made them more agreeable to everything I asked them to do.

At mealtimes, Mama refrained from complaining about the new foods I introduced them to. Rather than complain, she acted impressed. Money was relieved mostly because I was there and making their lives better. Money formed an intriguing bond with Margaret. They sat at the table, and Money held what she thought was Margaret's hand. The two old ladies talked together about their aches and also about how the renovation was going. They liked to speculate about how long things would take or what the colors of their bedroom walls would look like now that all the grime had been removed and new paint applied.

From time to time, their curiosity took hold, and they'd object to sitting still and wanted to watch the work in progress. They didn't know what to make of me at work, and their conversation turned into the sound of two pigeons perched on a wire, commenting on the life going on around them. These pigeons were noisy but not mean birds. They kept me entertained.

I've tried to capture what they sounded like:

FIRST PIGEON: Why's she gotta empty my room first? How'd she move that bed all by herself? What's that on the floor? Did I forget to eat something?

SECOND PIGEON: Yes, looks like you left a whole sandwich under there quite a long time ago.

FIRST PIGEON: Who put her in charge?

SECOND PIGEON: You did. You called her, remember?
     What is she going to do, fix everything in this
     lousy place?
FIRST PIGEON: Let's stop her before she fixes every-
     thing here.
SECOND PIGEON: Why do you want to do that? This
     place is beginning to be nice.
FIRST PIGEON: What happens when she finishes?
     When did she get so tall?
SECOND PIGEON: Yes, tall, that's for sure. Whose side
     of the family had tall women? Not mine.
FIRST PIGEON: Not mine either. And she's so skinny.
     And she dresses like a man.
SECOND PIGEON: Don't start with that, Bev. We have
     to let her work or this will go on forever.

Then they left the room. Mama pushed Money's squealing wheelchair, breathing heavily as she urged that old chair back to the kitchen for another cup of tea and a hand of canasta.

The two weeks became three and then more. My schedule was fine. The work went fine. We didn't need to finish on time.

In the midst of that work and caring for the old ladies, I met a woman named Helen. She was often at the track, but I hadn't noticed her until one morning, after I finished running, the skies burst open. This was a typical Midwestern trick. Get a person's hopes up for a beautiful day and then spoil it by sending it a storm that doesn't clear the air but makes it heavier.

I never drove to the track and was in the midst of stretching after my run when the storm began. A voice shouted out, "Hey, get in my car!"

I looked around and saw a woman, Helen, in the driver's seat of her van, and I ran to it and jumped in. The rain pounded on the roof of her car while the wind and falling temperature made the windows fog up; it felt like we had been put into a storm chamber. I remembered seeing her at the track. She wasn't as committed a runner as I was, but she was there frequently. She always wore tight black shorts and sweatshirts with the sleeves cut off and a watch cap to keep her hair off her face. I had seen her but not thought about her.

The storm continued. We were trapped in her van. Both of us were soaking wet. She reached into the back seat and pulled out a couple of towels. We dried the rainwater from our hair and faces and placed the towels around our necks. Then we turned to peer at each other.

Helen reached out her hand. "Hi, my name is Helen. It's good to finally meet you."

I didn't know what she meant but took her hand and put my calloused one into hers and said, "My name is Scags. Don't worry, it's just an old name I gave myself that I refuse to change."

She laughed at that. With the rain still banging on the roof of the car, talking was more like shouting.

"Okay," she replied and then clarified her first comment. "I know you come here often because I have been watching you for a while now."

I looked intently into her face. She had a scar that ran from beneath her right eye all the way down to her jawbone. It was a deep scar that looked like someone had sewn up her face badly and quickly. She watched me looking at her. Her eyes had a deep brown cast to them, almost like mahogany. Clear, open and with laughter in them. She kept looking at me, but I had no idea what she saw.

I felt self-conscious. I was sweaty and had recently given myself a bad haircut. I thought I must look tired and burned out.

I raised my finger to her face and traced the scar all the way to her jaw. She was an attractive woman. I took a breath, and the next thing I knew she grabbed the towel I had around my neck and pulled me to her and kissed me. I quickly breathed that deep breath of arousal as her tongue entered my mouth and the warm air from her nose along my cheek sent the wisps of lust straight through me. She had caught me by surprise, and when she finished kissing me, I took her long hair into my hand and twisted it as if it were a rope. The feel of it, the weight of it, was exciting.

The sexual energy between us kept the windows steamed up. We didn't make love then. We kissed a lot and held onto each other and then, with the morning slipping away, I felt the tug of my routine, my responsibilities.

"Are you hungry?" she asked me.

"I could be. But . . ."

"Uh-oh. Did I do something wrong?"

I was embarrassed about the predicament I was in. But I was in a predicament, and I had to take care of it.

"I am staying with my mother and aunt right now. After my run, I make them breakfast. I need to get home to help my aunt out of bed."

We sat quietly and pondered what to do.

"I don't see that as a problem. We could meet for lunch then?"

I took a deep breath, amazed that there were other ways to proceed. My mind was a blank. Being thrown out of my routine, even with such a prospect as being with Helen, I was stumped as to what to do.

"There's one other thing I should mention. I'm a vegetarian."

I looked at Helen, and there was that laugh again.

"You too? Oh, that is too delicious."

I had hit the lesbian trifecta. An available, desirable, vegetarian lesbian. At least available for lunch.

The rain continued to come down hard, and Helen gave me a ride home. When I got out of the van, she told me where to meet her for lunch and when. As soon as I closed the door, she drove off. By the time I got inside Mama's apartment, my clothes were completely soaked. I was chilled and needed a hot shower. As I turned on the water, I tried to turn off my mind. There were too many things happening all at once.

I had arrived at the moment I knew returning to Skokie would lead me to. I had danced around those memories with Margaret, and that was helpful, but at the moment that water came pounding out of the shower head, I remembered why I had not seen my mother for all these years. I remembered in the way that cells remember deeply inside where the hurt still lives.

The daily chores to repair their lives had given me a place to live again with them and to get to know them. Getting the work done for them, however, was not the same thing as reconciling the accounts with Mama.

It wasn't anything more or less than having to say who I was and who I loved that had caused the rupture.

Standing in the shower, the hot water took the chill from my bones, and I wept.

When it was time to leave to meet Helen, I said nothing. They were accustomed to me coming and going during the day to shop, and this could have been another shopping outing. I said nothing about where I was going or when I would be back.

I washed up but left my work clothes on. Even to myself, I didn't want to say that this was a date. It was lunch. I was meeting someone for lunch.

But as soon as I walked into the darkened restaurant and saw Helen's eager face waiting for me to walk in the door, I knew it was a date.

We sat together in a corner. Helen was well known at the restaurant, and the chef made a big deal about serving his "two 'vegan' ladies." He smiled at us from beneath his drooping mustache; vegans were a rare sight those days, especially in Skokie, where most people lived on traditional Jewish food—bagels, cream cheese, blintzes, lox, along with all the chicken and brisket they could consume.

I had not eaten out except at diners since I had left New York the first time. Being served wasn't a familiar experience. I was uncomfortable with the interruptions of a waiter asking questions, wanting to make sure I had everything I needed.

I did like listening to Helen talk. She liked to talk. She told richly textured stories of her years in Afghanistan teaching English to young girls in the village where she lived. The cadence of her voice was odd to me. I got caught wondering what it was she was saying often and had to ask her to explain it again. Then I caught on, and with my brain attuned to the rhythms of her speech, I picked up much of the nuances of what she said. She spoke English not as a foreigner but as someone who had not spoken it frequently for a long time.

I listened to the chronicling of her life. The life she had led in Afghanistan was difficult, and the teaching was more difficult than she could explain to me at that first meeting. The girls were eager to learn and enjoyed being in class with her. But they weren't encouraged to go to school, and for some it was a dangerous choice. Helen wrapped herself in her story but was also present with me.

"You seem to miss being there."

As I finished that sentence, she looked right at me.

"I had to come home. My mother was dying. I came home to take care of her. My oldest sister lives in California, and while she is a doctor, she could not be with our mother 24 hours a day for the length of time it was taking her to die. My brothers live here, but they are not good at being still and quiet so our mother could be peaceful in her last days of life. It fell on me. My mother and I were not close, but we respected one another and the ways in which we lived our lives."

She paused and then burst forward into another story about her life.

"My mother was not a typical suburban Mom. She had been a scientist. She taught at Northwestern and did research there as well. This is years ago now because she retired to take care of my father in his last years.

"He, too, was not typical of the parents in Skokie. His medical training taught him very little of what he wanted to know. Becoming a vegan was a great choice that he thought everyone should make. My sister, in California, is a vegan, but not my brothers. And my mother, she went back and forth and since she did most of the cooking, she could cook for herself whatever she wanted. My parents enjoyed each other. My father's last years were marred not by illness, but from a fall he took on a hiking trail. He fell off the side of a mountain and hit his head. He suffered all sorts of brain trauma from that and someone needed to take care of him ever after. My mother stepped into that role and never stopped being there for him. She accepted better than any of us the amount of damage his brilliant mind had suffered.

"When he died, I was sure she would go back to work, but she said she didn't want to. She wanted to spend time doing other things. Those other things included working with a radical peace movement here in Chicago and going off on retreats with them to study nonviolence."

While watching her talk about her parents, I saw in her gestures and the way she slyly laughed about what she was saying, the younger Helen rise up out of her face. I assumed growing up with such remarkable parents, she absorbed much of what she had seen of how they lived and adjusted it to her own life. It was mesmerizing to watch a woman's face glow with the love she felt for her parents. I had never seen that before.

I admit, I was jealous. The degree of intellectual poverty in my parents' lives caused me to try and fill it up in me. That ache and emptiness have motivated me to do lots of things I might never have done without that need to spite them for their lack of mental prowess.

"Of course, someone did try to kill me, so that too was an incentive to return home."

She looked at me and we both laughed. The non sequitur, I learned, was typical of Helen. At times it felt like a strange form of forgetfulness, but then it always fit in somewhere. In response, I put my hand along the scar on her cheek.

"Yes, that was a wake-up call for sure. I had never felt fear before. Then I did. That sort of killed the adventure."

We finished eating and the table was still full of food. Helen had ordered enough for a second meal.

She motioned to the waiter to pack up the food.

"Please take this home, Scags. It is a tradition with me. I would come here for lunch when my mother was alive and bring home enough for our dinner."

I didn't pause to think about what I then said.

"I'll only take it home if you will join us for dinner tonight. I can supplement this if we need something that the old ladies will like." I paused then, and then said, "Please join us. I would love for them to meet you."

"Okay," she replied, but it sounded a bit like a question.

"Around 6 okay with you?"

And there it was, a dinner plan. And a guest.

As I drove home from the restaurant, Margaret spoke up after hours of silence.

"Don't expect it all to be smooth sailing. But having her to the house is a good way to be with Helen."

Her comment confused me, and she seemed to want to confuse me. I was willing to let that be. I wanted to get home to finish painting Money's room. Whatever Margaret meant about me and Helen could wait.

Precisely at 6:00, the buzzer sounded. I opened the door, walked into the hallway and let Helen in. She arrived with her arms laden with more food and a bottle of wine. She also arrived wearing a teal-colored shirt that deepened the darkness of her complexion and the sheen of that long black hair. She may have arrived laden with food, but her presence was a feast for my eyes.

As I walked with Helen into the kitchen, trying to relieve her of some of her gifts, I saw how her eyes sparkled when I introduced her to Mama and Aunt Money. Had there been a better way to introduce her to the old ladies, I couldn't have imagined it. They were swept off their feet by her charm and warmth. It was as if we had been dining all these weeks by a weak, unshaded lamp only to have a beautiful candelabra rise above us, its warm light highlighting what was best in all of us.

I don't remember what I had said to Mama about Helen other than we had met at the track and become friends. Mama's behavior towards Helen came as a surprise. I had expected Mama to sit in silence for a long time, judging and criticizing to herself everything she saw and heard. But instead, Mama was as ebullient as the rest of us. I almost cried with relief.

Margaret's observation that it was not going to be smooth sailing made me realize that if this new relationship was to work, they would all have to get along. The wine helped to open us up. The wine also helped Mama and Aunt Money overcome their fear of new foods. The spices and the textures were new to their palates, but if wine was good for anything, it was great at making fears subside enough to allow the new sensations in.

Helen had fun asking the two old ladies questions. She wanted to know how they had managed to stay together so long. Mama laughed. I couldn't believe it, and Money made a joke about her name and her having all the money.

Money asked Helen where she was from. "I grew up not too far from here, right on the border between Evanston and Skokie. But I haven't lived here in a long time. I came home to take care of my mother."

"Ah, like our Scags," Money said.

"Not quite the same," Helen said. "My mother was dying."

"No, not at all like our Scags!" Mama burst out. And we all laughed. What a surprise that we could all make a joke about that. Helen looked at me, and with fresh tears in her eyes, something opened up in me.

I was not the only one looking to belong and seeking love. The love affair between us didn't begin as mine and Margaret's did, in the lobby of a theater with the scent of a woman and the mystery of her being, but with the look of sadness and loss, the tears of finding a place to rest.

The wine put an early end to the night for the old ladies. Not accustomed to any alcohol, they nodded off at the table before dessert. I looked at Helen, dressed in her beautiful teal blouse and asked her to stay and help me with them and the dishes.

"If you could get a start on the dishes, I can get them into bed quicker. I have some old work shirts if you want to protect your clothes."

She followed me into the hallway where I had hung up my clothes. She unbuttoned her blouse and took it off, hung it up in my closet and took the shirt from me, an old clean but spattered shirt representing years of work and numerous attempts to remove the stains. They were stubborn reminders of the sweat and the grease and the blood of life on farms.

"Not quite as colorful as what I wore here, is it? But it's fine. I can make it work."

I shook my head at her. "It is a work shirt, Helen. It's meant to look like that."

"Don't worry so much. I am fine. Do you want me to help with them and then we can work in the kitchen together?"

"I just want you to know that I don't ever ask anyone out on a date and not expect them to work right alongside me."

"You are funny, Scags. I'll wheel Money into her room, if I knew where it was. . . ."

"I'll show you. Untying her from her chair is a bit complicated."

We worked side by side getting them into bed. A charge passed back and forth between us as our hands brushed against each other's, and it singed me, like entering into a world protected by energies I didn't see.

Once every dish had been dried and put away and the silverware and plates put out for breakfast—the three everyday chipped plates, the large glasses for water and the tea cups, also chipped and mismatched—we were free to stop working.

We hadn't chatted much while we worked, but we had breathed deeply and smiled a good deal.

As I put away the wet dish towels, Helen walked back to the closet to retrieve her shirt. I followed her and helped her remove my now-wet shirt. Before I let her put on her clothes, I kissed her shoulders and her neck.

"Thank you for the help. That made everything so much easier. And fun. I don't want you to think I didn't have fun."

"I bet you say that to all the girls you bring here to help with your housework."

We walked outside and stood near her car, talking about absolutely nothing, and I felt as much sexual energy as I could allow myself at that moment. I wanted it to fill me up, to flow from the pit of my pelvis into my throat and engorge my lips. I wanted to feel that surge again as I had so many years ago when I was first dating Margaret.

Then she drove off. I knew I would see her again at the track in the morning. Margaret neared me. She, too, filled me up with energy. That energy came from the spiritual taps of my being. I needed her that night.

We didn't walk and talk though. The two old ladies were asleep, pleasantly buzzed from the wine and from the arrival of Helen in our lives. We sat quietly in the living room. I turned on the radio and we listened to music, a recording of an older Chicago Symphony concert. Mahler's First Symphony. Fitting music for the awakening of a new life. This was how Margaret and I nested together, in silence, but communicating, totally invisible to anyone but completely known to each other. I held onto the sound of the cuckoo from the symphony over the next few days as things began changing.

The apartment looked so different from when I had first walked in the door. The work had been easy but time-consuming. Mama and Aunt Money looked better too from when I had first arrived. They'd had lots of healthy food and better sleep; they hung out with their neighbors outside so they got lots of fresh air; and the excitement of the changes occurring all around them energized them. Life had entered into their lives.

Mama had decided one day to paint her and Money's nails. This one simple activity made them laugh together. They couldn't stop admiring the bright redness on the tips of their twisted arthritic hands. They kept adding on new interests like people who cannot stop decorating their homes. When I called the doctor they hadn't seen in years, they hung around me on the phone as if I was going to unearth a wondrous treasure. I couldn't believe they were eager to see a doctor. Maybe it was the prospect of a car ride, something they hadn't done in years.

I didn't know what getting them to the doctor would involve. We prepared to get to the doctor's office and then, as we got to the car, it became obvious immediately that putting the two of them and the wheelchair into my VW Bug was impossible.

Neither of them said a word as I walked around and around the car, trying to figure out how all of us could get into it. No matter how much I examined the doors and the seats, it was, as I'd seen from the first moment, entirely impossible.

Aunt Money spoke up first: "Scags, dear, our savior, you're not going to be able to fit us in that car."

I circled the car and circled the car. It had been established that I would not get them to the doctor that day. Finding the solution to taking them places was what plagued me. What was I to do?

I looked for Margaret. She sat on the roof of a van parked across the street. It was a good solution. Margaret could have told me this, but then what fun would we be having?

I took my charges back inside, muttering to myself and Margaret that I should have been more aware of what I needed. Mama was silent but looked perplexed.

"Don't worry," I said to her.

I had to make two phone calls. The first to the doctor's office to cancel the appointment. Mama listened but didn't stop looking perplexed. "I don't have to explain to the doctor what happened. I'll fix this."

They were worried. Nothing like this had happened since I arrived. I had seemed to them endlessly resourceful but with a minimum of work. This was an insurmountable problem to them; I could see it in their huddling next to each other, not believing I could fix this.

The second phone call I made was to Max. Margaret huddled now too with the two old ladies. I anticipated that explaining what was about to happen to Mama would be difficult.

I called Max on his private line, bypassing his secretary. He picked up on the second ring.

"I need your help, Max."

"Aha! Good afternoon to you too, Scags."

That's what people say to you when they want you to feel bad about how you have neglected them. They point out how impolite you are.

"Nothing to worry about Max. I'm with my mother and aunt. I drove here, as you know, in Margaret's old VW.

Turns out I need you to buy a van for us, with a ramp, and get it to me here in Skokie as soon as possible. Please."

He asked some practical questions and the address, and I knew he would do this for us.

"Nice to hear from you, Scags. Any idea when I can see you again?"

"No, not at this moment. I will know more once we have the van. Thanks again, Max." I hung up.

I sighed with relief that Max would know how to get the van quickly and that I had avoided answering any questions about what it was I was doing. I sat with my head in my hands for a few moments, thanking Margaret and Max and the money for making this possible. At no time in our conversation did we mention what the price of this new vehicle would be.

When Money spoke, it was a reminder of that.

"Scags, dear, I hate to be throwing a wrench in this plan, but buying a new car is very expensive. I'm sure you know that, but there aren't enough pennies in this place to buy a car for us all to use. Are you sure this was a wise thing to do?"

"Don't worry, Money. I've got this covered."

Mama's suspiciousness rose into her cheeks and eyes. She didn't believe that I had the purchase of a new van covered. She suspected foul play of some kind, but it was clear she didn't know what that foul play was.

"Who is this Max you called, Scags? Why would he buy you a van?"

I started to tell them one story and found myself telling them another. I wanted to talk only about the money. But then I needed to talk about Margaret too, no matter what the risks were. Margaret's plan would move forward no matter how Mama reacted to the stories. I had to learn to trust that.

"Remember when Pops died, and you told me to leave your house because of my relationship with Margaret?"

Aunt Money perked up her ears and looked at Margaret with new eyes.

"Yes," Mama said, but more as a question. She was not sure where this was going or why asking about Max had taken us back to that "ancient history," as she called it.

"Max is the lawyer who handles Margaret's estate."

"So, handling an estate, that means Margaret is dead?"

"Yes, she was killed in prison."

Mama looked more certain that her suspicions were correct. Money's ears perked up; she always liked a good story.

Looking back and forth between the two of them, I told them, "Margaret was killed in prison by a woman she was tutoring. It happened very fast, and there was nothing anyone could do to save her. At that point, Margaret and I had been together for more than 10 years. She had been in prison a couple of times for her anti-nuclear activities. She was due to be released, and we had planned on building a farm community in upstate New York."

"Good," Mama said. I didn't know if she meant good that we were going to start a farm or good that Margaret was getting out of prison.

"Margaret and I couldn't be married."

"No shit there," Aunt Money said.

"In her will, she left everything she owned to me. It's a lot of money. Max handles it for me."

"Can you just pick up the phone and ask Max for anything you want?" Mama asked.

Mama processed my story through her balancing system of need and remorse. Her eyes turned to an inner place where she went to tally the pros and cons of this information. Maybe she felt remorse that she had abandoned me but then calculated that I had been adequately compensated for my pain. From her perspective, having money sufficiently rewarded a person for all kinds of pain and suffering.

Aunt Money said nothing. She waited for more; she was sure there was more to this story.

Mama asked, "This woman you loved, she loved you?"

"Yes, she did."

"And when you lived all those years in Vermont with that other woman, she loved you too?"

"Yes."

"After Charles, you never wanted to be with a man again because he died on you?"

"I wouldn't say that."

"What would you say? How come this woman left you the money? What do you have to do to keep it? Does it mean that you can't marry a man?"

KA-BOOM! An explosion had gone off between me and Mama.

Mama looked at me with tears streaming down her cheeks. That balancing sheet had finally been thrown away. She saw pain when it sat before her.

Mama said, "Don't tell Money." She forgot Aunt Money sat next to her. She may have been thinking we were alone in the living room of our old house with Pops in the basement at his desk, drinking too much and yelling for her to come downstairs and dance with him. She had that same look on her face that there were things going on that were forbidden. That knowledge lodged in her cheeks, a swollen face, a cheekbone aching with fear and remorse.

"Don't tell Money what? She's right here beside you and knows I am a lesbian."

Mama cringed at the word. Calling a girl a lesbian in Skokie in the 1950s was like telling the world you would never fit in, that you were defective and your entire family was tarnished as well. In that age of conformity, both misogyny and homophobia came together and caused irreparable harm.

I had lived in fear in Skokie. I had lived in fear too while on the road. I had gotten out of Skokie fast enough to not get called out for being a lesbian. I barely knew that I was a lesbian then. But by the time I was on the road, I knew and almost anyone looking at me knew too. There were ways to stay safe while traveling. But on occasion, I wasn't safe and had to run away as fast as I could. I once hid in a field in Wyoming. The night's cold temperatures may have turned back the men following me, but I took no chances and dug a small hollow in the ground to lie in. I covered my car in branches and dug that hole not far from the car. I "belonged" to no one. To them, I was a smart-ass woman and therefore could not be trusted. Eventually, the good old boys smelled a woman who was content without them. Their "master plan" for making my life miserable followed the same playbook no matter where I landed. First, they got their women to shun me. When I ignored them, the men took over. I didn't own anything but my car, and that meant everything to me. So, when they began vandalizing my car, I ran. I learned lots of survival techniques. One of them was to run at the whiff of any danger. Danger had its unique smell. It's like knowing a man is nearby because his lit cigar precedes him.

Mama grilling me that afternoon about Max and Margaret triggered my safety concerns, but I was not intimidated by her. The arousal mechanism only served to remind me of how much strain it could be to run from danger and have to find work elsewhere all the time.

While our little drama unfolded in the living room, the sun disappeared. It was not as late as it looked. I went into the kitchen to see what was going on outside. Just as I stuck my head out the window, rain fell hard, steaming up the air. Thunder and lightning followed, setting the building shaking. Tornadoes caused such disruption in the Midwest and had a way of sneaking up on you.

Standing at the window was not a safe place to be with lightning in the air. If a tornado was heading our way, however, we were on the ground floor of a two-story building. We were as safe as we could be from the forces of nature.

We were also as safe as we could be with each other. The storm of my sexual coming-out had passed. All that remained was to let the debris settle in everyone's mind. That meant letting Mama, now that the actual storm had arrived, go to bed. She needed to sleep with the effects of change and see where they left her in the morning.

Coming out to Mama at my age was so long past due that I couldn't help but laugh. What was Mama to do with this information? She had nothing to add to my knowledge of it, and she couldn't warn me. I had wanted to share something of my life with her, but she'd built a wall. She was like a marshal intent on shutting down a business for nonpayment of taxes. My storytelling was way past due, and there was no need to try.

Mama carried inside her that disgust of lesbians that I could smell wherever it appeared. Yet she was dependent on me. She suspected I had played a trick on her. Her only option was to go to bed. No dinner, no time with Money, just a quick wave of the hand and off she went to her almost-completed bedroom. She carefully closed the door, and we heard nothing more from her. That was the most graphic example of what our relationship had been when I was a child. We said things to each other, and she walked away. The last walking-away had lasted 15 years.

Money and I ate dinner, said nothing to each other, and then I helped her to bed.

Margaret and I took our evening walk. I was exhausted, so we didn't go far or for long. The air had gotten warmer. The storm had not removed the moisture but intensified it. When the streetlamps went on, networks of moisture hung over us like vast tentacles holding us in place, but the day's drama had drained me.

As we got back home, I turned to Margaret and said to her, "Don't you think it odd that Helen and I are dealing with a similar problem with our mothers?"

"That's not true, Scags. Your mother and aunt are alive. You're not in mourning for them."

"I'm assuming you approve of Helen."

"What makes you say that? Do I have to approve of the woman you fall in love with now?"

"Yes, you do. You want to have a say in who I start a new life with."

"Maybe. But for now, we need a plan to move Mama and Aunt Money."

We hadn't discussed this yet. Having focused on the apartment's rehabilitation, I lost sight of the longer-range plan. I didn't want to think about it. The general outline hadn't provided the details for how to get them from their apartment in Skokie into an apartment in New York City.

I didn't know how to proceed, and so the bright idea was to call Irene and hash it out with her. In a rush of clueless nostalgia, I picked up the phone and knew the number without looking it up. Even though it was one hour later there, she answered the phone and when she said, "Hello," I heard another voice in the background. My impulsiveness ran its course. Not sure if I should proceed with the call, I said, "Hi, Irene, it's Scags. If you have a minute, I need to talk to you."

I heard her put her hand over the mouthpiece and then when she removed it, there was silence in the room.

"Hi, Scags. How are you?"

So far, so good, I said to myself. She wasn't angry and was willing to talk.

"I know this is weird to call out of the blue like this."

"Not weird, but certainly uncharacteristic of you."

She paused, and I didn't speak.

"But if you want to talk, I can listen."

There she was, the gentle soul I had hurt so badly.

"I'm calling because we, I mean, I am in the process of moving my mother and aunt with me back to New York. Don't ask me why I am doing this, please, but . . . I am having a hard time getting my mind around how to do this."

A silence greeted my remarks. She must have been thinking to herself why I had called her and not Max.

"Don't you usually call Max with these questions?"

"Yes, of course. Why didn't I think of that?"

I knew there was something more plugging up the works than just the practical side of this move.

"I don't know what else is bothering me, but there is something else going on inside me, and I can't call Max without figuring this piece out."

"I don't know what you mean."

Her voice reminded me of Margaret's. I heard it distinctly then. She had a particular way of saying "mean" that was how Margaret emphasized the word too. The lilt at the end of the simple, single syllable that gave it something other people didn't add to the word. What else could I say? Was I calling her about Helen? No.

"I am sorry, Irene. I should have said that to you sooner. I apologize for running off and not saying a word about where I was going or why."

"Yes." She meant "yes" the way Margaret would mean "yes" too. Yes, it is accepted. Yes, you are forgiven, Yes, you are still loved. That gave me the courage to continue.

"I didn't need religion after Margaret died so much as time to be without her. I needed you to . . ."

And I couldn't say it, but I wanted to say, not be so much like Margaret.

"What, Scags? What is it?"

"I don't know really. You gave me so much, and I took a great deal and never thanked you but abandoned you. I know you missed her too. You loved and grieved with me."

"What can I do now? Did you call to apologize because you are returning soon?"

"Yes. I called to say that I would be returning with Mama and Aunt Money and that I'm sorry I treated you so badly. I'll call Max about the particulars. I'll let you know when we are planning on arriving. Thanks again."

A silence filled the entire space between New York and Skokie. We said more with that than we ever said with words.

We hung up.

Margaret watched me talking to Irene. When the conversation ended, she sat and watched more. I had nothing to say to her. Inside me, something new tried to find its way to behave, and it did a terrible job. I didn't need her to tell me so.

The next morning, I arrived at the track eager for Helen and her smile and the way she looked at me. I wanted to run up to her and ask her to move to New York with me, like a little kid asking her best friend to do something crazy and necessary because that was what best friends did. Her van wasn't in the parking lot. I saw the word "crestfallen" written large in front of me.

The world moved fast both inside me and around me. No firm decisions had been made. The start button to this new life was not ready to be pushed. I held my finger over it.

Helen didn't know enough about me, I told myself. She didn't know Margaret's story. She didn't know how she died and what she left me. She didn't know Margaret was a ghost or that I had been given the gift of knowing the future. Helen didn't know that I was one of the wealthiest women in the world. I took a deep breath at that list of things Helen didn't know.

I stretched slowly and carefully. In the midst of so much anxiety, I didn't need any pulled muscles. I had enough pain walking beside me. I began my run, and the Stroller Ladies and I behaved cordially toward each other.

I ignored them as best I could and gave myself the time to breathe and cruise around the track with a shorter gait and less energy pushing me to go fast and go long. When I began the slowdown, and the Stroller Ladies pushed their ways home, that was when Helen arrived.

As I ran the last lap, she pulled her van into the parking lot. My head had been emptied while I ran but seeing her, it filled up again and too quickly. It was as if my head could get a cramp.

She didn't get out of her van. She sat in the driver's seat waiting for me. With a sweaty body and face, I slid in next to her in the passenger seat. The AC was on, and I shivered from the wet clothes turning cold against my skin.

I looked at Helen. She had a new look on her face. I liked it but didn't know how to read it.

"What's up?" I asked.

She turned to me and held a check in front of my face.

"That's my reward," she said, "for being the one who raced home from Afghanistan to take care of my mother. My brothers sold the house and gave me most of the money. And they promised to take care of clearing it out for the buyer. My work here is finished."

I looked at the check in her hand. It had her name on it and was written out for a significant amount of money.

I sat as close to her as I could in the bucket seat. "You're set, aren't you?"

"Oh my, yes, I am. What should I do with this?"

I seized the opportunity because she looked at me with such anticipation.

"Move with me to New York."

"What?" She looked surprised, pleased and worried all at once.

I might not have said it exactly as she wanted it said, but if faces can reflect the inner world of their owner, then hers broke out into the reddest of flushes and the wettest of tears and the most engorged lips I had ever seen.

"What a day I've had," she said.

"It's still early. It could get even better."

"Don't tempt me, Scags."

She put a big kiss on my cheek and sat back against the window looking at me.

"Helen, I hate to break up this moment, but I am freezing. Please drive me home so I can shower and change."

"Oh my. Of course." She turned off the AC, opened the windows to let the hot sticky air in and pulled out of the parking lot. Driving slowly and quietly, she passed into her own world. I'd seen her do that before. She is happy there and holds onto her happiness inside her for a while.

Then she returned to me. "Are your mother and Money moving to New York too?"

"Oh, yes," I said. "They'll have their own apartment. I will see to that. We're going to live in my apartment. If that's okay." Plans finally formed in my mind. All I had needed was to hear Helen agree to move to New York with me. Then all the energy needed to build our new world came out, and I saw it as it was supposed to be according to Margaret's plan. I didn't resent the plan that day.

Then Helen said, "Everything is okay with me. We'll take care of our old ladies, and that is fine with me."

I said, "What a funny way to put that."

"Yes. It came slipping out of my mouth."

I felt Margaret's presence hovering around me. Was she making sure I got things put in order, or was she merely enjoying what was happening now?

Helen and I laughed. Neither of us had said a word, but merriment surrounded us. I was not a bit surprised when she pulled up to the curb to let me out that my new van had arrived. A man with my van, smiling at us as we pulled up, waited at the front of the new vehicle we would drive to New York. It looked much like Helen's van except it was spiffier, with all kinds of accessories that were needed to keep Aunt Money safe in her wheelchair, and with a ramp to get the wheelchair into the van. The front bucket seats were plusher than Helen's, and the back seats were equipped with drop-down trays and surrounded by many pockets to put things into. The old ladies always carried many things with them, but I never knew what they were for. I teased them that they were like the Queen of England, carrying a pocketbook with probably nothing in it.

I hopped out of Helen's van and shook the hand of the man with my van. He had me sign some papers and handed me the keys. Another car pulled up, and he jumped into it and waved as he left. The New York plates were on it, the car was registered and had passed inspection. The insurance card was also in the glove compartment. It had a full tank of gas. Leave it to Max to take care of everything in this fashion. When I had been on the road, these were the pesky things I had to carefully skirt the law to provide for myself. I never had a clean license or legal plates or a car able to pass inspection. That was one of the features of living without any ID or credit cards or a home address.

Helen parked her van and got out to inspect the new one.

"Mighty impressive." She paused. "Why couldn't we have used mine?"

I took her hand, and we stood next to the new vehicle. All I wanted was to talk about anything other than the van, but she was right. We could have used hers had I known her that well when I ordered the new one.

"I don't know," I said. "Does it matter?"

She touched the pocket on her shirt where she had folded up the check and said, "No, there is plenty of money. I could sell mine, I guess."

I kissed her cheek and then ran inside, calling over my shoulder, "I have to shower. Follow me. We'll tell the old ladies we're moving together."

I had so much work to do. I liked that feeling of so much work to do. We were leaving Skokie for good. We all had to fit in the van. That was all I could think about.

I began thinking of Mama and Aunt Money as small pieces of furniture that had to be packed carefully. Helen was the large valise I had to bring with me but didn't know where to store. The "celebration" had shown me generally what was going to happen but not how to make it happen. For example, how was I to convince Mama, who had a lifelong hatred of New York, that she must move with me and that she had no choice?

I hoped Helen could help. I stood in the shower, with water cascading off my back, smiling with a new glee. The three women I knew there were the three women making up my family. I had never felt what it meant to have a family. This was it, and I had so much work to do!

I wandered out of the bathroom with the clean clothes sticking to my body. The humidity had descended on us like it does in the Midwest, and there was no escaping it. Mama and Aunt Money sat with Helen in the kitchen. Their rotating fan was on high, and they sat at the table playing cards. I went immediately to the refrigerator and pulled out the large pitcher of cold water and began cutting up some fruit to keep us all hydrated and vitaminated. I was extremely proud of how good Mama and Aunt Money looked.

"You look flustered, Scags," Money said. "Stop feeding us and sit down."

"Good idea," I said, pulling out a chair to sit next to Helen. She turned to smile at me, and that gave me the courage to plunge into the news of the day.

"I have some news I want to share with the two of you. Helen and I are moving to New York together, and we want you two to come with us."

Mama's head jerked up as if a spring had been released. Money continued to smile as if she had known this all along.

"New York? All four of us?" Mama asked.

"Yes," I said.

"Okay, then. Sounds like a good idea."

That was that. You could have wiped me off the ceiling, I was so flabbergasted by Mama's swift, positive response.

"Right. So, there are some things we have to take care of before we can leave. Not a lot of work actually, but it won't be until next week or so that we can make arrangements for the day we leave."

"Whatever you want to do is fine with us, Scags," Mama said. She looked at Money, who nodded her agreement.

Not having to spend any energy convincing Mama of the need for her to leave with Helen and me, I found myself with an excess of fuel racing around inside me. My first impulse was to suggest to Helen that we get a hotel room and have some fun together. But then something inside me kicked in that took me in another direction. I asked the old ladies if they wanted to take a drive in the new van that had just been delivered.

"What? Why didn't you say something, Scags. Of course, we want to go for a ride. We haven't been out of the area in years."

Mama left the kitchen to get her and Money's pocketbooks.

Helen stood up. "As much as I'd like to join you on this maiden voyage, I have things to do and—"

Money interrupted her. "You'll be back for dinner. And there is no 'no' allowed."

Helen bent down and kissed Money on her forehead. I walked with her to the front door. I had no cares at that moment. It felt good to have no cares while having a new woman in my life.

"I want to get this check into the bank and find out what I can get for the van."

"Sell it soon. We still have the VW, and we'll sell that right before we leave town. You can use that if you want."

"I had no idea what my day was going to be like when I got out of bed this morning. All I knew was I would see you and show you this check. It must have had magic powers."

I threw my arms around Helen and held her close and then let her go. "See you for dinner. I'll make some cold salads to help us deal with this weather."

She kissed me hard and long and then left.

The old ladies stood back in the shadows but had seen it all. I turned to them, my cheeks ablaze, and helped Aunt Money in her wheelchair roll out of the apartment and toward the new van.

They were like children at first. The sight of its clean white exterior, matched by the new-car smell and the plush seats, the mechanical ramp and the ways in which Money's wheelchair got held in place in the van, not to mention all the other niceties of the big new vehicle, had them enthralled. They buckled up, and I pulled away from the curb and headed north. I wanted to get us away from the suburban sprawl and into the country for a day away.

The two of them were beside themselves with excitement. For the first time in years, they were being taken out of their day-to-day lives and on an excursion to see the world they had not been able to see. All the transformations that annoyed and upset me were things for them to take notice of with immense interest. Like the mismatched tea cups and saucers in their dining room, this new/old world was a mismatched set of perceptions that had nothing to do with them, and they moved through it with me as if they were in an amusement park. I didn't share with them my frustration that we could not escape the suburban sprawl. No matter how far north we pushed, it was all the same as it had been for the previous miles. Farmland had been sold, developers had put in sets of identical townhouses that combined the urban with a faux rural façade, and the roads had been expanded and more strip malls added to make the shopping easier for those living in the new exurban world.

I eventually turned the van around. As I did so, Mama spoke up.

"This van has to have cost a fortune, Scags. How did you pay for it?"

Just as the way out always seems to bring out new ideas, the way back retraces what has not been sufficiently completed.

"Yes, it was expensive."

"That is all you can say?"

"What do you want me to say?"

"How you paid for it."

"Why?" I didn't want to have this conversation. It aggravated me that Mama believed she could ask these questions.

Money would be no help, I thought to myself as I lined up what it was I wanted to say at that point. Aunt Money may not enter into the conversation, I reminded myself, but she will remember every word said. It was time to be honest but not overly forthcoming. In fact, not forthcoming at all.

The real fact of this conversation for me was this: it didn't begin to cover the issues that were of importance to me. I could give a reckoning of Max buying this van in a simple, straightforward way that was truthful without exposing the deeper issues. Yet it was the deeper truth of this money that was of the most importance to me, and I had no way to share that truth with the old ladies. What also pushed against my desire to be as open with them as possible was having a ghost living with me. I had no idea how to explain this phenomenon, and I doubted that there were even any clues in the literature of ghostly appearances to guide me. I had the plan that Margaret gave me, along with her presence in my life from almost the moment that plan was revealed to me. She had distanced herself from the estate and that work. Her plan included nothing, that I could see, about what I was going to do with all that money. The lion's share of my life once we returned to New York would be working with Max. I knew that then, and it felt like going back to school to me. I didn't want to go. I didn't want to be back in that kind of routine.

"I can tell you this, Mama, I have more money than we will ever need. You don't have to worry about anything on that side of life."

"Bev, I bet you want to find something to worry about. But we've done really well since Scags came home. Can't you trust her on this?"

Mama sat in a huddle within herself. Her long silence followed us home. She didn't want to be dependent on me, but there was no way not to be dependent on me.

Mama had a new dilemma, and I had learned to let her have it. She shuffled off to her bedroom when we got home. I pushed Money into the apartment and then onward to the kitchen. I wanted to make a meal and wait for Helen to return. And I wanted to make lists of all the things that needed to be done to get us all home.

The moving day arrived. We sat buckled up in the van and crossed the Skyway out of Chicago. Unanimously, we had decided to drive straight through to New York. A nonstop drive with no scenic side trips. We all agreed we were too excited to start our new lives to dawdle on our way to it. Mama crawled out of her cave and joined in all the activities. She didn't want to miss out on anything. I had never seen her willing to work as a team member before, but sometimes the promise of change is too enticing to be passed up. Helen and I were as nervous and eager as newlyweds to arrive at our destination and enjoy each other in a way we had not yet had the privacy or time to do.

I continued running every morning until we left. Helen skipped meeting me at the track and came straight to the apartment in the morning for breakfast and to see what her work assignment was. She had no prejudices against any work. So long as the work helped us move on, she and I were in total agreement about what needed to be done.

By the time we crossed the Skyway, leaving Chicago behind and driving straight into the former industrial hub that was Gary, Indiana, all of us had become settled into the comfort of the van and were each, I think, saying our own farewell to the city that had nurtured us for some time. It was there that we had become a family that could work together, but saying goodbye to Chicago felt good. We took I-80 straight across Indiana, Ohio, Pennsylvania and New Jersey before sliding through the tunnel into the city that was going to hold us in her arms.

Helen drove us into New York City. She didn't hesitate a moment. From the middle of New Jersey, where we had stopped for gas and a long bathroom break, all the way down Fifth Avenue to our new home, she gladly and confidently drove along highways and streets she had never driven before.

Long car rides put those not driving to sleep, and the gentle swaying of the van and its very good stability kept the two old ladies snoring away almost all night. We ate and sang to the radio as Helen took us in for the home stretch. Mama and Aunt Money, once awake, became a bit restless until we got out of the Lincoln Tunnel and began the drive downtown.

The van turned into a big movie theater. For the first time, all of them were seeing the city I had known for years. I didn't say a word. I didn't want to act as tour guide. Their impressions were theirs, and they deserved to see it as they could. Mama was amazed that the pedestrians waited at stoplights to cross the street and how many of them there were. Money loved seeing lights, and when we passed near enough for them to see the Empire State Building, they were disappointed that the lights hadn't been turned on yet. Helen never got rattled by the cabs swerving in front of her or tailing close behind her. The noise on the streets and the congestion served to keep her focused and happy. She wore her wide smile all the way to the building at One Fifth Avenue.

She slid the van right into the spot for loading and turned off the motor. The sudden quiet took all of our breaths away, and we sat in silence for a couple of minutes until the concierge, George this time, came to the window and knocked. He had a large dolly with him, and we slowly unfurled ourselves from the seats we had occupied for several hours.

We got Aunt Money out of the van first, and then I went to help Mama out of her seat. I guided her to the curb, not because she was frail but because her head was tilted so far back I was afraid she would fall over.

When Mama got to the curb, she went straight to Money's chair and held the handle. Her head swiveled around and around. She was like a beacon of light, her eyes trying to take in everything near and far. I had never seen her so happy.

George emptied the van quickly and handed the keys to a porter who had been hired since I had gone to Skokie. He drove off with our chariot that had brought us on a magical trip to this new land where life was brand-new for this new family. We proceeded into the lobby, George with the dolly holding all our possessions, Helen pushing Aunt Money, and me guiding Mama into her new life. We exuded joy and anticipation. Taking the elevator to the top floor, we could have used the energy of our smiles to push it faster.

George led the way to Mama and Aunt Money's apartment, which was next to Helen's and my apartment. We all walked into the new home of our old ladies to discover a woman sitting on the couch waiting for us. This was Alice. Max and Irene had hired her for the old ladies.

Alice stood up to greet us. She had been knitting as she waited, and her basket sat at the foot of the couch. She dropped her needles into it and was ready to take charge immediately. She looked to be about my age but less ruddy or outdoorsy. She smelled of good soap and not-too-spicy food. The apartment's AC was on, and it was a bit chilly, so she had on a very beautiful sweater that I assumed she had knit. She wore a skirt and sensible shoes. Given a different personality, Alice might have disappeared into the woodwork, but she had a robust nature that was attuned to the needs of women like Mama and Aunt Money. I knew right away that we were lucky to have her with us and quickly counted her in as the fifth member of our family.

Mama and Aunt Money needed to shower and eat and sleep. Alice shook my hand and Helen's hand and then led the old ladies into their bedrooms and started helping them to get ready to do as she had proposed—shower, eat, sleep.

Mama looked back at me, almost asking if this was what she must do. I went to her and kissed her on the forehead.

"Don't worry, Mama. If Alice does anything you don't like, we'll take care of her." I laughed. Alice laughed too.

Aunt Money, always attuned to what was going on around her, yelled from her room, "Get out of here, Scags. You have better things to do than hang around with us."

Helen and I said goodbye quickly, like they were two children who needed to accustom themselves to the babysitter. We left quickly.

I was eager to show Helen our apartment. George waited outside our door with the remaining bags on the dolly. As he put the key in the door, I told him to stop. I didn't want George ushering us into our home. I don't know if he understood, but like lots of people who have to serve others' needs, he seemed to take the hint and left, telling me to leave the dolly in the hallway so he could collect it later.

We were alone. In front of the locked door. I turned the key and opened it. I told Helen to stand just inside while I took the dolly into the living room and pulled the luggage off it and rolled it back to the hallway, locking the door behind us.

"Don't move yet," I said, and went into the apartment opening curtains and turning on a few lights. I wanted Helen to see it as I saw it, the kind of light and the views we had as well as the comfort of the place.

"Okay," I said. "Step in, and let's take a little tour and then go to bed."

I walked back to her side and took her hand. I brought her into the living room, where she could see the large bookcases and the comfortable chairs for reading in as well as the big window facing south, where at the end of the horizon, the World Trade Center stood out against the sky, which had been brushed with the last of the sun's light. We stood side by side, admiring what we had to look at, and then we turned around and walked through more of the apartment until we reached the bedroom.

When we arrived in the bedroom, Helen said, "This will do."

We laughed. The room looked lovely at that time of day, when the white bedspread and the dark mahogany furniture picked up the soft lights of the small lamps on the bedside tables. The room's gauziness helped set the mood for that first night of lovemaking. We undressed together for the first time and got into bed. We touched each other, thrilled not to have to stop.

Sex and love became their own feedback loop. We touched and talked until we fell asleep next to each other. I knew Margaret was around. This was her furniture and her room, and we had made love here too. But I wasn't making love to Margaret or a surrogate for Margaret. Sex with Helen was its own reward, and it led to a sleep that also felt like a reward for living well.

Margaret was still her ever-present self but in more accommodating ways. Not as intrusive, and yet she helped me in ways I learned to rely on.

Bodies at rest tend to stay at rest. My story began with me in motion and continuing to be in motion for so long that when I finally came to a resting place for five years, it awakened me to other ways of living.

This at-rest being also had a wealth index that made me one of the richest people in the world. The money I controlled—well, "controlled" was the wrong word—the money that came into my possession and needed to leave me was also out of control. Adjusting to that work, which I needed to learn how to do quickly, often competed with the adjustment to having a family and a new lover.

While I wouldn't say we lived a stable life, it was more stable than any I had lived for years. I understood that being human, we exist alongside the biological systems that regulate all life on this planet. Evolutionarily, we have learned how to accept and adapt to the constant changes we face. History taught us that those who can adapt and accept these struggles have a better chance of living worry-free lives. That promise of inner peace had not yet been granted to me.

Having more money than I knew what to do with might have seemed like one of the best ways to achieve that inner peace, but it wasn't. Trust me on that one.

We moved into the two apartments and grew together as a family, as I had wanted. Alice, too, integrated herself into the workings of this strange amalgam of women. Having sufficient funds to do as we wanted gave us all a freedom that most people moving to New York don't have.

I often amused myself with the stories about what my life had been like when I first moved to New York. I had arrived with very little of anything. I had had more books than money. It wasn't until Charles' mother reached out and gave me an allowance that I had had enough in the bank not to worry about food and rent. Once I had been shepherded into Margaret's life, I never thought about money again until she died. Then money became the whole focus of my being. I rejected Margaret's estate and made myself become totally dependent on cash-paying, menial work.

Returning to New York meant that the weight of wealth became my primary concern. Those facts, Margaret's ghost and her estate, were the two big secrets I walked around with. Carrying secrets in my pockets all day long made me a not-very-nice person. I turned into an ogre. I grumbled to myself about the things I had to do and what it meant to me to have to do them. It was a far worse daily existence than anyone else in the family had.

Even Max insinuated himself into our family by becoming the doting son Mama and Aunt Money had never had. Their faces lit up whenever he visited, and when we all had dinner together, they needed to sit on either side of him. As for Max, there was nothing he wouldn't do for our old ladies.

Max took over their lives. During the week, he found something special to do with them and on Saturday afternoon, the three of them went to the movies in Times Square. He bought them popcorn and soda, and they sat through a movie more than once if they wanted to. They could not believe any of this was possible. Mama had not trusted Max when she only knew him as the man who managed my money. When he showed how he could do similar things for her, she turned to him with more trusting eyes.

When he set up their apartment so they could each have a computer, life changed immensely for the two old ladies. He taught them how to use them, how to stay safe on them. Mama, for reasons I never knew, began investigating butterflies. Aunt Money researched the stock market. Max set up a trading account for her, and she began making trades and following her earnings.

Alice was always nearby, mostly silent, well dressed and observant. I don't know what Alice thought of all these arrangements. I didn't know then where Max had found her or why she worked as she did. What I did know was that she liked to knit, and Max made sure her knitting bag was always well supplied. Money wanted to knit too but her hands had become too arthritic. Watching the stock market and keeping track of her research took up most of her time, that and watching old TV shows.

Mama's interests in butterflies expanded. I was surprised at how quickly her knowledge increased and then spread to the study of bees and then to plants and then to the future of bees and butterflies, and soon Mama was studying botany and agriculture. Little did we know then what her research would do for us in the coming years.

It was clear that good health agreed with them. Having so much to think about and a new family eager to hear what they were doing allowed them to have separate lives for the first time in years. I almost didn't recognize the Mama who walked into our apartment some mornings for a cup of coffee. She lost her constant scowl and her negativity. With so much to think about and to share with her growing family, she had no time to sulk.

Irene and her new lover, Carole, became a part of the family and shared dinners with us often. I liked Carole. She and Irene worked at a new social service agency where men with HIV-AIDS came with mental health problems. They were not caregivers but the development team that raised money for the agency. They never suspected that the grants they wrote went through the foundation Max and I set up to award money to as many of the nonprofits that we could fund as possible, given the amount of money we had to find a home for, so to speak.

My life had developed into so many networks of money-laundering activities, all of them based on giving money to those who would make good use of it, that I often found myself in some moral agony of one kind or another. For some reason, all that pain took Carole as its target. Every time she and Irene were in heaven because they had been able to secure more funding for their agency, I wanted to wring her neck.

Carole was a sweet person, funny and easy to talk to, yet I avoided her as often as I could. I told myself I was jealous of her. I was jealous that Irene now loved her and was no longer waiting for me. It didn't matter that I loved Helen. I found that my aversion to Carole kept me away from dealing with the stones I carried in my pockets.

Our circle of seven women took turns cooking for our dinners together. This nightly occurrence altered everyone's life. Family growth always causes some new stress. But we assimilated that into our rituals. We cooked, prayed, ate and cleaned up as a unit. We paid attention to the work and to our gratitude for that work. This was something Margaret knew I needed. She was always with us, always observing.

Helen had walked onto the island of Manhattan and had everything handed to her. Her new life mirrored what I had hoped to find when I moved to New York City. I quietly seethed with jealousy.

Margaret intervened. She reminded me how ambivalent and uneasy I had been to claim my place at the table.

"You see, Margaret," I said as we walked home from an appointment I had had uptown. It was an eerily quiet Monday night early in the fall, when leaves fell to the ground, swirled about the feet, and reminded everyone but me that ghosts might be real. "I am convinced that I could have found my way had things been different."

"You mean, had we not been lovers and I had not gone to prison?"

"Yes, you could put it that way. I suppose that is the best way to put it. I'm not saying, 'I could have been a contender.' I was lost then. I know that."

"But you aren't lost now. Your life is clearly directed now."

"That's enough, Margaret. I didn't ask you to step in and take command of things."

"Not in so many words."

"Right." It was best to concede at that point.

We were almost home. I whispered to Margaret and waited for a response and came back at her as quietly and unobtrusively as possible. To an observer, I might have needed help. But what I really had was an annoying ghost who wanted to take credit for everything that was happening. I couldn't accept that.

The odd looks passersby gave me made it a relief to slip into One Fifth and find the lobby empty and my short walk to the elevator unimpeded by anyone wondering what my overwrought demeanor might mean. However, walking into my apartment, Helen was wandering about the rooms, thinking her own thoughts, and when she took one look at me, she knew something was wrong.

She came to me and took me in her arms. I smelled something strange on her. There was news, new news about her. She was excited but from the way she held me, I could feel how carefully she approached sharing her news.

"What is it, Scags?" she asked as I threw my coat onto the bed and sat down with my cheeks flushed from the walk and the talk with Margaret.

I could feel that screw tightening around me again. Too many secrets had carried me to this very moment, when all I wanted to do was cry to relieve the tension they placed on me.

Though, looking at Helen in that light, with her face radiating her happiness, I paused, took a step back from my desire to spill out everything I had been holding inside me for centuries, it seemed, and became magically still to listen to her.

Margaret too placed a hand on me, so to speak, to quiet me down. Inside me I heard her saying, "Be patient, please. Find a better way to tell her your secrets, preferably not now."

Helen could no longer hold back her excitement. The popping brightness in her eyes reflected the fireworks going off inside her. I needed her to look at me like that, with the expectation that the news she had would lead to even more love.

Helen worked at an agency in New York that helped relocate Afghan refugees here in the US. She dove into her work with great enthusiasm and knowledge. She understood more than many at that agency what it meant for these refugees to be safe here. Her compassionate approach to her work led to finding a network of others equally as concerned but who lacked Helen's in-country experiences. They urged her to write about her life in Afghanistan. Then she was invited to give talks. Helen was a good writer. She knew how to write about her personal connections to the women she had worked with and to share the political story too of what her life there had shown her. She had no apparent agenda. That gave her work a seeming objectivity and fairness that could get lost in the polemics of the day. She became what our family loved to call her: our resident pundit.

Watching her about to share her news, I floated above us both and wanted to see how we both would behave. I did know what she was about to tell me.

"I can't hold this in any longer, Scags."

"You don't have to. Tell me."

She took a deep breath and blurted out, "I have a book contract." She might have been close to tears, but I grabbed her and held her close to me. I felt her heart beating against my chest. I knew how much this meant to her and how it would change our lives. But from my out-of-body perch, I also watched as I stood up, holding her even closer to me, and whispered into her ear, "I am so proud of you."

I was proud of her and happy for her. Her success, though, shone a light on my life. I was a money-laundering machine. We had so much money coming in and there were so few places we knew yet to trustingly place it. I lived like a faucet that I had to open to various degrees of fullness. But that was what I did. That was what my life was like then. Everything had to be evaluated through the filter of the money, where to put it, and then where was the next place to put it.

Helen untangled herself from my hold and told me she needed to speak to Max about an agent to handle the book contract. She dialed him immediately. She was like that. Why wait? What was going to change by waiting?

I left her in the bedroom on the phone with Max. When I walked into the living room, Mama and Aunt Money were there, along with Alice, of course, and they had furniture rearranging on their minds.

On the surface, a trivial thing to handle. I've observed that we think moving furniture will give us some much-needed change in our lives.

Mama had her ideas. Aunt Money had hers. Alice sat on the couch while each presented her ideas, and continued knitting.

I zoned out of the talks. I knew if the two of them kept talking, eventually, either one of them would give up her objections or the other one would find a way to compromise. I had learned from these previous discussions to be with them but not enter into the fray, which allowed the dynamic of their negotiations to come to a peaceful resolution.

But Mama surprised us all and got very angry. She slammed her hand down on the table we all sat at for dinner and one of the legs gave way. It split and collapsed. The noise jolted me. Helen ran from the bedroom where she had been talking to Max. I don't think Alice dropped a stitch. She stood up, though, made sure Mama was not hurt and then returned to the couch and her knitting. It was not her job, she often said, to interfere in these discussions.

However, we were now left with a table with three legs that needed four if not more. The weight of all our elbows on the table along with the food and books that accompanied each meal had made the table feel precarious almost from the start of our daily dinners. We had to decide: repair it or replace it.

Helen said, "Wow, that sounded like a gunshot." None of us questioned how she would have known that sound. But the wood had been dry and grown weak. Now it was shattered.

Before returning to her call with Max, Helen said, "I vote in favor of replacing it with something bigger and more sturdy. We will grow as a group. Let's plan for that too."

By that weekend, Helen found a table suitable for our needs. At dinner on Saturday night, we held a vote to authorize Helen and me to act for the group and to visit the table. It was our first substantive vote. We often voted on what to cook or how we might change the shopping and washing rotation. But this was a milestone for us.

We were in urgent need of a new table. The circle had grown. Women from the building as well as the surrounding area had joined us. It became more than a supper club. We gathered at the Table to work on helping food pantries and to support the AIDS project that Irene and Carole worked on. We also offered help and support to the homeless and had just added a new tutoring project. Our decision to replace the fractured table reverberated into the neighborhood we lived in.

The motion passed unanimously that Helen and I would go see the table she had found. Since we were now such a large group, Helen and I decided to go see it that Sunday.

On Sunday morning, we drove upstate to see the monster table someone we knew who knew someone had decided would be perfect for our needs. Good car trips require the proper weather. That day, the sun did not shine too brightly, and the traffic leaving the city was very light.

Helen loved to drive, and I loved to be the passenger. Helen liked to talk while driving, and I liked to listen while staring out at the scenery. Helen had plotted out the route, and I served as navigator.

I watched the map, I listened to Helen talk, and I thought, this trip might be the perfect time to tell Helen about the money and Margaret. We rarely had time alone, except when the day ended and we were falling asleep.

That was why, on our way to Sullivan County, Helen took the time to tell me her plan for writing the book.

"It's a pretty simple plan, if I do say so myself. I will quit my job and write full time. You have room in the foundation office that you can rent to me for those two years, and I promise not to bother you or nag at you to take me to lunch or to hold my hand when I get stuck."

She looked at me and smiled.

"Do you already anticipate that your book will be hard to write?"

"No, I think it is always a temptation to take breaks from writing."

I agreed, and we proceeded to fantasize about scheduling sex meetups during the workday. We fantasized taking holidays and staying at bed-and-breakfasts in the country, pretending to be working but really just hanging out together.

"Are you saying that we don't have enough time alone?" I asked her after we had gone into multiple versions of how we could spend time together while she wrote her book.

"I'm saying that I like making love to you."

"I do too."

We stopped at a diner to pick up a cup of coffee for her and a cup of tea for me. Then we pulled the car into a field off the road and had a picnic in the car from the cooler we always carried with us, filled with food we could eat. Being vegan made that a necessity.

In early afternoon, we arrived at a farmhouse that was similar to Ruth's farm. I had been gathering my thoughts about the talk I was determined to have with Helen after we bought the Table. This talk had been on my mind for too long. I should have told her before we left Chicago. Now, years later, it was past time. But being out in the country gave me the emotional room to say what I needed to say.

"Margaret and the Money," was the title of my talk. But first we had to buy the Table.

We met our Table as soon as we walked into the farmhouse. It could not be avoided; it was a monster of a table. We were greeted at the farmhouse door by a young woman dressed like a hostess in a country restaurant. Once she had taken us to the Table, she left us to look at it. The room was dark because all the lights had been removed. All we had was sunshine gleaming off it to assess if it was right for us.

This entire farm had been sold to a developer who was creating yet another country club golf course with a surrounding housing development. Nothing much in the way of imagination was involved in that plan. The Table too would be destroyed if no one wanted it.

It truly was too large for most homes and most apartments. We would have to empty the living room of most of our furniture to accommodate it. In its present location, it seemed that the house had grown around it. The surface had stains, burns and whittlings reflecting the generations that had gathered around it. Helen and I walked around its large circumference, placed our hands on it, felt the sturdy weight of it. It would be impossible for Mama to slam her hand down and shatter it. It wasn't rectangular but round, the perfect shape for us all. We arranged to have it shipped to our apartment almost immediately.

Helen didn't want to stay too long in the house. She said it upset her that it was about to be torn down. I wrote a check for the table and its shipping, and with one last touch of it before it would be in our home, I felt the same sturdy sureness of a farming life, of Ruth's life, as I had known it, and took Helen by the elbow and walked her into the fields.

Helen said, "The movers'll have to take the table apart and roll it into the apartment. It is a beauty."

"It is perfect," I said.

There was lots of daylight left, and we took a walk into the fields. The stubble of the mowed field was rigid; soon it would freeze. Fields in the winter before they get covered with snow look like the faces of old men whose whiskers have grown out of their chins and cheeks. I smelled fall ending and winter approaching. Was I homesick for the road life? Standing on that mowed field, holding Helen's hand, an urge to get back on the road came billowing out of me like a sail that had been lost to the wind and then found it. Then I lost myself again. I saw

Margaret and me sitting on our porch, watching the rain come down, resting from a day in the fields of our farm.

"I like farms," I said to Helen. "I've worked on many."

We stood facing each other in the middle of a furrow.

"I once had a lover. We were going to own a farm and live on it forever. We talked about it in such a way it was as if we already lived there."

"Who was this, Scags? Who was it you were going to live on a farm with? I don't know about any of this."

"I had a lover—Margaret. You and I live in her apartment. Yes, it's now ours, but it came from her. So much of what we have came from her. I've never had to tell anyone about this. Irene knew her, and of course Max did too. They have been most considerate to leave it up to me to tell you about her. There are things about her even they don't know. But I am going to tell you it all now because I cannot live like this with you and not tell you this story. I have wanted to tell it to you since we met. I have found so many reasons to postpone this that I am now embarrassed and afraid that you will leave me."

"Leave you? Because you had a lover before me?"

"Margaret was the love of my life then. She was also an anti-nuclear activist who went to prison for her actions, and as she was near to being released, she was murdered by one of the inmates."

I paused. I had to. I was on the path to telling Helen that Margaret's ghost lived with us.

"Oh my, Scags. What the fuck? I mean, wait a minute."

Helen didn't look too good. I wanted to stay in that moment with her.

"I had no idea, Scags."

"That's because I haven't told you about Margaret. If that were all there was to this story, I might have told you sooner, and it might not be the agony it is to tell you the rest. But I have to say it all now, or I am afraid I will find more reasons not to tell you. Please, let me go on."

I meant it too. I wanted her permission to say what I had to say.

"Of course. Whatever it is, please tell me. I love you."

That was true. Helen was a lover. Even if we had not been romantic partners, she would have said the same thing. Love, for her, opened up all doors between those who loved.

When I started to tell her my story, I wanted all the guilt I carried with me about what Max and I were doing, about not having told Helen about me and Margaret, to magically disappear.

Then as the words came out of my mouth, one after the other, I looked at her face to see if she was with me. I started talking, and I could have been in the shower talking to the water splashing onto my head. Words glistened like spray as I talked about the things that were as important to me as breathing.

"Let me back up and start again. I had a lover, Margaret, when I first came to the city. We lived together, and it was one of the most important times of my life. Margaret was an anti-nuclear activist, went to prison for her actions and was killed in prison shortly before she was to be released. That was when we were going to buy a farm and leave the city behind us. I was visiting her when she was killed.

"Staying alive after she died was so difficult that I did a lot of awful things and hurt the people who were there for me the most. I left town for three years, disappeared, and then one day returned.

"Before I left town, I learned that Margaret's estate, the whole of it, had been left to me, and it was more substantial and well, criminal, than Margaret had ever revealed to me. I wasn't supposed to have to handle it. She was not supposed to have died in prison. Max and I were left in charge to manage it, and at first, I could not deal with that amount of money or how it came to be mine to manage.

"And there is more to this story than I have ever told anyone, so please stay with me and listen, just as you have been. I know this is a lot to take in, but I need you to know."

She gave me a big hug as a way of saying she would listen. We continued standing face-to-face in the middle of the field.

"I couldn't do anything after Margaret died. I tried, but it was useless to count on me. Then Irene and I became lovers. She was very kind to me. She took care of me and made me get out of bed and try to live. She missed Margaret, too, of course. She and Margaret had been lovers in the convent—Margaret had once been a nun too—or maybe even before then. We each loved the other's body because it had been with Margaret. After several months of this kind of love, I had to leave. I didn't plan to leave. When I left, I took nothing that could help them find me. I ran away from Irene and Max and the money. I worked menial jobs and only for cash. I lived on the road and kept my distance from any kind of real relationship.

"After a while, I couldn't find any place that didn't make me feel miserable. There was nothing I could do to relieve the pain of losing Margaret, until, one night, hanging out in a motel, Margaret's ghost appeared."

I paused and waited. Helen looked at me. "You're not going to stop there, are you?"

"Do you believe in ghosts?"

"I might. Keep talking."

"One night, near my 45th birthday, I had gotten to that point where I could either go on or I could die, when Margaret's ghost appeared next to me and offered to take me home. She meant back to the city and to the life I had there. Or so I thought.

"We did return to the city, and that night, on my birthday, she gave me a present. It was unlike anything you can imagine. She showed me the entirety of my life from start to finish. It wasn't a road map about how to make everything happen, but it was a set of signposts that showed where all of my life was headed.

"When Margaret was alive, we often talked, at length, about how aimless my life felt and how rootless I was. Part of that was because Margaret needed me to take care of her business affairs, not in real terms but in the language of structures and trusts. Without reading them, I signed a lot of papers that Max handed me.

"Margaret and I lived with constant surveillance. The FBI and other legal enforcers listened in on everything they could and read our mail and so forth. I didn't know what Margaret was really doing and I didn't care. Margaret was an amazing person and she loved me. I did as she needed me to do.

"But my life was at a dead end. I couldn't find the traction to move forward. By the time I got on the road, I thought that experience would lead me to a better understanding of who I was. But I wasn't on the road for that reason; I was on the road because I was in mourning.

"Margaret rescued me from myself and turned me in the direction I needed to go. When you and I met, I had come to Skokie to help Mama and Aunt Money, who had need of great help. But before I showed up at Mama's, we hadn't spoken for fifteen years. Mama had thrown me out of her life when she found out I was a lesbian. So, you see, you and I met during that period when the fragile detente between me and Mama had just begun. I believe having you appear in my life helped to cement it."

"Wait, Scags, you're going so fast that I have lost the story about Margaret being a ghost."

I laughed. I had never told this story, and I lost track of the threads. And maybe having to talk about Margaret's ghost with Margaret's ghost right there with us was more than I had the skills to do then. But I tried.

"Let's get in the car. I am getting cold."

We walked back to the car, and as we buckled up and headed back to the road home, I relaxed, having accomplished more than what we had been commissioned to do. The worst of it was over, as far as I was concerned. The story in most of its outlines had been laid out. Filling in all the details would take time, but there was lots of that before us.

"Don't you want to wait to hear the ghost story for when we are home and in bed? I can make it all the more entertaining that way."

"Stop teasing me. You opened up this whole mess of a story before me. You better damn well finish it."

Helen pulled into traffic. I watched the way the sunlight played on her face. So many times before that afternoon, I had wanted to be in this exact moment, flowing with the traffic back into the city, with a full tank of a story to still share with her. Helen relaxed too. She could keep track of all the cars around her and the line of my story. She kept smiling throughout the entire drive, so I knew, and had always known, that she had been picked by Margaret for me.

"Margaret is always with me. I see her as she moves about and she talks. She is invisible to everyone else, though I think that Aunt Money can see her too."

"That makes sense. Money is like that."

"Yes, she is. Funny how she is actually living up to her name, isn't it?"

"Don't get distracted. One story at a time. For now, I want the ghost story."

"I've told you about as much as I know about that. Margaret is here, with us, all the time. As long as I am around, she is too. She and I have become inseparable."

"Can you make love to her?"

"Aha! Now the real reason for your interest comes out."

"Seriously, is she able to have sex?"

"No. She has no form. No physical being."

Helen relaxed more.

By the end of my story, we were almost home. She said nothing more. We left the car at the garage and crossed the street, with Helen holding my hand as she usually did as we approached home.

I mentioned going to the park to sit on a bench, but Helen pulled me into our building. We continued quickly across the empty lobby and into the elevator and up to our apartment.

I unlocked the door. The whole place was dark, and we left it that way and entered the bedroom.

"Is she here now?"

I took a deep breath and felt the room and knew that in some ways, Margaret was always everywhere, all the time. But as far as being a witness to us at that moment?

"I don't think so," I replied, "but I'm not sure where she is right now."

"Can you see her?"

"Not now. And I don't want to see her. I want to be with you. She isn't your competitor, if that is what you're thinking."

We sat on the bed, still in the dark and holding hands.

"It's always something with you, Scags. I mean that in a very good way. Surprises seem to be your way of life. Yet, we always end up having a good time. No limits here to what we can do or imagine. Then you tell me about a supernatural being who was once your lover and whose home this is. I feel a bit lost now.

"I came here at a very odd moment in my life. I had nowhere I had to be and no one I had to be with. I saw you on the track and thought, that woman looks interesting and is cute, why not see what's up with her? Then we became the typical lesbians-fall-in-love-and-move-in-together couple, and we have no real problems, and we never fight, and we live in this magical place, and I am doing everything I ever dreamed about.

"Then you throw in that the money comes from these tainted sources. Sweetheart, you are talking to someone who lived in Afghanistan, a place where the economy is based on heroin. I'm not about to get my purist self on a soapbox with you. You add a ghost to this too. What? You think that frightens me or that I, what . . . ? Will go running scared back to Chicago?"

I got up from the bed and lit the candles sitting on each of our bedside tables. The scents rose up as did the shadows of the flames flickering on the wall. Helen was thinking out loud with me. I took that as a very good sign.

"What were you doing during those three years you were away? I know what you were doing. You were in mourning."

"Yes. True."

"You must have really loved Margaret."

"Yes." That was true. I loved her, but what we had was so different from what Helen and I were developing. "It was very different with Margaret."

"You mean than it is with me?"

"With anyone, I would say. Sometimes I didn't believe she was real even when she was alive. She and Irene had been nuns before I met her and were in the convent together and left together because they were lovers. Strangely, their love didn't survive the freedom. But they were involved with the same work and shared so much of their lives while living separately.

"It was hard to know what Margaret actually thought of me. I know she loved me. I loved her. I often suspected that she could put up with me because my love was like a puppy dog's. Maybe she expected me to age out of this life with her. But I couldn't have done that. While I was away, I began to see how deeply ingrained in me she was. I couldn't breathe some days because of the loss.

"I did things to take care of myself that took me into the lower levels of my soul. When it was time to come home, it was Margaret's ghost that came to guide me. She swept me up, and I was caught again in this web of her past, her father's crimes and all of this money, and against all of that is you and having Mama and Aunt Money to care for. That's where my heart sits now."

Helen and I then lay back on the bed. For the first time, I had no idea where my arms ended and hers began. I don't know who was undressing or needed help undressing. I did know that her hands on my skin had a three-dimensional impact. That is, I wanted those hands on my skin. My skin wanted to be against her skin. Something happened that gave our sexual encounter that night a grace that had not been there before. We kissed without time. We finally came without any reserve, and when we repeated and repeated the gracing of our bodies to each other, we had crossed a new threshold where our bodies knew the other so well that before we went to sleep, I knew where she was cold, and she knew where to cover me up.

The next morning, I woke up to see Helen resting her face on her hand, staring at me. She smiled when I opened my eyes and said, "We bought a table."

I laughed. We had bought a table and now our circle could be seated comfortably together.

Helen's presence in my life was extraordinary. Having met in midlife, we had had enough forming of ourselves to know what we wanted.

Helen, though, had an experience of life and a perspective that made her feel implacable. If there were things that could shock her, they weren't the things that happened with the people she loved. And she was generous in her loving. She laughed a lot, which crinkled her face, and the scar on the right side would make her cheek look like the slats on vertical blinds. Her joy disfigured her face, and yet she retained her open acceptance of fun without any self-consciousness.

When I touched her scar, I never thought of how bad a job the stitching was but of how lucky that she had survived. I touched her scar and was grateful for whoever it was who'd been there for her.

I tried to talk to her about it. But she assured me that it didn't matter.

I often thought of her acceptance of that scar as representative of her attitudes about life. To her, that scar was not her. Someone else had done that, and his actions were separate from who she was.

She had survived his aggression. On some days, as I wandered through airports waiting for a flight or decided to walk to a meeting in Manhattan because transport was a mess, in those rather unfilled times when I was not connected to my surroundings but filled with time to think, the contrast between Helen and Margaret rose up in images of their wounds. I saw the hole in Margaret's neck where she was stabbed. Helen's scar grew on me because we lived in such intimacy.

Intimacy did that. With Helen, I floated into those places where we experienced love's buoyancy. We shared a similar view of the shimmering lights that guided us forward. This intimacy was not what I had known with Margaret. Margaret had seen the emptiness of me and loved me entirely. With Helen, all that I was could be shown, and we shared the everything we were without reservation. Through our lovemaking and daily living, I no longer missed Margaret or required her. Yet it took me many years to realize that.

I'd never known Margaret in this way. Margaret had a different way of being in love. She had a beautiful body, but she barely noticed it. She loved my body but was not sure what to do with it. She wanted me, but her interest lagged because she always felt drawn to higher purposes. The tension of sex, though, was too hard to resist. Our love grew out of the New York sidewalks. We walked away the anxieties of the day and talked without fear of being listened to.

It was wonderful to walk and talk as we each held a cup of coffee growing colder in one hand, the other holding on to each other. At some moment that we had not planned, we'd turn back toward home. We'd go home to make love. At dawn, Margaret would rise to pray, kneeling alone in her alcove, silent and peaceful. Then she'd shower, dress, kiss me and leave for her day.

We had met when that need for physical contact overwhelmed Margaret. We never talked about how that sexual connection grew into love. Since our life together was one of constant interruptions, separations, secrets and surveillance, I was not surprised at how little time we had to talk of love.

I lived with that aching regret after Margaret died. Why hadn't I been brave enough to tell her how much I loved her? I ached too much for physical contact after she died. Irene was the perfect lover because she was the perfect substitute for Margaret. She had had sex with Margaret. She had memories of her body too.

As I tried to explain all of this to Helen, I saw her listening to me with the ear of the lover.

I loved Helen for listening to me. I loved her for finding these talks arousing.

When I met women on the road and wanted to sleep with them, that was sometimes all I wanted. No sex. Just the closeness. For some, this was sufficient. They'd wake up in the morning, and I'd be gone. I blamed them for these sexless encounters and made fun of their sexless lives. I'd show no pity and no sympathy.

Some women I met became aggressive and even dangerous, threatening me and playing lots of games of control. Knowing there was no hope of connecting with them, I played some of the games too. I picked up those bad habits easily.

I always knew I could leave at any time. All I wanted were moments of release from missing Margaret. What surprised me for all those years was that I never stopped missing Margaret.

"You lived to survive," Helen said as we talked in bed one night. "You weren't even able to feel pleasure, I bet."

She had her hands on me. Her touch had been to so many places on my body and had recorded so much sensory data; it knew so much.

Helen had a special sensory participation in life. Before buying a fabric or a leafy green, she needed to touch it and smell it. I loved watching her bring the item to her face. I could tell by her expression whether she wanted to buy it. As I learned more about her, as our lives merged, I dug deeply into the ever-growing library of Helen's habits and history.

Margaret had not fascinated me. The degree of danger we lived with made me stay away from that kind of intoxicated love. Trespassing on her secrets was not possible. Keeping my distance didn't hurt until she was gone.

And as a ghost, Margaret had no interest in her past. We didn't sit around and discuss those things we had shared. That meal that is the whole of loving someone, those memories that keep the flame going, that was not of any interest to Margaret. It had all evaporated.

Thus we entered into the stable portion of our lives in New York. It slipped up on me, but it happened. Helen, Mama, Aunt Money and I lived our lives in ways I had never lived mine before. I had to travel with Max, which took me away from them, but we were a family that I returned to.

When the new Table arrived, Mama looked at me with awe. I didn't know what the Table had to do with her changed attitude to me, but whatever it was, I enjoyed it.

She took her seat next to me when we sat down to a meal for the first time at the Table. It barely fit in our apartment, but it was a beautiful piece of furniture that needed to be with us.

Mama came the closest to saying the obvious. "This is a huge table, Scags. Are you planning on inviting the whole building to eat with us?"

Everyone laughed. We had made the Table a part of the family. Helen got up and brought in the place settings. Irene followed her into the kitchen and brought out the food. Unexpectedly, Max joined us that night, looking as haggard as always. He pushed Carole to one side so he could talk to Aunt Money. He had come to talk to her about her stock portfolio. They sat huddled together. No one bothered them.

The end of the 1990s ticked by for our large extended household. We were aware of the forces outside our sphere that were at work destabilizing everything. But we were also busy and that ticking of the clock was annoying. The fears of a Y2K meltdown blared from the rooftops. President Clinton embarrassed himself and ordered the bombing of Iraq to divert attention from his own sexual deviancy.

Max and I worked double time at the end of the 1990s trying to alleviate hunger, and it was a bad game. We had to circumvent too many governments to even get close enough to push some food—in particular, baby formula—across an Iraqi border heavily patrolled by a moronic force that considered feeding babies subversive. We risked an enormous amount of capital to get food into Iraq, and it was never enough. We couldn't advertise it either.

But we were like so many in those days. We were, in fact, like too many in those days. We worked beyond what was humanly necessary, causing me, for one, to come down with a bad flu. I lay about the apartment with a high fever and no energy to do a damn thing. I was thoroughly disgusted with myself. I tried to fight off the flu, to deny it any place in my life, but then it toppled me.

Max and I had been to Switzerland, the land of money, too many times that year. We had been doing more than counting our money. Max kept his ear attuned to the news from multiple sources. He knew many more people than I. My name was kept off the accounts as best we could, and I stayed silent because it created less friction for Max. At Max's urging, we hired a game-theory consultant. It was a wise move. He kept us way ahead of all curves when it came to strategically placing the money.

I settled into the steepest learning curve I could handle. I attended seminars and cocktail parties. I learned to listen and to learn while keeping as quiet as possible.

A few people we saw repeatedly came to interest me. I watched how they moved into the rooms and where they set their attention even while not speaking. I used the bite-my-tongue approach at all cocktail parties. Eventually, no matter how hard we had worked to keep a low profile, appearing repeatedly at these top donor events gave Max and me a mythic standing. Stories circulated about who we were and where our money came from and where it went. Most of the stories were untrue.

However, it soon became apparent who the recipients of our awards were, and they were more obvious than the sources of our cash. Humans are curious beings. Given a situation where there is no information, stories are made up to fill the void, or at least the initial two minutes of a cocktail party when everyone finds the person or persons they must talk to and then leaves.

Max and I flew in and out of places so often that we learned how to travel very light and without carrying many details of our work. It became a point of pride how much we kept memorized, including account numbers and their passwords.

In the midst of all the Y2K chatter, we were aware that none of it was credible. I became adept at listening to the supposed soothsayers of finance and knowing that they were not the ones whose ideas mattered. It was like running a maze. Every new idea had its reliable proponent and then a flotilla of those who were set out to deceive and subvert.

I was often bored out of my skull at these get-togethers where wealthy people deluded themselves into thinking they were using their money for the good of mankind. Travel became a skimming-on-the-surface-of-life experience. It was only when we were back in New York that I felt at all like I was a real person. I began to believe that the life I lived with the wealthy was more a novel of intrigue, a spy novel in which the forces of evil met the forces of goodness and always won.

I had no illusions that doling out money to organizations was the best use of my time. As the conflict about this grew inside me, so did the tensions in our political world. For the first time in my lifetime, a presidential election result was not known within a matter of a few hours or days but went on for weeks. The conflict in the body politic grew large while the conflict inside me grew to horrendous proportions. I took this nasty feeling I sensed in the world and lashed out at everyone, until one day, sitting at my desk in my office, I fell over and hit my head, then passed out and became deathly ill. All the ill will I felt around me had backed up inside me.

The year had changed. The election had been a sleeper and then a nail-biter.

By the summer of 2001, I felt overwhelmed. I talked to Max about it. He was preoccupied with how the political arena was affecting economic growth. What this was going to mean for those who depended on the money we distributed and where it had to be placed so it could do the most good.

Max engaged Money to track the markets. They both had concerns about the government's actions in the Middle East. Too many variables were at play, as Money often muttered under her breath. Strange things happened offshore, away from the prying eyes of the press, Money reminded us.

The election results shocked us all. But it confirmed something Money and Max talked about endlessly but didn't want to take the time to explain to us.

When I asked Mama what Max and Money were discussing, she looked at me and said, "I'm almost afraid to say. If Money were going on about this without Max, I'd say she was senile."

"What is it, Mama?"

"Really, Scags, I don't understand it. Such a lot of talk about Arabs and they talk about studying 'lines of power.' Those are their words. They come up with stories and then plot the probable market response. They seem to be paranoid, Scags, but only when they are talking to each other. I don't understand a word they say. I can repeat it, but it means nothing to me."

She began twisting her hands, a sure sign we needed to change the conversation. Despite the better times she was having, Mama seemed restless and that worried me.

I asked her what I could do to help her feel better.

She looked at me as if I had caught her in her most private place.

"What do you mean, Scags? Do? For what?"

She stared at me with her green eyes pooling over with tears. She wiped them away, but couldn't stop them.

"What's wrong, Mama?"

I didn't know anything about her new life, I realized then. Our old ladies had seemed so happy. What changed?

"Is Money upsetting you?"

She looked at me as if that was the strangest question. It took her a moment to finally respond.

"I don't want you to think that I am ungrateful."

"Okay. I won't. Tell me."

"I miss living in the country."

That took me by surprise then. If ever there was a non sequitur, that was it.

"Mama, you never lived in the country."

"Yes. That's the problem."

"I don't understand."

"I don't expect you to understand, Scags. When did you ever live in the country? Really. How could you appreciate what I'm feeling?"

At that moment, I too began to cry. I didn't miss living in the country. Not at that moment. I had missed something developing in Mama. That made me sad but hopeful that she trusted me enough to tell me her worries.

"If you want to visit the country, we can go, or Alice and Money can travel with you."

"I don't want to travel. I want to be."

Mama walked away before we could talk more. I had never heard her talk like that. She lived inside something she still hadn't told me about. But I heard her heartsick tone. It made me love her more.

Then I got very sick. I picked up a bug on my travels. I passed out at work, and because Helen also worked in my office suite, she was there to help me get home. I developed a high fever. I had bruised my forehead when I fell over, which gave me a bit of vertigo that was exacerbated by the fever. All that meant I couldn't walk without assistance. The intensity of my illness lasted a few days. But the recuperation went on for weeks, it seemed.

I had gone from being a person who never got sick to becoming a complete invalid. I had delirious dreams. No appetite. No drive of any kind. All I could do was sleep and when not sleeping, lie in bed with the radio on. My body ached, chilled and then sweated. I thought I was decomposing. The illness came on so fast that I had made no preparations for it. I struggled to talk, to manage our lives, but I learned quickly to do nothing, absolutely nothing. It had to run through my body until it had had enough. As I began to feel better after a few days, I saw that I had to let my own system do the fighting. That autonomous part of our being that we have no control over, that part needed the energy to do its job.

An array of nurses took shifts to watch over me. I was never left alone. Helen stayed with Irene and Carole so she could get some rest. Everyone at the Table pitched in. Whenever I opened my eyes, I saw someone I knew and trusted at my side watching over me. I had never been so sick or needed such round-the-clock care.

Then, as my mind had more energy to reflect on what was happening, I caught glimpses, almost like snapshots, of something I wanted, that Margaret and I had wanted and that may have been in that life Margaret laid out before me on my birthday over five years ago.

I slept and woke. Slept deeply, and the pain in my body receded. Like a tide that was, for now, leaving the shore and taking with it all those rocky shards that had been plaguing my body. Whose sharp edges had been poking into my gut and throat and even the backs of my knees and behind my eyes. My entire body had, at one point or another, suffered their piercing. As they left, as I could speak without them shredding my throat, I had another strange rush of emotion run through me, as if those feelings, all of them, had become liquefied. They coursed through my body, checking on the status of each organ, soothing the tissues and bones; even my fingers and toenails were bathed in this restorative touch.

While I had been well looked after, Margaret, too, never left. It must have been easier for her to be with me then. She could monitor me in ways no others could. I held fast to her throughout the time when I was most unable to move or communicate. She was a presence, the essence of herself, making up for all those years since she had been gone.

It was a brief but intense sickness. Much of my work that the foundation relied on had been abruptly delayed. Once I was able to sit in the living room and eat whole but smaller meals again, Max and I decided that I needed to take one of the trips to a pick-up point where cash was stashed from our "friends" in Canada. It meant having a car and driver take me to Sandusky, Ohio. Our cash flowed along old Prohibition routes. It was hidden in an old bunker, a safe house from those days, and the time had come to retrieve it.

It may not have been smart to travel. I thought Helen and I could go together and have time alone after so much time apart. No other solution seemed reasonable to me. I didn't hear what Max thought. I knew best, and we agreed to take two drivers, Maurice and Martin, our double team, so we didn't have to stay in a motel. It would be a quick two-day trip, there and back, with an opportunity for dinner at the Italian restaurant that had been built almost on top of the safe house.

Having put the structure in place, I asked Helen to join me. Even if all we did was hold hands and rest in the back of the limo, that would be enough for me. Of course, there would be time for dinner too at the Sicilian's. That was the lure after all, a wonderful Sicilian vegan dinner prepared for us. And then there was the kitschy charm of the restaurant, with its *putti* and half-dressed women flowing out of their clothes while dreamily fleeing across marble staircases, so intent on arriving in their lovers' arms that their clothes leave them in anticipation.

How many young boys had sat at those tables slurping in pasta while gazing at the bare-breasted women? Probably a couple of generations of boys, if not more. And in the basement, in the women's room, was one of those cheesy gags that comes with the mobster motifs. This was where I took Helen on our round-trip ride to pick up a trunkful of cash. The cash was secretly placed in a vault behind the restaurant. The vault was known only to those who had read the old deeds to the original buildings, much of them having been torn down to build the restaurant.

Max and I had found the papers in Henry's archive of holdings, lots and lots of small businesses in out-of-the-way places, which he could visit as a silent business partner. Who probably was not all that silent, given what I knew of him before he got sick.

I tried to imagine Margaret and Henry driving to Sandusky, Ohio just as Helen and I did on that September morning and wondered how they would speak to each other. If they spoke. Margaret had not attended to the estate at all because of the constant surveillance. Now, I was overwhelmed with the amount of money and the amount of work it took to keep it available to hundreds, if not thousands, of organizations that needed this cash support. All over the world, we were depositing lump sums, no strings attached, and if I were creating a misery index for our planet, I would have to say we barely touched the surface of the misery, poverty and hunger that grips billions of people.

I acknowledged that fact to Helen while we sat in a lovely corner of the restaurant enjoying a tasty pasta dish and a carafe of wine, but I knew I was doing what I could. I lived an absurd life. Helen had accepted it better than I had.

She went down to the bathroom when Maurice came in to tell me the money had been transferred. He said he'd received a strange message from Max. We were to get on the road immediately.

I had the waitress pack up our food as well as food for Martin and Maurice, and before I could finish paying, it happened. Helen had removed the cardboard covering the large cock of the leering muscled man in the women's bathroom setting off a set of alarms guaranteed to embarrass any women climbing back up the stairs to finish her dinner. There would be no peace now. Everyone mocked and laughed at the prurient female.

We were helped out of the restaurant by Maurice and Sid, the owner, who enjoyed that stupid prank. Martin was at the wheel of the car. Sid carried our food and set it on the seat between Helen and me. He told me to say hi to Max, and he went back inside to join the wisecracking crowd waiting to see the face of the embarrassed woman who had removed the swim trunks from the Italian stud standing in the ladies' room. We had to leave through a back doorway to get to the car without anyone noticing us.

"That was a surprise," Helen laughed. I grabbed her hand and squeezed it. I still felt weak from the illness and wanted to sleep. The ride back to Manhattan was long and circuitous. Maurice, Max and I had discovered a variety of routes in order to stay safely away from anyone suspicious who might want that trunk filled with cash we were transporting back to New York City.

The ride that night was beautiful. A big full moon lit up the fields. As we approached each small town, I wanted to stop. I wanted a bed and to stop moving, but we couldn't stop. Max gave the order to get home fast. It wasn't wise to ask why; it was necessary to do it. Martin and Maurice got us through to I80 near Paterson via the back roads. They knew where to ignore speed limits and where to be extremely cautious. We had to trust them.

I slept most of the way home until the sunrise filled the car with the golden light of pollution-tinged air. Max kept checking on our location, and as we took the lower level of the George Washington Bridge, crawling into town with the earliest of commuters, he told Maurice to use a different phone. Maurice looked at us in the back seat. Helen slept. Something was wrong. He got out of the car and headed downtown on foot.

Max gave the driver several instructions, and as we headed toward the door of One Fifth, the first plane hit the World Trade Center.

Maurice was meeting someone who would be able to pick up the money. Martin got us out of the car and then was on his way as fast as he could go, given the tumult of that morning. I would have gone with Maurice to make the drop but I had Mama, Money, Alice and Helen to look out for. Chaos was just foaming up around all the corners of downtown Manhattan. As the lines of communication fried up, Helen and I rushed upstairs to take care of our old ladies.

Mama fell into a hysterical fit, and it took many hands to soothe her. Aunt Money wept. Alice kept her hydrated and warm. Helen and I took turns helping Mama calm down. Her hysteria, which erupted as quickly as the Twin Towers went down, kept us up many nights as we paced the floors with her, helping her to breathe. For hours on end, Mama cried from fear and anger. We tried as best we could to keep her away from the windows that looked south. There she would see the smoke rising from the giant hole in the ground. That smoke lasted for 99 days. None of us counted them, but we were always aware of the smell and the sights.

As the days went by, the Table filled up with a growing community. In a series of moves whose order I can't recall, people started moving into our apartment. We took turns using the bed and couches. We cooked together, cleaned together. Carole and Irene organized our spiritual health by spending time with each person in some form of meditation or prayer. The psychic wounds of having watched the towers fall were different for everyone. The bellicose nature of the government's response also pained everyone who sat at the Table. We all felt in need of each other.

This may sound like we lived in chaos. But it was an organized chaos. We all wanted to do something and began talking about it. What could we do? What was the best response we could come up with in order to understand both what had happened and what we could do to maintain peace?

Irene and Carole first brought up the need for a calling. Again, we were in the midst of chaos, and the chaos led us to abstract ideas that had no practical basis yet.

I felt the hairs on the back of my neck rising as I entered into prayers with our group. This was what prayers were for, I thought. We offered prayers for our immediate concerns for Mama's health, for enough food for us all, and for rest. Living on top of each other, we were aware of how unfocused this catastrophe had made us. We also shared everyone's nightmares.

We started the practice of holding hands at the Table before each meal. Each woman spoke her concerns.

The three-times-a-day repetition of worries changed us, and the worries changed too once we knew everyone listened to us. The circle at the Table expanded to fourteen women. Then we had to stop any further additions. We ran out of room and the ability to care for anyone beyond that number.

We grew so fast without having planned for it. We had the money to take care of everything, that wasn't the problem. But there was not enough space to hold everyone who wanted to be a part of the group. Even utilizing both apartments, we couldn't live like we were for very long. But we didn't want to evict anyone either.

Everyone we knew was traumatized and for good reason. Max's family was not exempt from the trauma. There was also the foundation to worry about.

Max was scared shitless about what was going on in Manhattan. The varieties of federal agencies now running around town were like a Wild West movie. The government absently forgot and then dangerously ignored civil liberties; even the concept of habeas corpus was being thrown out the window as if it were just too complicated and antiquated for the times we lived in. It was too hard to work in that environment.

We had a secure location on Long Island. It was Margaret's old childhood home. We found the deed to it and moved the foundation and Max out there. Any of the staff that wanted to move there also had to be moved. The grounds and the buildings were in good shape. Margaret had long ago set up a trust for it.

Max and his family moved out there. The foundation office headed out there along with the staff. I didn't want to move there. I wanted to take the Table group somewhere else.

It seemed to me that crossing that boundary between the Table and the foundation was dangerous, but I couldn't describe it better than that.

Helen didn't agree.

"Doesn't it make sense for you not to be commuting to the island when there is so much land there? And it is so pretty and we're near water. It's idyllic."

"Yes, it is beautiful, and it would be a wonderful place to retire to. But we're not retiring yet. And that property was meant for privacy and exclusion. I thought we wanted to be in a more open environment."

"Well, you are correct there. It does have that old Gatsby look to it."

"Another reason not to move there."

"So what do we do? Where can we go?"

"What would you think about living on a farm?"

"Oh?"

"We own a farm. Upstate, in the Catskills. It's a bit run down, but it is large enough to hold all of us and more. What do you think?"

"Why am I not surprised that there is a farm ready to move into?"

"Wait, I didn't say that. It needs work. It's not like the place on Long Island. It's not a picture-perfect glamorous mansion. It is a farm."

Helen and I had that conversation in Washington Square Park, away from Mama's prying ears. The park bench became our private room. We used it often. I was worried about Mama and her reaction to the chaos we lived in. I wanted Aunt Money to feel safe too. We would have to have Alice with us, as long as she wanted to be with us.

When Max and his family left town, Martin and Maurice became my staff. We did a deep clean of the foundation office, making sure nothing was left behind that would incriminate anyone. They hired crews that knew nothing about us but knew how to be discreet and to move sensitive documents out of Manhattan without attracting anyone's attention. This need for secrecy and covert action made me anxious. I hadn't felt anxious like this since I had been on the road.

I tried to remain calm, but I could not keep it together even after the office had been moved.

Irene, Carole, Helen and I retreated to the park for a talk. It had already become too cold to sit outside for long. Early November carried a chill into every part of my body. It was also the anniversary of Margaret's murder, which for the first time I was keenly aware of.

Irene took my hands while Carole and Helen hovered over us. "It's time to move," Irene said.

"I know. I have a farm we can go to. It is in need of work, but it can be moved into now."

"But you don't want to go, do you?"

"No, I don't. I am paralyzed with anxiety about it."

"Yes, I know."

Everyone took a big breath and let out the name, "Margaret."

Within the month, we had left New York City.

Chapter Six

When we left the city, it was winter. Upstate New York had had an early fall and now was having an early winter. The cold sat on everything we touched when we walked into the farmhouse, now renamed Margaret's Farm.

The move had been a sterile exercise for me. Some may have been disheartened that they could not join us, but there were just too many complications to be overcome. Others felt that we had been too unilateral in our decision-making. The group was smaller, and yet we were cohesive. I just had no feelings left when it came time to start boxing up the lives I had lived in New York and take them with me to the farm.

I put most of everything I owned into storage boxes. I planned on leaving them in one of the outbuildings and thinking about what I had taken with me at some later and less fragile time.

I remember sitting one afternoon in the living room, where Helen and I had set up our workstation for packing boxes. We had gotten all the books off the shelves, and she was dusting them. The apartment had been on the market for a couple of days, and we had no idea who, if anyone, would be interested in buying either of the places we owned in One Fifth. We were both pretty grubby, and I had an ever-present look of doom and gloom on my face. Helen didn't feel as morose, and for that I was grateful. Her writing was going well, and she could write, surprisingly, even with all the work we had to do before the move. She felt motivated and happy. We didn't fight, but we weren't as close as we had been.

The doorbell rang. We knew someone was on their way upstairs because the concierge had called us. Neither of us stopped what we were doing. It was a point of pride that we finish each day's assigned work so that we would be ready when the moving van arrived within the next week.

Max no longer lived close enough to spend time with Mama or Aunt Money or to help me sell these apartments. He gave me advice if I needed it, but he had his hands full out on the island. He was happier living out there. Everyone was happier but me and Mama.

A knock at the door reminded me to go open it and see who was visiting us. As I opened the door, a young couple, not much older than 25 or 26, strode right into the midst of the mess we had made. They looked exceedingly clean. I remember comparing how immaculately dressed they were and how grungy we were. They smiled as they entered the apartment but wouldn't shake our hands.

I saw no need to apologize and started to give them a quick tour when the young man pulled out a checkbook and asked if they could make a deposit for both apartments and return when we were not as distracted.

"You mean—I'm sorry—you have already seen the place?"

"No," said the woman, who looked as if she had met me somewhere before but couldn't place me. "We know we want the two apartments, and we're willing to meet your price. There's nothing to see as we're going to redo them. You know, make them our own?"

"Ah," I said.

Helen climbed down off the ladder to watch this event unfold, but it was over faster than the ink dried on the man's check.

"I'll have to talk this over with my lawyer," I said.

"Of course, we expected that. If he has the papers drawn up for us to sign within the next week, we would much appreciate that."

Without any further comments, other than a thanks, they left. I held in my hand a check made out to me—though how they knew my formal name I didn't know—and the door closed behind them, leaving not much trace of their presence in our home except the lingering scent of their perfume and cologne. The scents didn't clash but complemented each other.

"How long do you think that relationship will last?" Helen asked.

"Whose money do you think it is?" I asked her and put the check into the folder where I kept all the important papers we had to drag around with us everywhere.

"That was fishy."

"I agree. Let's see if the check clears before we figure out who they are. Though I have a feeling, Max will know. Didn't she look like she knew me?"

"I didn't notice. Maybe you met her at one of those big money events in Switzerland. She looks like someone who might show up there. At least for the skiing."

Margaret rustled around in me. This turn of events may not have surprised her, but I thought she must have some feelings about me deciding to give up the apartment. Ghosts are so immaterial that not even her home being sold could affect her.

"I still don't know why you had to sell these apartments. It isn't as if you can't afford to keep them."

"If we want to come into the city we can stay at a hotel."

I didn't know why I sold the apartments either. Now that it was a done deal, I didn't want to know.

"I should call Max."

"Email him," Helen yelled from the kitchen. She returned with two bottles of beer. "Let's toast the going out with the old and the moving on."

All the legal parts of the deal were handled by Max, as he always took care of that part of my life for me. I tried not to mention his name in front of Mama or Aunt Money as they were in deep mourning at not seeing their buddy, their loved and loving son, and knowing they would not see him as much as they were used to seeing him. It was time for a new life.

Mama and Aunt Money arrived for dinner. Alice brought them in. It was just the five of us for dinner. We had so much work to do that we decided to forego the group meals until we were at the farm. It felt lonely now, the five of us; not even Irene and Carole had time to eat with us.

The Table was too big for five, but the kitchen table was too small. I wanted to tell Mama that we had sold the apartments, but I never knew how she would respond to anything I said. But Helen blurted it out, not knowing my thoughts.

"We've sold these two apartments today. No turning back, I guess."

Mama looked up at her and smiled a weak, slightly upturned-mouth kind of smile. "I am glad. We can't stay here. I don't want to be here."

Alice took her hand, and we all sat in silence while Mama grieved for a life she had had for five years and now wanted to leave as soon as possible.

When the old ladies silently left us, still trailing their fears and grief, I no longer wanted to yell at Helen for telling them we had sold the apartments.

Helen loved living in New York. Leaving had not been her first choice. She would have gladly stayed in the apartment and visited us on the weekends. We had agreed to that. Then one night, while cleaning up the kitchen, she told me she had changed her mind.

The sentence came out of the blue, and I had no idea what she referred to. I had been talking about a farmer I had met online, who lived not far from where we would be living, and how he had volunteered to help us in the spring if we needed him.

I wanted to talk about that, but she interrupted with that non sequitur. I looked at her, waited, and then she said, "Living here alone is not a good idea. I don't know what I was thinking. Maybe I thought if I said I would live here during the week, you would say, 'Oh, that is a good idea, I'll do the same, and then we can both commute.' But obviously, that makes no sense whatsoever, does it?"

"No. None."

"Maybe I'm having separation anxiety too. It's been five years here, and they have been very good ones."

"I think so, yes." At that moment, I felt Margaret coursing through me. She was a river that never froze or overflowed. Steady and reliable but always a mystery too. How else can one describe a life with a ghost? Maybe all of life should be like that, I thought.

"Would you please listen to me and stop listening to your ghost?"

On occasion, Helen found my communing with Margaret too frustrating or irritating. That night was one of them.

I took her by the hand, and we sat down at the kitchen table, where memories of Irene-and-me and Margaret-and-me still lingered. But the most important memories now were of Helen and me, and we were leaving that behind. With the growth of the Table, though, the kitchen had become less and less a place of meeting and more a place of cooking. The kitchen table was used for food prep rather than late-night sharing of ice cream from the pint container. Still, as was always the case with moving, with change, I regretted everything, every decision to move away from what had been ours in order to try to be that same thing but different in the new space. Having settled all discussions by selling the two apartments, there was no going back. Helen didn't regret her choices.

I went through spasms of grumpiness that upset Helen. But Mama's distress was the most worrisome because she could not be cajoled out of it. Even when the big moving day arrived and we were settling her and Aunt Money into the van, she was inconsolable. She wanted to leave but leaving was proving as difficult as staying.

I was no help. I had the moving blues, and the day started off badly. We were late getting out of bed. I lost the keys and then found them and lost them again.

Then Helen, who had prepared the food to take with us, forgot to put it in the refrigerator overnight. Her embarrassment added to the weird chorus of mute women seated in the van, ready to head up north in time to be there when our furniture and clothing arrived.

Once we left the city, I saw Helen's shoulders move back into their normal position. She was the first of us to feel the reduction of stress by actually being on the road to our new home. I sat stiffly in my seat, watching the city recede from the side-view mirror. Once I could no longer see it, sadness fell on me.

Why did I sell the apartments? Helen was right. The reality was, we could not turn back. Mama was still in her strange state but returning to the city would not cure that. She would still be traumatized out of her normal self. Aunt Money, of us all, had continued with her research as we packed up and kept talking to Max about what she was seeing in her market research. We had to finally add her to the payroll for the foundation and name her an advisor. She took all of that in a silence that made me realize what a life she might have led. The what-ifs of life came crashing down on me, but when we arrived at our new house and began the arduous work of setting up an entirely new life, I had no more time to think about any what-ifs, only about the what-nows.

One morning in the first week we had moved into Margaret's Farm, Irene and I were alone in the early morning light. Still trying to find the way toward an efficient use of our space and what it had to accommodate, we made tea and coffee for everyone. We were testing the places to put the cups and teaspoons and where to plug in the kettle and so forth.

Not yet having found our way to as smooth a working relationship as we had had in Manhattan, we kept bumping into each other. We needed to be as quiet as possible. Mama and Aunt Money slept in the living room rather than in their own rooms because their rooms were not habitable yet. Everything about our new life on the farm was a shambles. Irene kept reminding us, "It can only get better."

Aunt Money always replied, "One can only hope that is true." She was worried about Mama. We were all worried. Mama had sunk into an unspeaking world. We weren't sure she knew we had moved. Alice assured us that she did and was only processing what was going on and would return to us soon, but the estimated arrival time was not yet determined.

Irene and I whispered to each other in the kitchen. We were both happy about the quiet. From the start, the wonders of living in the country had startled Irene. She hadn't spoken to me about leaving the city, but I knew it had not been her first choice.

"Do you think Margaret would have really liked living here?" I asked Irene.

"Yes, I do. Margaret was a big fan of silence and she loved looking at the sky at any time of day or night. The clean air and even the cold would have made her happy. I'll tell you she would not have liked the bad plumbing. Margaret had little tolerance for things like that."

I heard Margaret chuckling while Irene described her like that.

"I'm surprised you never mentioned that this is the farm Margaret and I were to move to. Are you being careful?"

She bumped my hip as she walked past me with the pot of tea filled with hot water and tea steeping in it.

"Are you looking to make trouble?"

And that conversation ended with the arrival of Helen and Alice and Carole and the others, all of them doing the scratch-your-head-in-the-morning routine because the house was cold except for the kitchen and the front room where Mama and Aunt Money still slept. Alice picked up cups of tea for them and left the room.

I looked at Irene and said, "To be continued."

I put my arm around Helen and gave her a kiss and took my cup of tea into the living room to check on Mama, and so the day started. Many, many days began almost the same way. Irene and I were the early risers and set up the morning's food. Helen's office was in a renovated pantry off the kitchen, and she retreated there to write almost all day long. She had her communal work assignment too. She ran the laundry and the dishwashing at night. In time, when we all had found a better footing, she offered to help us in different ways. We each took a turn at trying to organize the farm life.

Carole and I left the warmth of the kitchen and went dashing around the property, trying to figure out what work needed to be done as well as what we needed to do to the house.

Carole's job included making phone calls to find contractors to get estimates on the work. She found no one willing to come to the farm. There was so much to do too. We needed a plumber and an electrician. With some restraint from me, we decided to forego the outdoor work until we got the house in better shape. We all needed a safe and well-functioning house to live in.

The farm buildings needed new roofs and there were buildings falling down that needed to be put back up. We also had a fleet of farm equipment that needed looking at.

Then it became Carole's turn to organize the work. We gave Carole an official clipboard to carry around. She began to look like the person to talk to about what needed to be done and when. Each attempt we made to organize the work got us closer to doing it the best way we could.

One of my jobs was the grocery shopping. I chose the old local store rather than one of the big-box stores farther out on the highway. While standing in line to check out, I began a conversation with a young woman who had commented about the amount of food in my cart.

I laughed. "I know, we are a large group of women and we eat. We're trying to fix up the place up the hill from here and having trouble finding workers to come help us."

She laughed too. "I know what you mean. Up here, there is a certain shyness about new people."

"Shyness? It seems more than that." I wanted to say something more. "But we really want to find some local labor. I can call on people in the city to come up here if we have to do that, but I'd rather use local workers."

"I'm sure they'd be glad of the work." She paused and then said, softly, "We've had trouble getting paid."

I looked at her. She counted out her money for the groceries and then handed over her food stamps as well. I wondered what to say to get her to say more.

"Can I buy you a coffee?"

"I've got to get these groceries home. My husband needs the car. If you've got a piece of paper, I can give you his number. He can do the work you need."

No business cards, no money, and we couldn't find people to work for us. I had much to learn, I could see that, and it was a good way to begin. Person to person. She wrote down the number and handed it to me.

"My name is Penny. My husband's Robert. Call him tonight."

"Thanks, Penny. My name is Scags. Our farm is out—"

"I know where you are. Take care."

She wheeled her groceries out of the store. The bumpy wooden floor gave the cart some resistance. The cashier, in addition to ringing up the groceries, took orders for groceries and sandwiches over the phone. She had her eyes going everywhere at once. The folks looking to fill up their cars with gas also had to pay her.

"Got anything else in your cart?" The cashier, eager to move the line along, bagged up my stuff and yelled at someone I couldn't see to pick up the orders she had taken over the phone.

An old guy, limping because one leg was noticeably shorter than the other, came to collect the order slips in her hand. No one but the cashier seemed anxious about the line or the slowness of the man with the uneven legs.

The groceries filled up many bags, and when I got them into the Jeep and myself into the driver's seat, a woman came to the window. I opened it.

I should not have been surprised. This encounter, much like the one in the grocery store, had all the stinging memories of my life on the road. Then, however, I needed work, and women often stopped me to alert me to something. Now I was being given recommendations for their husbands or boyfriends.

When she began talking, I had a hard time following her. But she wanted me to know I should put signs up with our phone number, and she would make sure that people saw them. This casual, shy helpfulness had saved me on the road and began to be a start to solving our problems at the farm. Though, as we learned, getting workers out to the farm—that was the problem. Once they arrived, they worked, but it was a two- or three-hour wait for them to arrive. How to manage this problem became our first priority. Then we realized we were going to have to learn how to do most of this work ourselves. We wanted, as we repeated daily during our Table talks, to have a good working relationship with our neighbors. We needed to find other ways to make that happen.

Our farm was building-rich; nothing had been sold off to developers to keep the place in a family. There were acres of orchards, mostly apple trees but some peach trees, and a small vineyard. The previous owner had held this land for decades and tried to make a commercial success of it.

Owning this large piece of land demonstrated what a mess Margaret and I would have walked into had she lived, and we had moved here as we planned. We knew nothing about farming, and living close to farms, as I had done in Vermont, was not the same thing as actually working on one. Margaret and I had lived in a fantasy-land of farming. Even when I worked for Ruth at the start of my road trip, my ridiculous desire to have her keep me there as her heir had been a distinctly fantasy-infused idea.

It required tenacity to hold on to land. The market for land was ruthless, and the ever-escalating development of housing for those wishing to raise families or retire away from the city made that ruthlessness tie up some farmers in court for years.

Land cravings had changed too. The attack on the World Trade Center had triggered a panic to get out, to live in a rural setting that would not be in the line of fire by these crazed terrorists. This new exaggerated belief that owning land not too far from a city guaranteed a better way of life had not reached into the reality of what it was like to actually live outside one's comfortable urban existence. Even with the cash to invest in a new home in a rural setting, the change in lifestyles rarely matched anyone's fantasies.

I had seen this so often, and it was a tragedy. Owning a home in the country takes a lot more work than owning a home in the city. Most former city dwellers either rented or owned an apartment. Their skill sets and expectations of how to take care of a rural property lag so far behind what is actually needed that they mostly give up on the whole notion of a country life. They have spoiled relations with the country people they tried to fit in with, and then they pull up stakes, owing lots of money to people who are unable to absorb the unpaid bills left behind.

I was not surprised that we had trouble finding labor and keeping them or even getting them to the job site on time. We practiced patience and incentivizing them.

One night at dinner, Joanne, one of the fellows who had traveled with us to the country, asked a simple question.

"Is it possible that we do this work ourselves? I know nothing about working on a farm, but I want to learn."

Mama sat and watched the back and forth of the comments everyone made. I listened too. I probably could do most of the work, but it was too much for me to do alone. I said that.

"You know how to fix a tractor?" Irene asked me.

"Yes. And how to repair a roof and plant seeds and . . ."

"Tell them the story," Helen said.

I looked at her.

"Well, not all of it, just the relevant parts. Like why you can fix a tractor or repair a roof or any of the jobs this place needs done. Go on. Don't be shy." She squeezed my hand and got up to get herself some coffee. That was how she indicated she was ready to listen.

I began to tell them the relevant parts of what I had done while on the road and what I had learned. "I spent three years on the road and survived by doing almost every menial job you can think of. I am not an advanced plumber, for example, but I can unplug a toilet. I'm not licensed to fix pipes or replace the bad wiring in this house, but if I have to repair something because we are in desperate need, I can do that.

"Also, I learned carpentry skills as well as auto mechanics. None of this was formally learned, but it was on-the-job training. It's amazing what you can learn to do when you need to make enough money to sleep somewhere that has a shower."

I paused and looked around the table. Every eye was on me. We sat cramped around the table because the rooms meant for Mama and Aunt Money weren't finished. If we wanted to put the Table where it belonged, we had to get the work done.

Carole spoke up. "Is it possible you could teach some of us these skills?"

She pulled out her clipboard.

"For example. The snowplow is not working. We need to plow away the snow so we can get to the other buildings. If you got the plow to work, then one of us could learn to use it. Then there is the work to move Mama and Aunt Money into their rooms. I know we need to find an electrician, but getting the rooms painted and the new carpeting put down would make things better for the two of them. And the bathroom that connects the two rooms also needs nothing extraordinary but paint and cleaning."

"As far as we know," I added. "But you are correct. Waiting to get a work crew here seems to put us in a precarious position, and we all need to know how to do some of this work."

Carole put out her list of priorities as she had determined them. We then began talking about how we could involve the locals in our work from a different perspective.

"Work" became the operative word. Borrowing from Ruth, I taught Carole how to assign work and how to set reasonable deadlines for completion so that each part of the work could be broken down into its essential parts.

Lois spoke up. "I'm going to create a work chart for us. I want to see something beautiful in here when I get up each day. I'll hang it on the wall, and we can all see the progress of the work and what our part is in it."

She produced a beautiful board. Everything we needed to do got its place on the new board. It stood out like a large yellow-and-green flower on the unpainted kitchen wall. We designated the decorating work that the kitchen needed as a last-tier project. The big board gave that wall enough sprucing up, and then Kate cut out flowers from magazines and seed catalogues to add to the decoration. It looked primitive, but slowly, as we registered the finished work on the board, and added photos of the work, we could see how everyone began to take ownership of the farm. That led to another period of thinking about that very word, "ownership."

Alice needed to be available for Mama and Aunt Money and couldn't participate in the daily work assignments. But on her own, she wrote to Max for wool to knit caps, scarves and gloves for the workers.

I hadn't yet talked to Max about my new ideas. I needed him to come to the farm to see what we were doing and to show him how I wanted to change the terms of ownership.

Meanwhile, our self-sufficiency had become worthy of gossip in the village. Word went out from our farm that these crazy women were taking matters into their own hands. The people-powered news machine had caught wind of our deliveries of materials and the questions we asked at the hardware store. This news fed a new form of neighborliness that none of us could have foreseen.

One evening, while I was struggling, again, to fix the carburetor on one of our trucks, a neighbor stopped by. In a manner unheard of by us, he drove right up to the barn where I was covered in grease, trying to find the cause of the truck's constant failure. He, too, was in his dirty work clothes and hauled a big tool kit with him to join me in peering into the internal works of our otherwise reliable truck.

"What's the problem here?" His name was Bud, and he smelled a bit sweet from the tobacco he chewed.

"I can get the carburetor to work, and then it doesn't. I now believe it's not the carburetor that dies out, but I can't see why the spark plugs are acting up. I just replaced them."

Bud was about as tall as I am, and he stood with me, craning his neck, looking at each cable and connection with an eye to discovering the problem before committing himself to further action.

Bud found the problem easily, and it was so easy that it embarrassed me.

After he tightened the spark plugs, which had become loose, and put away his tools, we sat on my two barrel chairs and talked for a short while. We sat side by side, wiping our hands off with a rag. Engine grease was always a mess to remove, and it came off best if I used a rag to get as much off as possible and then used a cleanser to remove the rest. It took time. It took the kind of time it takes to sit and talk.

That's when he told me about his problems at home. The talk between us went from how nice it was to have a neighbor to help out to the problem he had at home with his eldest daughter.

"Lisa is smart," he said, "and should go to college, not stay stuck at home waiting for some local boy to marry her."

Bud's wife, he told me, was ill, and Lisa thought it was her job to take care of her.

"If that was why I had kids, I would say so. But I want her to do more. My wife is sick and has been sick for years. Years," he finished up saying.

He stood up. I did too. "If you've got some work you could give her, I don't mean she needs lots of money, but she needs to get out of the house and do more than take care of her mother and talk on the phone with her girl-friends?" He ended that in a question as if asking if that were even possible.

"I can ask," I said. "Let me see what the others think or have need of that Lisa can do."

"I appreciate that." He got into his truck, and before turning on the motor, he asked if she could come over to us for dinner tomorrow and see what we could use her for.

I had no idea what we could do. Adolescents were not our favorite people. It wasn't that we disliked them, but none of us had been parents, and our own teenage years were far in the past, better left forgotten.

However, Lisa arrived the next evening for dinner with us, and it was not as any of us had expected.

Lisa joined us at our crowded kitchen table, and as soon as all the food had been passed around, she put her two hands together and began a prayer. It was a short one, thanking us and God for this opportunity to be together.

Lisa was a short and rotund girl. Her clothes were neatly ironed and her nails sparkling clean without any polish on them; they were clipped short. I noticed them first because her hands, as she put them together to pray, looked more like an adult's hands than a young girl's. Sometimes a part of a person speaks for them and in Lisa's case, it was her hands. Every time she spoke, I looked at her hands to see if the words she spoke and her hands were in sync.

Carole told her of our board. She then noticed it. Though it was the loudest part of the room, and I thought it would catch anyone's eye as they entered the kitchen, Lisa hadn't seen it. Her eyes had gone straight to the table where the food sat.

Lisa's eyes never left the surface of the table as we passed around the food. It later occurred to me that she was waiting for the meat dish to come out of the oven. Of course, there was none. She kept looking around as if we had forgotten something and wanted to speak up, I think, but was too polite to ask.

Despite the fact we served no meat, Lisa had enough to eat and seemed pleased with the meal. Carole and Alice both asked her questions about what it was she thought she could help us with. They had to assure her a couple of times that there was probably no job she could do that we wouldn't need help with.

Her eyes wandered around the table and looked at all of us women with this strange furrowing of her brows and wetting of her lips that reflected how seriously she considered our question.

"I've only had experience with my Mom, who is sick, and taking care of her and my brothers and sisters. You don't have any children here."

"No, we are just adults," Alice spoke up. Turning to Mama and Aunt Money, she asked Lisa, "Would you like to help me care for our two old ladies?"

"What?" Lisa blushed. She had never heard us talk about Mama and Aunt Money as we did, and it sounded strange to her. Her hands fluttered around her face, try- ing to hide her blushes.

"Dear," Aunt Money said, "it's a term of endearment. I'm stuck in this chair most of the day. I need help with my exercising. Do you think you could do that? I could pay you for the time you spend with me."

At the idea of money, Lisa turned her full attention to Money. Then she laughed, realizing what Money's name was and suspecting we had played a joke on her. We assured her we hadn't. It would give Alice time to recover some of her own strength to have Lisa help her with Mama and Aunt Money.

When it was time for Lisa to go home, Helen volunteered to drive her. I moved into her job as dishwasher and joked around with Alice about what benefits Lisa might add to the old ladies' lives.

"If nothing else, she is a young person, and that might be a good thing for them to experience every day," Alice said.

She had a point. I thought about that too and was on my way up to bed when Helen returned. I was exhausted and wanted to sleep. Helen said she wanted to write.

She liked her office, and her work was proceeding quickly. She had not needed two years to finish the book. She was working on the edits. Nothing was going to be more timely, she said, than her book on Afghanistan. Before we had left the city, the US had declared war on Afghanistan, and her publisher pushed her to do interviews and write articles about the situation as she understood it. She often had interviews late at night with journalists in other parts of the world, wanting her analysis of the situation in Afghanistan.

I had gotten into bed and was almost asleep when Helen came bursting back into the bedroom. Startled, I sat up totally awake when she said, "I forgot to tell you. Oops, sorry, I should have looked to see if you were asleep."

"It's okay, what is it?"

"Two things, actually. First, it took so long to return home because Lisa had 'to talk to someone,' as she put it. It had to be me, the one person who had nothing to say to her. Anyway, she told me that she had a boyfriend, Lance, and she either was pregnant and had lost the baby or is pregnant and wants to lose the baby. I could not figure out which it was. She is very glad to work for us, but, as she kept repeating, due to her condition, she is very tired all the time."

"Oh my." I sat up fully in bed. Helen had left the door partially open and not turned on a light. Standing in the doorway, I could only see her head in silhouette. "That may prove to be a problem. How does one ask for clarification on this subject?"

"I don't know. Give it a few months and see what happens? In any case, that will not be my problem. I got a call today from the State Department."

"About our driver's licenses?"

"Not that State Department. The US State Department."

"Oh. How did they find you here?"

"My publisher, of course." She looked at me. "You know what I am about to say, don't you?"

"Oh, yes, I do, and I am shocked that you would help our government at making war."

"You know my position would have nothing to do with the war. They want me to come to Afghanistan and be a liaison with the women's groups. It is a fabulous opportunity, don't you see, Scags? I have so much to offer. And what do I have to do here now? With you so completely tied up with making the farm viable, I feel cut off from everything that makes me happy."

"Okay," I said.

"Wait, I didn't mean it that way. You know what I mean. I am not and never claimed to be a country girl. And I'll be back."

"I need to sleep." I fell onto the pillows and closed my eyes. Pretending to have fallen back to sleep, I waited for Helen to leave the bedroom and then sat up again to think this news through. In my mind, I traced the scar on her face and thought of all the horrible things that could happen to her. If they were to happen, I said to myself and to Margaret, who was sitting there with me, they would have shown up in the cards. But she comes home. I know she does.

I knew before she knew, of course, that she was leaving. I walked around with a small and secret ache. I decided to be more attentive. My idea of attentive was to leave her alone to finish the book.

I wanted something then, but I had no idea what that something was. I knew she would say yes to going to Afghanistan, but I wanted her to say no. But saying no would have been completely out of character. I didn't want her to be who she was not.

We moved to the farm in the winter and Helen left us in the spring. She packed her bags and her big backpack with her laptop and passport and all those other double-worded essentials of travel hanging off her shoulders, and where was I?

I was lost both in the work of the farm and in missing her even before she walked out the door. We had a party to say goodbye, but the party fell flat. Not even the champagne gave her the right send-off. Helen wanted me to go to New York with her to spend a last night alone.

Thinking back on how pissed I was at her leaving me, I know I wanted to punish her, but I couldn't help thinking about how terrified I was of her leaving and not returning; of her leaving and not wanting to return; that she would be killed. Even though I knew she would come home, it did not matter. I had lost Margaret with all the good intentions and plans in place. Maybe a cruel joke was about to be visited on me again.

That made the fight between us inevitable, and the lack of closure of that fight a long-term, long-distance writing campaign where I worked to win her back—only if she acknowledged that I was right to be worried, even when I knew not to be worried.

That first morning after she left, when the emptiness of her study hit me harder than her walking out the door, I sat down in her office, smelling her, and her absence hit me. I cried and cried.

Alone in the small room that had once been a pantry, I ran my hands over the top of her desk. Her energy already fading, her work still lived in the grains of wood, but it receded with her life now in a country far away. I missed her mind and how silly she let it be. How did she find such a turgid soul as I to take up her heart? She'd find someone new, I believed at that moment. I began the slide into the deep waters of doubt and despair when someone knocked on the door.

I opened it to find Alice needing my help with a small emergency with Mama. The day began. Having a meltdown was not on the job board. Since I knew as well as Margaret knew about the happy ending waiting at the end of Helen's time in Afghanistan, why should I cry? I clearly needed to prepare for a happy ending. But none of us is ever prepared for a happy ending.

In Upstate New York, late winter/early springtime weather can be dangerous. One minute the temperatures are warm, all the buds are popping, and you are emotionally prepared for spring. But just as the snow is gone from the ground, then damn it all, the snow returns in its heavy, wet way and smacks you harder than you were ready to be smacked.

This storm hit us a year after Helen left. Our whole area was badly affected by it. The fruit trees had budded, but entire limbs snapped off. Early spring flowers came out of the ground full of color, until the snow stomped on them and killed them. The sunlight and warmth had tricked us. Winter had not completely left.

The storm hit us, without warning, on a Sunday night. I drove every Sunday the short distance to the local postal substation to put a letter in the mail to Helen. The storm rocketed its way out of the northwest. It dumped wet, heavy snow out over the mountains like some large dump truck full to overflowing with avalanches of snow. It was a thunder snowstorm. That scary kind where you can die of hypothermia because you get lost walking from your car to the front door.

I drove home from the post office as the first flakes began to blow in. I should have stayed in the parking lot and waited it out. I wasn't that smart. I decided, since home was so close, to keep driving despite being able to see nothing in front of me. In that zero-visibility storm, the air temperature dropped fast, so the snow and the ice fell in equal measure.

I drove slowly, but nevertheless, I hit a car. I couldn't see it. I wasn't driving fast but the force of the impact caused me to hit my head. I passed out. When I came to, I was convinced that the car I had hit was in the ditch in front of me. I tried to force my body from behind the steering wheel and pushed hard to open the door. That minimal work exhausted me. I sat back and waited a couple of minutes to summon the energy to walk to the car I hit.

When I next opened the door to get out, a dog came bounding out of the snow and into my lap. I yelled out, "Kaboom!" The dog sat in the seat next to me, her coat covered in snow and her blue eyes staring at me, wondering how we two had met. It was love at first sight. I threw my arms around her neck, and even with the wet doggy smell, I knew I had found the dog of my dreams.

Hanging onto Kaboom, I tried to be still and close the door to keep the snow from engulfing the interior of the car. The storm continued to blow, and lightning continued to light up the sky. When the blasts of thunder came, Kaboom shuddered and moaned. I held her tightly.

Kaboom's moaning reminded me of Mama's moaning when she had seen the Towers collapse.

I turned to Kaboom and said, "That's why we left the city in such a hurry."

She looked at me with understanding eyes.

"We need to get out of this car and attend to the people in the car I hit." It was comforting to have a dog to talk to in the midst of the storm. She was more frightened than I was.

I remember the two of us getting out of the car. We had to fight against the wind and the snow blowing at us. The snow was too deep for Kaboom to walk through so she jumped on my back. When we got to the car I hit, we found two elderly nuns inside, sitting wrapped in each other's arms. They were not hurt, they assured me, but were so cold.

I found blankets in their back seat and wrapped them up as best I could. Their farm abutted our farm and they too had been caught by surprise in the storm. I could barely hear them speak, the winds howling about us were so loud. But what I understood was they had parked their car in the middle of the road out of fear of moving forward or back.

We were all frightened. I held to Kaboom. They prayed. I had no idea where Margaret was. Why wasn't she watching out for me and the nuns?

The might of the storm hurtled on and on and then dissipated. I fell asleep in the back seat of the nuns' car with Kaboom still firmly nestled in my arms. When I woke up, I was in my own bed.

Completely confused, I reached out for the dog, and there she was. Now dry and looking at home on my bed, I also saw Irene staring at me as if I were a ghost.

"You're awake?" Irene asked me.

Nothing but my eyes worked. My skin burned, and my head felt like a coal furnace was working overtime right behind my eyes. My legs and arms had a strange numbness, and if they could move, they hadn't told me yet. I closed my eyes to rest them from doing all the work, and when I opened them again, the room was lighter, and there were more people standing around, including Max. Where the hell had he come from, and why was he in my room?

Kaboom remained where I remembered her to have been. The light from the sky outside hurt me and burned me. I tried to speak but couldn't, and closed my eyes again. Opening them, I found the room lit by a single lantern. Carole sat in a rocking chair, and she had taken on some of Alice's knitting, it seemed. Then I noticed it was Alice, which meant it had to be late at night after my old ladies were asleep.

"Where are the nuns?" I asked Alice.

Alice screamed my name. "Scags! You're awake." She stood up, dropping her knitting onto the floor, and Kaboom was startled out of a dream and began howling like the beagle she was.

Suddenly, the room filled up with all the people I knew. It was like the ending to the *Wizard of Oz*. Everyone had been someone else but now had resumed their roles, and we were one big happy family again.

Though I wasn't lost, I had only fallen asleep.

I looked at everyone standing around me, and some were crying. What happened?

"I only asked where the nuns were. Why are you all staring at me like that?"

Then the story came out of Irene's mouth until she began to cry, and it was taken up by Carole, who said, "We thought we lost you. You were stranded in the storm and suffered hypothermia and some frostbite, and except for that dog, who seems to have gotten lost and found you and the car to stay in, you were all alone for hours."

"Where are the nuns?"

Everyone laughed. There were a couple of former nuns in our community, but there were no other nuns. I had not hit another car. I had been blown into a ditch. What saved me was staying in the car and the bellowing of the dog the next day that helped them find me. I hadn't moved in several days, and neither had the dog.

From that moment on, I had a companion who never left my side or allowed anyone near me unless I said it was okay.

It took several weeks to recover from my imagined car wreck. Max had never shown up at the farm. There were no nuns. By the time early summer arrived, I could walk again and decided to take a full tour of the farm to see what it was we actually had to take care of.

I realized as Kaboom and I walked from one end of the property to the other that from the time we had arrived, I had not given myself the pleasure of knowing the land we owned. Walking alone gave me time to think and see all that lay around us. We jumped into our work, and it was necessary. But here we were too, with all this gorgeous land about us, and none of us knew it and how it changed from moment to moment. Max had frightened all of us by his dire warnings about moving in the winter. So we had chosen a path to get the work done that had been quite successful but had robbed us of this—of *being* on the land we owned.

"Well," I said to Kaboom, who loved being addressed as we walked, "we were also in a panicked state. Too much danger. We'd all freaked out from the attacks on the World Trade Center. But Max and I shared the panic of the tightening of all kinds of surveillance protocols that were making our work more dangerous.

"I can see it now," I said to Kaboom, who really had no interest in the story, only that I was talking. I continued, "Imagine that, Kaboom. Max and I being arrested as we left the city, caught with those large amounts of unverifiable cash that we were racing to take to the farm and to the estate. Don't tell anyone, Kaboom. We were really risking a great deal."

Kaboom took off; she had seen a rabbit. She never caught one, but she loved the chase. I kept walking and came to a stump in the middle of a field and sat on it. The sun was so bright that day that my eyes teared from the glare. Mud caked on my boots and on Kaboom's entire body. I closed my eyes and smelled the soil and the air.

Margaret was with me. I didn't ask where she had been. I probably wouldn't have been told.

"It's beautiful here," she said.

"Oh yes," I replied, as if we were sitting on the porch. I imagined the squeak and the whine of the metal of our porch swing. I felt the cushion on my butt and the way in which the sway of the swing kept time to the sentences we shared with each other.

"This might have been otherwise. Though now it seems superfluous," I said to her. "Would we have made of this place what it is developing into? I don't think so. I would not have been on the road long enough to learn the lessons I learned. I even question whether our love could have weathered such peace and so much time together."

"You are a strange one, Scags. You wanted to critique the media. Then you set that aside. Now you've been handed a large set of stories, real stories that can't be told about people and events that are criminal and dangerous. Use your imagination and make them into your own stories."

From the moment she spoke those words, I knew something had flipped forward on that large deck of cards that was my life. We had entered into a new time. The transitions from that card deck, from one way of being to the next, had never been easy, but this time, something more appealing loomed on my horizon. Did I want to write? She never asked me what it was I wanted to do. Each new way of being seemed to just arrive. Not always in its fullest form. But we were getting closer to another moment of change. Margaret moved on. The conversation ended.

Kaboom returned to my side and sniffed around as if she smelled something new, then she pushed her nose under my arm as if to nudge me up.

"Time to move. Use the legs God gave us." She enjoyed the rhythms of human speech.

Time was on the move. I heard from Helen frequently, and she was getting more and more upset about what she was seeing on the ground in this new kind of war that seemed to be war for war's sake. After the bombing of Iraq, she had become seriously disturbed with the war world she lived in but also felt too guilty to leave. Women's lives were once again being altered by war. It didn't matter who bombed them; they were being bombed and displaced.

Helen's letters piled up on my desk. I let them drift across the other papers I had so I always knew that no matter what Max and I were up to, there was a war going on, and the woman I loved was in the line of fire.

Max and I did some of our best work then. We met at his estate on Long Island; we no longer traveled to Switzerland to find ways to put money away from prying eyes. We didn't trust that process of investment anymore. We accepted our fate as farmers. We built a legal system for Margaret's Farm that we could then use as a template for cooperative farms anywhere in the world. We poured the money into them. We planned all of this out with a group of young lawyers who Max had found and enticed to the estate to live and work. We put together a plan that we were to offer first to the men and women who worked at Margaret's Farm.

We became the sponsors of much work connected to the feeding of the planet. We sponsored soil studies. We gave money to animal sanctuaries and to seed farms. We funded magazines, and we funded urban farms. We spread the money around the world to make sure that people could eat. We finished the plan; it had taken us a couple of years, and we were sitting in Max's office when his wife came into the room with a bottle of wine. It was time to celebrate the brilliant completion of a long but really important project. I felt more alive than I had in the years since Helen had gone away.

Max and I, his wife and the "legal eagles," as I called them, took the bottle of wine outdoors. We sat on a blanket staring at the stars, drinking the wine.

"I'm no revolutionary," Max said. Then he chuckled. "I've spent my life protecting those who are. But now I feel like we created a revolution and figured out how to make it grow."

"Thanks to Henry," I said. Then we all laughed. We knew how important this money was to protecting seeds and hiding them in seed vaults. Away from the predatory men who thought they should own all means of growth. We had created ways to protect the basics of farming behind some of the most sweeping new technologies for storing data and for making it inaccessible to anyone who was not a part of the circle we created. We had to. The future of farming had become that precarious.

The foundation became an investor rather than just a bestower of funds. It wasn't how I had envisioned my life, but it was what I had settled into with Max's help. We called the plan the Farm Subsidy Action. Henry would have been appalled, but his daughter, I knew, was pleased.

Margaret's Farm was in good shape and no matter who lived or died, it would live on. Helen was still alive in Afghanistan and had found her way into the heart of her work. Margaret was with me at the estate and everywhere still. I had no idea that all of this was going to change. I was at peace on that blanket on that early summer evening.

The wine made me sleepy. I walked back into the house and made it as far as the couch on the porch. I fell into a dream that looked a lot like the dream I had had on my 45th birthday. But this dream was about a different type of work. I didn't see a future so much as a number of stories. Just as I woke up from that dream and wanted to talk to Margaret, Max entered the room.

"Not the best place to sleep, Scags," he said.

I stood up, and Kaboom arrived at my hand looking for a pat on the head. I obliged.

I turned to look at Max. The morning hour looked good on him. The wheat colors that were his basic palette looked better on him in early morning light.

"You're looking healthier, Max," I said.

He turned his back to me and walked to the large windows looking down to the pond at the bottom of the hill. He stood with his hands behind his back. Both of us felt energized that morning. We had so much more than we had ever dreamed of having. We had more than we could ever use. For people like us, who had not grown up with the privilege of great wealth, we were always amazed at what it felt like to not worry about anything. At least not worry about where to find the money to fix anything that needed fixing.

"We're finally doing good work," Max said. He turned back to look at me. His smile was refreshing compared to the old dour Max I had traveled with and worked with so many long months on one project after another.

"Yes. This is actually fun," I said. "I hated being so tortured about the amount of money we had to work with. Being able to trust people to help us has changed everything. It was a good thing to buy the farm while Margaret was in prison. Getting there was too long a journey, but it has worked out."

"We're good here, on the estate. It suits us. How could it not, right?"

"Right, and it is the perfect place for the Farm Subsidy Action group. I am so happy we figured this out. Too many years were spent being tortured gazillionaires."

We laughed. I gave Max a big hug. "Once I set things in motion at Margaret's Farm, you'll have to visit us and put the paperwork in order."

"It'll be a pleasure to do that. You're right, this is a relief in so many ways. These younger legal wizards have been so helpful. Who knew that employing people at salaries that were actually far beyond their wildest dreams could be the ignition for such imaginative legal work? I will sleep better, and I am sure you will too."

"No more trips to Sandusky for us."

"Sadly, no," he said. "Though I did like the time on the road, with Martin driving and the two of us in the back seat barely awake and arriving with the sunrise and getting right to work. I felt, for a few moments, like a gangster. Now those were the 'good old days.'"

"What a change a good plan makes." I paused, not wanting to say anything more. My brain had emptied itself of what it needed to contribute to the plan. "I have to take Kaboom for a walk, and then I'll head back to the farm."

"Okay, my friend. I'll be here for the foreseeable future. As soon as you get the plan in place at the farm, call me and I'll arrive with one of my trusty new legal wizards, and we'll get the papers signed and into the vault. I think this will change how farming is done for a long time. And since we all need to eat, this is not a losing proposition."

I hugged him once more and left.

I wanted time with Margaret to talk about the new writing plan. It had been there, stuck away on one of those cards from my 45th birthday. I hadn't quite forgotten it as much as I had postponed remembering it until we had Max set up with lawyers living on the estate and with plenty of trust built in.

Margaret and I communed as I got Kaboom settled into the car for the ride home. I had so much hope for this new plan that I also forgot to say to her that I had another plan in place, but of course she knew that.

"If you want to write these stories, go ahead. I know where all this material comes from and what you have been allowed to see. Why not tell these stories and see what people make of them? You really have nothing to lose. You can write them under a different name."

Time meant nothing when talking to Margaret. It was an energy transfer, and this time I was not depleted by it but felt energized.

Driving back to the farm with Kaboom settled in the car beside me, I explained to her what I was about to do. She was the first to hear of this new plan. I wanted to tell her the first of the stories I had been working on. I was excited and as she settled in for the long drive and the story, she soon fell asleep, as I knew she would. But I told her the story anyway. It was the start of a long career as a storyteller.

Born Loser, Born Lucky, Inc.

Perry sat sipping a cappuccino accompanied by a glass of red wine. In his lap, his cell phone's timer counted down the minutes and seconds. He waited for Sophie West to walk across Father Demo Square to meet him at the cafe. On that cold December night in the West Village, Perry had his job to do. It would be over at 8:30 pm. He swallowed the rest of the wine and let the cappuccino hold his place at the table uninterrupted by a waiter's questions. It was time to press the code into the phone sending the message to the small bomb taped beneath a manhole cover right outside the cafe's window on Bleecker Street.

Sophie was always on time. If she said she was going to meet him at 8:30, she would be crossing the square a couple of minutes before then. Perry hadn't seen Sophie in a few years. They had dated in college. She was always on time and laughed at his chronic lateness. She couldn't understand it. She'd ask him, "How can you be late when you know someone is waiting for you?"

Perry's time had never been his own, but he couldn't tell her that. He had to do things for others, for the man, in fact, whom Sophie fell in love with and then swore never to see again. Tom Sinclair had owned them both for a while. Sophie knew how to get out, and Perry never had figured that out. That was why he was sitting with a timing device in his lap, waiting for Sophie to appear.

When Sophie left Tom, she had closed the door on all relationships with men. Perry never was able to catch her on the rebound from Tom. It became Perry's job to keep track of Sophie for Tom as best he could. But Sophie had gone underground for a long time. He had placed a tracking device on her, and it had been silent for years. But now, again, it began telling him she was alive and nearby.

The device's reawakening was a surprise to them all. Tom gave Perry the order to kill her. No more waiting around to see if she would play ball with them. Perry knew why she had to die. He could not understand why Tom had ordered him to do it. Perry often made up reasons for Tom's assignments because there was no use in asking Tom why he did what he did.

For this assignment, he told himself Tom needed him to kill Sophie because they both had loved her, and no one else should be given this job. It was a brotherly thing to do.

Sophie came up out of the subway on Sixth Avenue and walked toward Bleecker Street, under the marquee at the Waverly Theatre. Her long legs took a measured stride, pacing herself to arrive at the time she needed to appear at the cafe on Bleecker Street to meet Perry. She didn't really want to see him or Tom. It was her work that made her do this. It was always her work that made her take risks like this. Whatever it took to rid the world of men like Tom and Perry and Tom's father, Henry, the real enemies of this planet, she did. She knew that agreeing to meet Perry at this old haunt of theirs from years ago would let them all know she would show up. Both of them had a sentimental side. Tom never would have arranged to meet there. Henry, most likely, was the one who had chosen the spot. He played life like it was a large war game and left nothing to chance.

How Sophie had loved either one of them was a mystery to her. The only thing that excused her bad judgments was that having known them intimately, she had insights into their behavior she would not have had otherwise.

That December night, she needed to be as clear in her own mind and as calm as possible. If either of those two men could be used, it was Perry. Perry, at times, had something of a real human being struggling beneath his flashy suits and tough-guy talk that could be appealed to, if only for a few moments. Perry knew the chains he was trapped in. Tom didn't know and didn't want to know and that made him much more dangerous.

The outside lights of the cafe glazed the shiny wet road as she stepped off the curb from Father Demo Square. She knew Perry could see her now. Perry watched as Sophie stepped off the curb. He said a quick prayer for forgiveness as he punched the code into the phone, and the phone sent the message to the small bomb that was right beneath Sophie's feet.

Perry closed his eyes. He heard the bomb go off and then another loud explosion that he had not anticipated. He saw a car bursting into flames as its gas tank blew up. He had not planned on any collateral damage. He sat stunned like everyone else in the cafe and then got up from his chair, putting a large bill on the table and walked out the door to observe as the others were doing.

He wasn't prepared for the shock waves of heat from the car, or how they mirrored his own shock. He told himself that the car blowing up might be a good thing and would help to cover up Sophie's murder. He had just killed Sophie West. She was not a direct threat to him, but she was a threat to the people he worked for. He put his coat on over his shoulders and pulled a handkerchief out of his pocket to cover his face against the heat of the burning car. The smell of it made him feel sick and dizzy.

He knew to walk away as if he was upset and not to volunteer anything. He had to remain anonymous but to verify that Sophie was dead.

The bright yellow flames from the burning car rose up and almost reached the trees growing in the square. Perry skirted around it. The crowd grew and gave him more cover so he could look for Sophie's body. The blast and the resulting gasoline explosion had made everything one big black charred mess. He couldn't find any human remains, but the fire was so hot that that made sense. She was pure ash now.

The fire department arrived quickly. Their station was only a few blocks away on Sixth Avenue, just below Houston Street. As soon as they appeared, there was no further opportunity to look for body parts or even a scarf or shoe. She was gone.

"How could that be?" he asked himself. "And who had been driving that car at that moment the bomb was scheduled to explode?" These questions nagged at him as he walked away. He was to meet Tom and Henry downtown for a celebratory meal and for his payout for the job. Tom had chosen the Odeon. It was a long walk, but Perry was used to that.

Bleecker Street got noisy quickly with the fire department and the police cars racing to the bomb site. The area was cordoned off. People out on that Sunday night were both scared and curious about the bombing. They ran toward it as Perry walked away, head down and toward the church on the corner of Bleecker and Carmine.

He looked straight up, and looming over him, he saw the church's cross against the cold dark sky. The large cross stood out, as it was meant to do, like a beacon, saying to all, "Come here, no matter where you are or what you have done. Come inside this church for help."

Perry hurried down Carmine Street, ignoring the church's offer. He alternately stared at his shoes as he walked and looked into the glass windows to make sure no one was following him. He kept walking. His breath preceded him, his cheeks burned in the cold air. He hated the restaurant, but Tom had chosen it for the amount of noise even on a Sunday night. People hung out there because it was a great place to talk about their own importance. Henry thought that Perry would like it. He never knew a thing about Perry except that he always did what Tom told him to do.

Tom and Henry thought of going to the Odeon as slumming. They had no interest in the men and some women who showed up there on a regular basis. They wanted merely to borrow the ambience for their own ritualistic pleasures and then get on their private plane to Washington, DC, where they controlled the more substantial domains of power. Their evening plans were to make a payment, eat, run and get away with murder.

Perry walked into the Odeon and immediately saw Tom at a table in the back with his father. Their private security detail sat at the bar, and the hostess waved Perry to the rear of the restaurant. Perry paid no attention to the hostess. That was uncharacteristic of him. He was always on the prowl but that night, not as much. He walked straight to the table where Tom and Henry sat.

Both men barely looked up from their drinks as Perry pulled out the chair to sit down at the table with them. For a moment, Perry wondered if they even wanted him to join them. The family had never been all that welcoming. The father held a lot of influence over Tom so that when they were together, Tom treated Perry as if he were the hired help. What a bother it was to be friends with rich boys, Perry said to himself and to his mother whenever he felt tension about their friendship.

Perry had to be careful what he told his mother. She was so naturally curious and needed to know what these people did. She could not help but love their money and hope that her son would be paid handsomely for all he did for them. Little did she know how cheap the rich are.

Perry's drink had been ordered ahead by Tom. It sat a bit watery in the glass, but Perry didn't mind and took a long sip of it as soon as he sat down. Tom asked him how things had gone. Perry set his drink down and realized he had forgotten to dispose of the phone. His face filled up with shame. What a stupid, amateur thing he had done. He had walked all the way downtown, worrying about being followed, with the damn phone in his pocket, leading anyone who might be interested right to the table with the men who had ordered the hit.

Perry finished his drink and said everything went fine, but he had to leave immediately. Tom and his father looked worried but also relieved that they didn't have to sit through dinner with Perry. The food arrived at the table. Perry stood up. "Don't let your food get cold."

He reached out his hand to shake Henry's, who placed an envelope in it and then quickly took his hand away without saying a word.

Tom started to say good night, but Perry was already almost to the door.

The empty, cold downtown streets helped refresh his now sweat-covered face. Limos waited for their clientele at the curbs. Yellow cabs roamed the streets. Perry took off toward the river. He would cross the West Side Highway and hide the phone. He knew a spot that was perfect for it.

He walked quickly again, this time with more of a sense of purpose and pleasure. The fat envelope in his pocket made him feel safer. He had some big bills to pay. Trying to keep up with the wealthy who didn't work for their money but just removed it from an ATM wasn't easy. Perry had to spend a lot of money to look like he needed to look to be seen with Tom and the other men he worked for. They never understood that.

He paid his debts because he had to in the business he was in. He wanted to put some aside for a future that never seemed to be anything other than what the past and present had been.

He knew that Tom and his father were enjoying a big fat steak and some good scotch. That was how men like them behaved after killing a woman. Then, as if he were slitting his own throat, he ran his finger along his neck as if it were a knife. Perry knew the danger of talking about any of the work he did for Tom and Henry Sinclair. He knew he had really messed up this time too.

He walked faster until he reached the place along the river where he would hide the phone. This was better than having it be disposed of with tomorrow's garbage pickup. Maybe this mistake would offer him some safety if he ever needed protection from the Sinclairs.

Perry walked on to a ledge along the riverbank that he had often used as a hiding place. He pulled himself over a set of bars used to keep people off the ledge and was careful to protect his expensive coat.

He settled on the ledge and then bent over between his legs to find the little tin box where he kept letters he could not send and money he didn't want anyone to know he had. It was there he hid the phone that had set off the bomb that had killed Sophie West.

After returning the box to its hiding place, he sat back and watched the river. He was high enough above the water that he never worried that the box would be in danger from the river's tides.

For a couple of minutes, he relaxed and forgot he had killed her. He comforted himself with the thought that an envelope filled with money sat in his pocket. He thought he might buy his mother a new couch. She had been pestering him to buy her something with all the money he made. What a nice son he would be; he'd buy his mother a big leather couch and have it delivered this weekend and the old one removed. She'd give him a big, wet kiss on the mouth and then go off to tell her neighbors about her wealthy son and his gifts to her.

While soothing himself with thoughts of his generosity and filial duty, footsteps punched through his reverie. His training kept him alert, even in a place he believed was totally secure. It was not.

The footsteps came closer and closer. Perry decided to stay put on the ledge. No one could climb over the rails without making themselves known to him, and if this person wanted Perry's attention, Perry was prepared to get rid of him too.

Then the footsteps moved away, back the way they had come. Perry breathed. He thought, maybe just a vagrant out for the night, looking for a place to pee or sleep.

Silence returned to the night, and Perry took that as a sign he should get up and go home. As soon as he moved, he felt the cold air on his bare hands, and when he touched the railings to jump over them, he thought his fingers might freeze to the metal.

He leaped over them and began his walk back to the highway. He stayed alert, not completely convinced he was alone, but he saw no evidence of anyone else about.

He got to the opposite side of the highway, having crossed not on the raised bridge but by dashing through the traffic. He liked playing chicken now that the incriminating phone was out of his pocket. He walked along Murray Street and was almost to West Broadway when someone jumped him. His reflexes were quick but not quick enough to keep his assailant from pulling the money out of his pocket and running back toward the highway, too fast for Perry to catch up with him.

"Damned if you do and damned if you don't," he said under his breath and ran his finger across his throat again. There was nothing he could do. He sighed and turned back in the direction he had been going and walked right into Sophie West.

"That's all, Kaboom. You can wake up now."

By the time we arrived at the farm, I was famished. I had not eaten nor had I fed Kaboom. She was more forgiving of me than I was of myself. I parked the car in front of the house and went running inside with Kaboom right with me.

I was so excited. We had a plan, and we were going to protect and support this place and all the people connected to it. I wanted to run into everyone's room and give them a big hug and a kiss.

I fed Kaboom and grabbed an apple and ran to Mama's room first. Both of our old ladies had rooms renovated in keeping with the house's style and colors from the time of its building in 1933. But Mama's had not yet been handed over to the Mama treatment. She still was not well enough to do that work.

Lisa and Irene were in the room with Mama when I came barging in with my big, happy hello. I wanted to tell Mama and everyone how we had saved the farm from ever being sold or even parts of it being sold, and that we would all now share equally in it.

But Mama was having a bad night. I could tell from the look of worry on Irene's face and the way Lisa sat silently watching Mama sleep. Mama's face looked more relaxed than when I left for Max's estate, but she was still worrying us all.

We had been waiting a long time for her to want to speak to us again. I kissed her on the forehead. Then I went to visit Aunt Money. She sat at her computer texting Max.

I walked in, and she said, "Oh, there you are. Max said you were on your way back. He said you all did good work."

"You helped us, you know, Aunt Money."

"Max is outlining what it was you came up with. You are one smart kid, and so is he. I think this will work, Scags. I know your Mama will be so pleased."

"We'll see. If she ever speaks to us again."

"Yeah, and if she does and is her old self, she'll just complain about this. I can't wait. Come here and give your aunt a kiss."

I kissed the top of her head and told her to tell Max hi.

From there, I went to find Irene and Carole. They were back in their room, getting ready for bed.

I sat down on their bed while they put away their clothes from the day. I told them we had found a way to protect the farm and all farmers who wanted to join us. I said that Max would bring the papers to put this plan into its legal form.

"Does this mean we all own the farm?" Carole asked.

"Not exactly. It is more that we all own the corporation that owns the farm. And the way the corporation is set up, we can never lose the farm or have it sold to developers. It has to stay a working farm. Everyone needs to eat."

Irene came to me, and I stood up. For the first time in years, we kissed as we had kissed when we were lovers. I didn't know what Carole knew of our previous relationship, but she didn't look upset. She hugged me too as I left their room.

From the start of our life at the farm, Irene and I had taken a leadership role in organizing everything. Once we had the work ideas in place and had been able to learn as much as we could from each other, we expanded. We needed more people. The farm was large. We acquired more members of the group because we needed people who knew how to do the work and wanted to join us.

On some afternoons, the Table was not large enough to hold us all for a meal. But we had to keep growing. We needed to network with other farms to share in the distribution of harvests and the buying of supplies and seeds, along with the building and repairing of barns and houses. We formed a large communal farming cooperative.

The legal eagles that Max hired had studied our work and changed some of the processes we had jammed together out of expediency and made them more efficient and sustainable. But it was from the working methods that Irene and I had originally cobbled together to get us up and running that the grand scheme had come into being.

One night, as Irene and I cleaned up the day's accumulation of dirty dishes and pots and pans in preparation to start making dinner, Irene said, "I've been thinking, Scags, about how smart it was to move us all out here when you did. I like being in the country. The silence heals lots of wounds. I can see it at night, at dinner. We've all worked hard, and we are silent together, enjoying the food and the rest we need.

"I know I opposed this move. I was afraid. I had never lived in the country before and while I knew we needed to get Mama out of the city, a permanent move here seemed, well, foolish."

"I was scared too. This was where Margaret and I were supposed to move, retire from the anti-nuclear work and settle down for a long country life. We knew nothing about farming. But after she died and Mama needed to leave the city, it all fell into place, didn't it?"

I held out my hand to her. We stood side by side, admiring the clean kitchen. Taking a deep breath, we opened cupboards and began pulling down food from the pantry and dishes for the table. I had learned a lot from watching Ruth do all the work to keep her farm and its workers fed and clothed. Irene had become the work companion I had hoped to become with Ruth. Our ability to get a meal on the table together was a testament to how close we were emotionally. Despite the painful time we had shared, we had both healed, and her ability to love made me grateful for her every day.

I touched every object in the kitchen with gratitude. The renovations at the start of our stay in the house had been done well. We had a very efficient kitchen for feeding large numbers of people. As in every house, the kitchen was the hub. We even installed a chime to alert people when meals were ready.

I missed Helen. That always reared up when I felt good. Helen was not there with me.

I liked thinking of us in bed. I remembered a night when I had come into the room to get her sympathy because I had cut my thumb and it hurt. I had taken good care of it so it would not become infected and had been bragging to her about it, and she just laughed.

"What's so funny?"

"At this point, you should be more worried about what to plant this spring, hiring farmhands and buying equipment, and stop applauding yourself for surviving a cut."

I had turned to look at her. She was naked, on her knees on the bed adjusting the sheets and blankets. Someone had not made the bed that morning.

"Let me sit in that nice office and spend half my day ordering and studying how to make the farm work and the other half writing my book."

"Really?"

"Is there a budget?" She had looked at me with that silly grin when she knew the answer to the question.

"I suppose we should begin thinking about what this farm can be for us and for those around us. That would mean writing a business plan and deciding how much to invest now and over time."

"Do you want me to start working on that?"

"Irene can help you. Maybe put together a draft, and we'll all take a look at it with Max."

"Why does Max have to be involved?"

"Max is a stakeholder in the farm. He's needed when we make financial decisions."

The discussion had ended. Helen was curled up on the bed waiting for me.

"I'll be right back," I said. I'd been eager to jump under the covers beside her and be with her but I had other thoughts too. Always that set of other things to attend to.

First, I had gone downstairs to check on Mama and Aunt Money. I had found Irene sitting in a small circle of light, a cup of tea by her side and a book, closed on her finger, in her lap.

She had heard me coming down the stairs. "I'm not tired, so I thought I'd sit here a bit and keep an eye on them," she had whispered, staring at her book now. "Go to sleep, Scags. You can get up and get breakfast started."

There Irene and I were still, getting the meals ready while Helen was still in Afghanistan. She had often fallen asleep as I toured the house at night checking on everything and everyone.

"I wondered what Helen will think of our farm when she comes home?" I asked Irene as we set up the dinner.

"Is Helen coming back?" Irene asked.

"Yes," I said.

"Do you know when?"

"Not precisely. Why?"

"I worry about you."

I looked at her. I had thought of myself as so happy and at peace. What was there to worry about?

She looked at me.

"You won't want to be here alone."

"Who says I will be alone? Anyway, for now, with the Farm Subsidy Action Plan completed, I have new work to do. I began writing a novel. I am taking over Helen's office and writing it as fast as I can."

I would have said more, but we were now gathered to eat, and it was not the time to dig into Irene's worry about me. I felt terrific.

I felt terrific except when it was time to go to bed. Then, I missed to the point of pain the way Helen's and my body could cram together and become overcome with the sexual tension that made us so happy.

I began running again. The summer was not the best time for it, but it was necessary. And because it was necessary, it was like the time in Skokie when I met Helen.

I didn't have a track. I had a long dirt path out to the two-lane road leading off to the town. Those surfaces were more punishing on my legs than the track had been. I liked the heat, though, and it was easier to breathe out in the country, though I learned to run around dusk. Not having the heat of the sun on me, well, that was a good thing.

Running, my body processed the work I did at my desk all day long. It helped me see that I needed to put one foot in front of my other foot and keep the rhythm going, and all would be well.

On the last day of August, one of the hottest days of the year, I went out to run. I never before saw a car on our long driveway when I ran. Who would come to bother us at almost dinnertime? The car came straight at me. I jumped off the road, and the car stopped in front of me.

The door opened, and a woman got out of the car carrying a bottle of water and walked up to me.

I saw the scar before I saw the eyes brimming with tears.

"Oh my! You're home!" I yelled and grabbed the wonderfully dressed Helen in my arms and picked her up and swung her around.

"Yes, I am, my strong farmer. Put me down."

There is nothing more beautiful than Helen's face as she looks at me. In that moment, Margaret became a sweet breeze fading away, never to return again.

Happy endings are wonderful. They may not last as long as we want them to last, but they are among the sweetest moments of our lives.

Acknowledgments

Writing this entire Scags Series has taken me much longer than I had anticipated. But the good news is this: it is now complete and you are reading it or have read it to have found this page. If you've also read all the other volumes in the series, I hope this last one helps you, as it has helped me, find the resolution to Scags' life and her awareness of what life is.

On a more personal note, there have been writers and friends who have helped me more than they may ever know and so I want to say so here. Kerry Langan was an invaluable reader who added to *Scags at 18* and *Scags at 30* when others were not as enthusiastic about these books. Stephanie Dickinson too gave a great deal of her limited time to empathically connect with Scags and to help her grow. Both these women are outstanding writers and deserve to be read too.

Many of my friends who are writers or readers gave me support by buying my books and talking about them with others. That kind of support is invaluable.

I mention my wife, Suzanne Pyrch, at the end of this list because she is always the final voice and the first voice I hear urging me on to tell my stories. I spend my time writing and she spends lots of time practicing her flute. That shared creative energy is an anchor in our home during these pandemic times. Suzanne is the happy ending to my stories.